MADAME VOODOO
AND THE
VOODOO KING

A. W. JACKSON

CRANTHORPE
MILLNER
PUBLISHERS

First published by Cranthorpe Millner Publishers (2025)

ISBN 978-1-80378-324-6 (Paperback)

www.cranthorpemillner.com

Cranthorpe Millner Publishers

INDEX OF SPECIES

Please, before you delve into the mystery, I suggest you familiarise yourselves with the index of species. This is a guide to all the magical beings you will come across in this story. Here you will find their abilities, traits and heritage.

Voodoo Witches/Practitioners

The modern voodoo witches of America can trace their roots back to New Orleans in the 1700s, where their ancestors (most of whom were slaves) amalgamated their voodoo beliefs from Africa with the Catholic religion in their new-found home of New Orleans.

A voodoo witch's spell and ritual casting is limited to a meaningful word or phrase spoken or chanted in French. There are also many voodoo deities, the most regarded being Papa Legba, keeper of the spiritual realm and the barrier between the living and dead. Those who come face to face with Papa Legba are powerful witches or the idiotic and the damned.

The voodoo community usually comprises a king or queen to lead, guide and protect the community. A new king or queen can either be born into the role or win the title in a test of strength between them and the current reigning monarch.

Voodoo witches, in addition to spell casting, can perform talents such as possession, spirit manipulation, voodoo doll creation and ritualistic magic.

Common Witches/Warlocks

The common witch can be found in every corner of the globe. They are a separate species to humans, born with unique gifts. Each witch can spellcast and brew potions, as well as progress their natural talents. During the witch trials that took place across the world, they were often mistaken for satanists and therefore beheaded, drowned or burnt at the stake for crimes they did not commit.

Since the days of the trials, witches decided to stick together, forming covens to rely on the powers of one another, should any monstrosity such as the trials happen again. In these modern times, they have managed to thrive, now that the majority of humans no longer believe in such fairytales. The sheer number of witches has led to towns and cities having a main governing coven. A few of its members have decision-making powers while the rest are disciples. There is also usually a matriarch of the coven; the oldest, wisest or most powerful witch, who has the final say on all matters. Similarly to voodoo reign, to take a throne at the inner circle of a coven one must either be a blood descendant to a current seat member or contest for one.

There are two subcategories of witches: Marcidus and Indignus.

A marcidus is a mortal born of two witches. They have no innate talent and cannot spell cast, nor brew potions.

An indignus is a witch born of two mortals though, due to their origin, they lack the volume of magic coursing through their blood compared to a normal witch. Therefore, they must siphon energy from others in order to power their magic, making spellcasting twice as hard.

Hedge Witches/Warlocks

Hedge witches are also a separate species to humans, born with a connection to Mother Nature and the earth. They respect and care for the earth in return for control over the elements. Fire, earth, wind and water can all be at a hedge witch's will, if they take the time to harness their abilities.

Due to their ability to draw power from Mother Nature, they have no need for covens and usually live in solitude or in smaller groups of twos or threes. This also means there are no hierarchy of hedge witches unlike voodoo and common witches. They are usually a peaceful and caring person. However, they can become very passionate and therefore powerful – when necessary. They are not to be trifled with lightly.

Though hedge witches tend not to do much in the way of spell casting, it is still within their capabilities. As well as this, they have been known to gain control over the weather and be able to communicate telepathically with animals. They also often partake in holistic potion-brewing, purely for healing purposes.

Satanic Witches/Warlocks

Otherwise known as devil worshipers, satanic witches are humans who have given their soul to Satan, to serve him. The devil imbues them with hellish powers that allow them to exact his murderous repulse on the world, without having to lift a finger himself. Going back to the days of the witch trials, agents of Lucifer's would often kidnap and murder children, and place plagues on towns, crimes which, nine times out of ten, a common witch would've been tried with.

Some satanists are mouth-breathers who don't amount to much, instead focusing on lower level evil doings. However, there are some who seek to bring about the end of days – the apocalypse – where Lucifer himself would bring about hell on Earth. Satanists are usually lone wolves as the intelligent witches don't dirty themselves with the mouth-breathing type. Their homes are often normal, upon first glance. However, satanic runes keep their dungeons hidden, where they commit their heinous crimes against humanity. The cost of being an agent of Satan's is their appearance; a spell used to disguise their hideous new looks. When signing the deal, they begin to shapeshift into monstrous-looking people with horns and scales.

A satanist's abilities can vary from summoning demons straight from the depths of hell to a venomous touch and hellfire, though such abilities are often tailored to the individual when they draw up their contract with the devil.

PROLOGUE

A few days had passed since Nkechi had awoken from her coma, and as she sat on the step outside her apartment building awaiting Kosum's arrival, she couldn't keep still. She garnered the usual stares from passers-by due to the vitiligo across her face, but in that moment, she didn't bat an eyelid. She was too preoccupied with *him*. Her legs were shaking, her hands were moving from one procrastinating position to the next, and she could still hear his voice in the back of her mind, causing the odd twitch of her head. Even after his death, Nkechi still didn't feel free of him.

Kosum flew down the street in her flashy car and pulled up in front of Nkechi. She flipped her windswept hair over her head and popped her sunglasses on as the morning spring sun broke through the cloud cover. Spring was almost over though, which meant one thing: summer. Kosum couldn't wait for summer. It meant no school, balmy heat, and she could finally once again see her girlfriend. And yet, summer wouldn't exactly be the break Kosum was hoping for and deep down she knew that. Her mother was still in a coma, and her girlfriend was still in a town controlled by the infamous voodoo king. Nevertheless, Kosum wanted to stay strong and positive, if not for herself then for Nkechi's sake, especially today.

"Hey!" Kosum shouted to an oblivious Nkechi, followed by two playful honks of her car's horn.

Nkechi came out of her dazed state and lifted her head to see a smiley Kosum waving, beckoning her to come over.

Nkechi plastered on a smile as she slid into the car next to Kosum.

"You okay?" Kosum asked, seeing straight through Nkechi's attempted smile.

"Yeah," Nkechi replied, unconvincingly.

"We don't have to do this, ya know. Ana said that she doesn't mind doing it."

"No, it's okay, I want to," Nkechi muttered, her head tilted down, still unsure. Her thick curly locks hid her face a little from Kosum.

"Okay, but if you change your mind at any point, just tell me and we'll leave, okay?" Kosum lowered her head to try to regain some eye contact with Nkechi.

"Yeah, sure," Nkechi smiled, appreciatively.

"Right, let's go," Kosum said, before swiftly catapulting them back into the madness of the New York traffic.

"How are we doing this again?" Nkechi asked rather loudly, over the sound of multiple taxis beeping at Kosum's driving.

Kosum didn't care, or at least she didn't notice as she kept on drifting past each block as if she was racing for a podium place in *Mario Kart*.

"Well, there isn't a body, so we're going to clear out the apartment and leave a note to say that he's up and left and wants to be alone. Then, with any luck, his maid will find it and then we can all be done with that chapter of our lives,"

Kosum explained as her jet-black hair whipped in the breeze created by her open-topped Jaguar.

"Doesn't this all sound a little too simple?"

"What part of emptying an entire townhouse do you think is simple?" Kosum asked, laughing at her own sarcasm.

"You know what I mean," Nkechi replied, rolling her eyes, trying not to give in to laughter.

"Besides, isn't simple good after everything we've been through this year?"

"Yeah, I suppose so," Nkechi agreed. "How are we emptying the place, anyway?"

"Ana gave me a spell to use. Apparently, it will transport everything in the house into a volcano somewhere. To be honest, I think she used it on the woman who slept with her husband."

"Kosum! She put a woman in a volcano?"

"Oh, no, no," Kosum laughed, "just all of her stuff."

"I mean, that's still pretty—"

"Don't say crazy," Kosum interjected. "She'd probably hear you all the way from her house."

"She's just so nice to us that sometimes I forget how ruthless she can be."

"Well, we're like family to her now, and she'll do anything to keep us safe. Anything."

"Okay, stop it. You know I hate it when you say things in that weird tone," Nkechi cringed.

"I don't know what you're talking about," Kosum joked, using the same voice. "Hey, it got you to smile at least."

"Yeah, yeah, whatever, weirdo," Nkechi said, playfully.

The girls swiftly came to a holt in front of a familiar, grand townhouse. *His* townhouse. They got out of the car and slowly walked to the door. Nkechi stood before it in silence as the realisation of what they were doing and why they were doing it set in.

"Hey, Kosum, can you go in first?" a nervous Nkechi asked.

"Yeah, sure thing."

As Kosum edged closer to the door and reached out her hand to grab the handle, Nkechi had a thought and tugged at her, causing Kosum to jump.

"Jesus, Nkechi, you scared the crap out of me. What's up?"

"Sorry, I was just thinking that before we burn everything in the fiery pit of a volcano, shouldn't we look for his research findings from his experiments? There could be even more that we don't know about," Nkechi said, looking rather worried.

"I think it's best that we just let it die with him, don't you?"

Nkechi reluctantly agreed, a disappointed look on her face. "Yeah, I guess you're right. I think I kinda just feel guilty about it all. After all, he said that it was my blood that was the key. I'm just curious to know how."

"If you really want to, we can have a quick look around for anything obvious. But we can't afford to be here too long and risk anyone seeing us."

"Thanks, Kosum," Nkechi smiled.

"You ready?" Kosum asked, as she planted her hand firmly on the door handle.

"As I'll ever be," Nkechi confirmed, with a weary nod.

Kosum twisted the doorknob and used her telekinetic abilities to sense the pins within the lock, pushing them into the correct place one by one. This was a rather new talent Kosum had been practising. It made for a stealthy way of breaking into someone's house (not that she planned on doing it very often, just for when times such as this called for it).

As the door opened ajar, both Kosum and Nkechi's noses were punched with an overwhelming smell of bleach. It didn't make sense. None of the coven had been to clean up yet – there was nothing really to clean. As they had said, his body was no more, there was no blood, no crime scene, and certainly no need for bleach. All they were doing was destroying any evidence of his life.

Kosum continued to push open the door once they had accustomed their noses to the smell. As she did, it revealed an empty house that looked like it was ready to be sold.

"What? Where is everything?" a shocked Nkechi pondered aloud.

"This is the right house, isn't it?" Kosum asked, having never visited before. Nkechi, on the other hand, had spent quite a few nights there with him in the weeks leading up to his death.

"Yeah. There was a table here," she said gesturing to the empty space. "And a rug over here," she added, darting about the once palace-like interior. "Where has it all gone?"

Nkechi felt crazy as she began searching every room in the house.

"Hey, wait up!" Kosum shouted, running after her.

After checking every square inch of the building, it was clear that there were no remnants of *his* life. Even the furniture that Nkechi presumed was built-in was no longer there.

Nothing was making sense. Who had done this? And

why? Nkechi and Kosum had no clue. It was becoming too eery to stay any longer, Nkechi clearly upset. As someone had already done their job for them, there was no reason for them to stay, and so they departed.

As Nkechi hopped back into Kosum's car, she couldn't help but wonder who else knew about this place.

Who else knows about Charlie?

CHAPTER 1

Summer Break

Three weeks later, Nkechi and Kosum were at college enjoying their final day of freshman year. They had both been looking forward to the relief of completing their last assessment. Though they would only be swapping their mortal stresses for some supernatural ones over the summer.

In the few weeks since the Charlie situation, tensions had grown in New Orleans. Somehow, the voodoo king had learned of their visit and, as each day passed, the streets of Nkechi's hometown were becoming more and more like a warzone. Nicole and Anuli were holding down the fort, but it was inevitable that they would need Nkechi and Kosum's help soon. The voodoo king was too powerful for them to take on alone and his goons outnumbered them ten to one. Before they could go to New Orleans to help, however, Nkechi had struck an agreement with Kosum that she would help find a way to bring Kwanjai out of her coma.

Kwanjai still lay unconscious in Ana's infirmary, with Ana exhausting every effort to wake her dear friend. She had tried every herb, crystal and potion that she had available, but not a whisper or a twitch of a finger.

There would be nothing normal about Nkechi and Kosum's summer break…

"Hey, wait up!" Kosum shouted, chasing after Nkechi in the courtyard.

"I literally couldn't be walking any slower! Besides, I wasn't gonna leave without you – we've got to walk out of freshman year together," Nkechi smiled.

"Can you believe it's been a whole school year already? We've come a long way since that *eventful* first day," Kosum chuckled.

"I know, it's gone so fast. But I guess time flies when you see multiple magical suicides; find out about your family's history; have your best friend come out; kill a pervy professor, and send your killer boyfriend's spirit to limbo for all eternity!"

"*Ex*-boyfriend," Kosum corrected with a fake cough.

"Yeah, well, that's kind of implied, considering he's dead," Nkechi laughed.

"Yeah, I guess. And we still have no idea who emptied his apartment."

"I know, it's annoying. But to be honest, I think unless it was the devil himself, it's far down our witchy priority list this summer."

"Ain't that the truth." Kosum laughed off the rather pressing and dangerous paths that lay ahead of them.

"Anyway, forget about the future for a second. How does it feel to have at least survived freshman year – literally and in the 'cute teen chick-flick' sense?" Kosum asked.

"Ya know, it feels pretty awesome. And I'm so excited for next year. Professor Thompson seems like she knows what she's doing."

"Yeah, she gives off cool, older-cousin-from out-of-town vibes."

"That's so stupid, but annoyingly accurate," Nkechi laughed.

"I know, right! She's so young and pretty," Kosum said, her mind drifting off slightly.

"Hey, you're with my cousin – no daydreaming about hot women, please, or at least not in front of me," Nkechi chided, snapping her fingers in front of Kosum's dazed face.

"Sorry," Kosum said, rubbing her eyes and bringing herself back to reality. "I wonder what all the normal students will be doing during summer break?" she added, swiftly changing the subject.

"I don't know. But something tells me it won't be quite the same as what we will be doing," Nkechi said, looking around at the sea of mortals rushing to begin their summer vacations.

"You mean they won't be finding a magical cure for their comatose mother while also travelling across the country to fight a voodoo king?" Kosum said sarcastically, looking over at Nkechi until they both couldn't hold in the belly laugh anymore.

When the giggles died down, Nkechi asked, "How is your mom, anyway? Did that potion I made do anything?"

"Unfortunately not, but thanks for trying. Ana said everything she's tried so far hasn't made a difference, either," Kosum answered, defeated. "But she said she'll keep researching until she finds something."

"I'm sorry, Kosum. I'm sure we'll work it out soon." Nkechi half smiled as they came to the college exit.

"Here's hoping. I'm sorry, I know you're just waiting on me until we can go help Nicole and your auntie," Kosum said, lowering her head.

"Hey, don't worry. They understand, especially Nicole. And they're doing their best to fight back and find out some more information on the voodoo king and his men. Now come on, chin up."

"Thanks, Nkechi. Nicole's been a real rock these past few weeks. I can't wait to see her again," Kosum replied, cheering up at the thought of her.

They strolled out of college side by side and walked over to where Nkechi's bike was chained up to the bike rack on the paving in front of Kosum's Jaguar. Nkechi's bike had finally undergone a long overdue facelift. The bike that Charlie had once offered to help renovate, had been sanded and repainted, with a lot of help from Kosum. It was now a royal navy blue, kitted out with a fresh gear chain, a bell and a cute little white basket.

"Named her yet?" Kosum nudged, as she admired their handiwork.

"Who said it was a she?"

"Ew, so you're riding a guy around the city? That's pretty gross." Kosum couldn't help but laugh.

"Oh, ha-ha, shut up," Nkechi rolled her eyes as she strapped on her helmet and mounted the bike.

"Hey, don't forget about tonight."

"Tonight?" Nkechi looked at Kosum, confused.

"You know, the first open meeting for all the witches of New York."

"Oh shit, I totally forgot, though it's not like I have any

other plans tonight."

"Don't sweat it. Just don't forget again in the next few hours, okay?" Kosum chuckled.

"I won't, I promise," Nkechi answered, her hand on her chest.

Nkechi and Kosum moved off, both returning to their equally as empty apartments. Though Nkechi was used to living alone Kosum was not. She had mainly kept to her bedroom since her mother fell into the coma, not wanting to acknowledge she was alone in such a large penthouse.

After Nkechi had dragged herself up the depressingly worn stairs to her apartment, she reached her front door to find an eviction notice from her landlord attached with duct tape:

Dear Tenant,

I am sorry to inform you that I am selling the building and hereby serve your notice of eviction. You are required to exit the building by May 14th.

Sincerest apologies, and best of luck in your search for alternative accommodation.

Kindest regards,

Mr Carter

"'Kindest regards'! Well, that's the biggest load of bull I've ever heard!" Nkechi tore the notice from the door and entered her lonely apartment.

She looked around. The cat's food bowl caught her eye –

she had forgotten to get rid of it since Cece's (or rather her mother's) second passing. She'd missed the goofy antics they would get up to together and all the cosy morning visits. All she could do was hope that Halloween would come around quickly so she could see her mother again.

Nkechi made herself some dinner with the scraps from her cupboards. There was some pasta and a jar of creamy sauce. "Maybe carbonara," Nkechi voiced to the empty kitchenette, only to be disappointed by the lack of any meat in the fridge. "A veggie carbonara it is, then," she said, not so much as her own echo in return.

Nkechi took her creamy bowl of pasta and sat on the bed. She stared deeply into the open wardrobe at the lacklustre rack of clothes and slurped up the tagliatelle which kept flopping on her chin. She needed something to wear for the coven meeting. It was the first time she would be meeting the coven's members outside of the inner circle. 'Disciple' was Gweneviere's preferred term for them, but since the remodelling of the coven, they agreed that 'member' was a much less derogatory noun.

What does one wear to a meeting among witches? Was she supposed to wear something fancy? Or something you might wear for an interview? She wanted to look like she cared, but she didn't want to be overdressed. She settled on a pinstriped pantsuit which had an interview vibe. Luckily, Kosum would stop the fashion crime before it was too late, if that was indeed what she was about to commit.

Kosum soon arrived at Nkechi's studio to take her to the meeting. Nkechi walked out of the apartment building, and Kosum's head cranked round like she could smell the fashion disaster from the car.

"What *are* you wearing?" Kosum interrogated, pulling her shades down sassily.

"Hey, you're supposed to be my friend!" Nkechi moaned, knowing deep down the choice was a mistake.

"I *am* your friend. Hence why I'm not letting you turn up to the meeting like that," she laughed.

"Fine, I guess it's not the best fit for the occasion."

"Don't worry, I've got something you can wear. Now c'mon, we don't wanna be late for our first open meeting."

Nkechi hopped in the car and Kosum pulled away like the speed-demon she was.

"So, did anything happen in the last few hours since I saw you?" Kosum asked in jest.

"Actually, yeah."

"What?"

"I'm being evicted." Nkechi sighed.

"Evicted? But you're the best tenant ever, and an all-round goody-two-shoes. What did you do to get evicted?" Kosum asked, turning her gaze to Nkechi, perplexed, taking her eyes off the road.

"Nothing. It's not just me; it's the whole building. *Apparently*, the scumbag landlord is selling up. So, I've got two weeks to find somewhere else." she answered while keeping an eye on the road as clearly Kosum wasn't.

"What an ass! Can he even do that? Surely you should have more notice than that? Are you going to appeal?"

"To be honest, most of the people in that building are too high on crack to notice, let alone help. And since Cece – I mean my mom – died it's just not the same. It's just a shitty studio that's overpriced and falling apart. I'm going to start looking for a new apartment tomorrow, I guess, although on my budget, I'd be lucky to get a closet."

"Move in with me!" Kosum blurted, having a eureka moment. "It won't be like when I lived with you, I promise. You can have your own bedroom *and* bathroom."

"I don't know, Kosum. What about your mom?" Nkechi asked.

"Nkechi, my mom is obsessed with you. You're like the second daughter she never had. If she was awake, she wouldn't take no for an answer."

"Thanks," she smiled. "But I'm paying you rent. I can probably afford a bit more than I was paying before," Nkechi explained.

"No. You can buy half the groceries but that's it. All the apartment's bills are covered by the fact my mom owns the place. I'd just be taking your money to spend on nothing. Besides, this way you can still save up to look for your own place, if you want to."

"Okay, thanks." Nkechi humbly accepted.

"No probs, bestie," Kosum winked, pulling into the hotel car lot.

"What's this? You, Kosum Jenkins, parking the car yourself? Are you feeling all right?" Nkechi asked.

"Oh my god, Nkechi, shut up. I've been trying to, I dunno, be like a nicer person or whatever."

"So, you're taking away the poor man's job by doing it yourself? That's pretty mean," Nkechi teased.

"Only you would turn that into a bad thing! You idiot," Kosum chuckled. "That's it, you can drive yourself places now.”

“Okay, I’m sorry. I don’t want to lose car privileges. I mean, I know we spruced up my bike and all, but it is nice to ride in something that doesn’t have pedals every now and then.”

“Fine, you’re forgiven, but only because I’m still internally laughing at your outfit,” Kosum cackled.

“Bitch.” Nkechi feigned seriousness, before looking down at what she was wearing and laughing too.

“You look like a forty-year-old realtor or mortgage broker or something.”

“Okay, I get it. Let’s just go up so you can do your favourite thing and play dress up on me.”

“Ooh, yay.” Kosum clapped her hands together giddily before following Nkechi out of the parking lot.

Up in the penthouse, Kosum was sifting through her wardrobe to find a more suitable outfit for Nkechi for the evening.

“Now girl, don’t get me wrong I love a powerful pantsuit and I’m all about the workplace fashion, but let’s make you look your age, and hot, in case there are any sexy warlocks in the meeting. What about these?” Kosum asked, holding up a leather skirt and top. “Ya know, keep it casual. We’re trying to be different from Gwen and Margaret; we don’t wanna give off rich I’m-better-than-you-bitch vibes,” Kosum explained.

“Well, that should be easy for me because I’m not even rich,” Nkechi commented. “I’m surprised that you’re becoming so good at thinking about other people’s feelings. I guess you are becoming a ‘nicer’ person.”

"See, I can be nice and sensitive and shit."

"I know," Nkechi chuckled. "Give me a second to get changed and then I'll be ready." Nkechi went behind the paper partition screen to get ready and remembered what Kosum had snook into conversation a moment earlier. "Oh, and by the way, even if Micheal B. Jordan is in the meeting, I still won't be talking to him, or any other guys for a *long* time," Nkechi shouted over the screen, as she struggled to get her blouse off over her hair.

"Yeah, I get you. But you never know when the right one will come along. Plus, it doesn't hurt to play the field, so to speak," Kosum said sniggering under her breath.

"I'm not the 'play the field' kinda girl."

"You never know until you try!" Kosum exclaimed.

Nkechi didn't answer as she smiled to herself, unseen.

After her wardrobe change, the girls headed to see Ana and fellow witch Trish in the meeting room for a briefing, before they opened the doors to the witches of New York. It was the first time Nkechi had been back there since it all happened. She swore she could still smell the scorched wood and the earthy roots from her spell. Even the whispers of Charlie's last few twisted words wormed their way into her ear.

Kosum managed to distract Nkechi from such thoughts as she pointed out their very own thrones. Ana had had them designed and made by one of the local warlocks (who doubled as a carpenter in the mortal business world). Kosum's was silver and flashy of course, with each armrest having a rounded edge, which she grasped as she sank into her throne. It was upholstered with the finest plush black velvet, matching her hair colour to make it look like it surrounded her whole body. Nkechi's wasn't quite as ostentatious as Kosum's, but it was still beautiful in its own subtle way. It was made from an ivory-like substance that was hand-carved to represent each element over which she had control: fire, water, earth, wind and the spirits. It effortlessly combined her Voodoo and Hedge witch heritages into a stunning representation of her power and heritage. Meanwhile, Gweneviere and Margaret's thrones had been moved into storage, with other old coven memorabilia. It served as a reminder of the past and what the girls didn't want to become.

"So, gurls, do you like 'em?" Ana asked in anticipation, her eyes fixated on their expressions.

"Oh, Ana, they're amazing – thank you so much." Kosum gleamed from her throne as she shimmied her bum around to get comfy.

"Yeah, truly pieces of art, thank you," Nkechi added as she ran her fingers along the carvings, admiring the artistry.

"Aw, I'm so glad you like 'em. I gave him the inspiration and he ran with it. He's a handsome young warlock too!" Ana said, with an unsubtle look in Nkechi's direction.

"Well, you both did a great job – please thank him from us," Nkechi added, not taking Ana's hint.

"No need. He should be here tonight at the meetin', so you can thank him yourselves." Ana smiled.

"Right, well we probably should get to the business at hand," Trish said, appearing from behind Ana.

"Yes, Trish is right. We need to bring a unified front to the meetin'. There will be a lot of questions about that night and the fact that Gwen and Margaret are now AWOL. People are gonna want explanations and answers that, quite frankly, we don't have," Ana said.

"Well, what do we say?" Kosum asked.

"We should tell the truth, or as much as possible at least." Nkechi answered.

"Which is?" Trish questioned in a condescending tone.

"That Gwen and Margaret abandoned the coven, like the cowards they are, and that Nkechi stopped the crazed Marcidus," Kosum jumped in, sensing Trish's tone.

Kosum and Trish weren't the close friends they used to be; Kosum never really forgave her for trying to sneakily interrogate Nkechi. It was clear that Trish was just out for herself (though she still wasn't half as bad as Margaret).

"Right, come on now, take your seats, they'll be waiting outside," Ana respectfully commanded, naturally taking her place as the mother figure of the group. "Kosum, would you do the honours?" she asked, pointing towards the doors.

"Yeah, sure." Kosum waved her hands to open the doors where the witches of New York began to filter through and fill the meeting room. The room that had once housed only five thrones now had an additional thirty seats for their fellow members. Not every witch in New York was there as that would've been in the hundreds, but the main representants of each family attended. Once all were seated, Ana introduced the new coven leadership to the crowd of witches and warlocks.

Trish and Ana were already well known amongst the witches of New York. Nkechi and Kosum, however, needed introducing. They both stated their names, and Ana opened the floor up to questions, of which there were many. One of the first to voice their opinions was a rather handsome warlock who stood and towered over the room with his six-foot plus stature.

"Will Nkechi be the new powerhouse behind the coven, now that Gweneviere is gone? I mean, let's be honest, the main reason we put up with Gwen's crap all these years was because she was powerful enough to protect the New York coven from any threats," the warlock said, looking around at the crowd for reassurance which he received with a sea of nods and agreeing groans.

"I can assure you, that within the coven we have more than enough power to protect against any threats that may arise." Ana stated.

"Besides, Gweneviere and Margaret went AWOL during the last battle. So much for your almighty protector," Kosum sassily pointed out.

"Also, if I may, I would like to add something. Of course, we have the power to protect the coven, but we're also wise enough to use our words first to try to defuse a potential hostile situation," Nkechi added.

"Well said," Ana nodded in agreement.

"Understood," the attractive man conceded, smiling in Nkechi's direction.

"Well, I for one would like to know exactly what happened that night. Wasn't the perpetrator Nkechi's boyfriend?" an unknown witch shouted from the back of the room.

"I'll take this one," Kosum said to the panel. "All you need to know is that Nkechi was the one who defeated Charlie, and you should all be grateful that she did. Who knows where his vengeance would have taken him next? And yes, they were romantically involved, but Charlie was a sociopath and mass manipulator who had everyone around him fooled. But as soon as Nkechi realised this, she didn't hesitate to do what was necessary."

"Agreed." Ana once again nodded, seemingly allowing Kosum to take the lead.

"Does anyone else have any questions or concerns?" Trish asked, trying to move the topic of conversation away from Nkechi, jealous that she was getting all the attention.

"Yes, I do," a voice in the crowd asked. "Where is Kwanjai? Shouldn't she be in this meeting?"

Trish subtly rolled her eyes. Wasn't *anyone* interested in her?

"Kwanjai is currently in a coma. We are doing everythin' we can to bring her out of it and are open to any ideas to help," Ana answered.

"What?" another voice shouted.

"Oh my god!" a further witch gasped.

The room began to fill with the whispers and heckles, of witches and warlocks wanting answers:

"How have you let this happen?"

"How can you protect the city if you can't even protect yourselves?"

Ana could see that the constant questioning was getting to Kosum, and with no one knowing the right thing to say, she concluded the meeting.

"Now if that's all, this meetin' is adjourned until next month."

The sea of witches groaned. Ana wasn't scared though, as she coaxed them out of the room using her loud Southern charm.

"Well done, girls. I think we handled that rather well," Ana voiced, unconvincingly.

"Yes, I agree. What a success," Trish said sarcastically. "Anyway, I'll see you guys at the next meeting, I've got to go charge the old batteries, if you catch my drift." Trish alluded to another one of her model orgies and of course everyone did catch her drift.

"Are you all right, Kosum?" Nkechi asked, stretching out her hand for support.

"Yeah. I guess I just wasn't expecting so many questions about Mom."

"Hey, don't worry, darlin', we won't stop until she's back with us, okay?" Ana gave an awkward smile.

"I know. Thanks, Ana."

"So, gurls, what are you up to tonight?" Ana asked, before they too deserted her and she had to return to her unfaithful husband, and children. Though she loved her children, even she needed a break sometimes.

"We were just gonna head up to the apartment in a minute. Nkechi's been evicted so she's gonna move in with me," Kosum explained.

"Aw, I'm sorry to hear that, darlin'. If you need anythin' I'm just a call away."

"Thank you. I really appreciate everything you're doing for us both," Nkechi said.

"Not a problem. You gurls just make sure you keep looking after each other. I'm gonna head down to the infirmary to check on your mother, feel free to come by."

"Thanks, I might do a little later."

When Ana left, Kosum went to the bathroom and Nkechi was left alone. She stood looking around the meeting room where Charlie died and wondered if she'd ever be ready to move on. As she waited for Kosum's return, Nkechi felt a tap on her shoulder which scared her. She spun around and blew a gust of wind in the direction it had come from without seeing who or what it was.

"Ow," a handsome warlock moaned from the wall Nkechi had just pushed him into.

"I'm so sorry, I'm a bit jumpy," Nkechi said, heading to the man's aid.

"It's all right," the winded warlock said as he held his stomach and slowly walked back to meet Nkechi halfway. "Did you like your chair?" he asked.

"Huh?"

"Your throne. I'm the guy who made it, and Kosum's too."

"Oh, yeah, It's really beautiful."

"I guess you have that in common then," he said, sporting a cheeky smile as he flipped his blond, shoulder-length locks to the side, fully revealing his face. He had high cheek bones, dark eyebrows and luscious lips. But none of his good looks and charm were going to work on Nkechi. She was nowhere near ready for that. "So, are you single?"

"Listen, I really love the throne, but I'm not really looking for anything at the moment," Nkechi said, trying to subtly reject him.

"Well, that's great cos neither am I. I'm just looking for fun with a pretty girl, that's all," he said, as if that was supposed to convince Nkechi to change her mind.

"Well, I'm not interested. It was nice to meet you but I've gotta go," Nkechi said, turning in the direction where she'd last seen Kosum.

"Okay, but if you change your mind, Ana has my number. You know, we're not all bad, baby cakes," he pronounced loudly as Nkechi walked away.

Nkechi swivelled back round at the comment. "What the hell is that supposed to mean?"

"I'm just saying that just cos you couldn't satisfy ya last boyfriend, doesn't mean you couldn't please another guy."

"Do you hear yourself right now?" Nkechi asked, baffled by how brazenly rude he was being.

"Yeah, and I'm offering you something a lot of witches in New York are gagging for... A piece of me!"

Nkechi did indeed gag but that was from the chunk of vomit that had just risen to her throat.

"I suggest you get your ass out of here before I slam you into another wall!" Nkechi said, her voice louder and more pointed.

"OK, fine!"

Kosum returned just in time to see the guy leave.

"What was all that about? I could hear you shouting."

"Just proof that all boys are indeed dicks," Nkechi spat. Her arms were folded and her lips screwed up angrily as she watched the sleazeball walk away.

"Hey, Hakeem isn't a dick. You're always talking about your funny work stories with him... though I suppose that's because he's a man and not a boy, so yeah, I can agree with that prior statement now," Kosum said, in a light-hearted attempt at relieving Nkechi's anger. "Come on, let's go," she added, gently leading Nkechi out of the room.

"Ugh, I just don't get why guys think they can say whatever they want and it not have repercussions."

"I don't know either, but what I do know is that those kinda guys will ultimately end up sad and alone."

"Yeah well, here's hoping."

Nkechi and Kosum headed up to Kosum's apartment to unwind from an eventful first meeting. Kosum poured them both a glass of wine before they changed into some pyjamas and snuggled up in Kosum's bed.

"Now *that* was a first meeting," Kosum said, taking a well needed glug of wine.

"Yeah, well, I didn't need the encore from that douche afterwards. Even if I was ready to move on, if all the guys are like that then I am quite happy to live vicariously through you and Nicole."

"Oh, come on. I know we joke but not every guy out there is a total pig. Now drink, it'll help, trust me," Kosum said, pushing Nkechi's glass to her mouth.

Nkechi took a large gulp. "Ahh, you're right, that did help."

"See, I'm right a lot. And for the record, even though he was a dick, he was practically drooling over you. So, at least you know you still got it, girl. I think he was secretly scared of you – he might have a dominatrix thing," Kosum laughed, playfully pushing Nkechi on the shoulder.

"Oh my god, shut up, you idiot. How many glasses have you had?" Nkechi asked.

"One," Kosum hiccupped while holding up three fingers.

"You're such a lightweight," Nkechi laughed. "But thanks again for letting me move in," she added when her laughter had died down.

"Don't sweat it. You're like family, it'll be so much fun. Now, crash here tonight, and tomorrow I'll help you move all your stuff in properly. Then you can finally be out of that deathtrap. It's a wonder he got away with the building conditions for so long, anyway."

"Preach," Nkechi concurred, raising her glass sassily.

The two of them nestled down for the night in Kosum's room drinking wine, eating Cheetos and watching funny YouTube videos until they both fell asleep.

The next day at Nkechi's apartment, Nkechi and Kosum had created three piles of Nkechi's things: keep, donate and trash. The keep pile was significantly bigger than the other two because Nkechi was finding it hard to part with of a lot of items. She hadn't realised just how many seemingly trivial items reminded her of her mother.

"Hey, what about this? It should be trashed," Kosum said, holding up a moth-eaten scarf.

"No!" Nkechi shouted.

"Okay," Kosum replied, a little shocked.

"Sorry, it's just that was my mom's favourite. She wore it all the time," Nkechi explained.

"Oh sorry, Nkechi, it was just so battered, I thought…"

Nkechi took the tattered scarf and held it to her cheek.

"Yeah, I know, it's okay. God, I wish I could go back to

the day she first saw it in the store window. She loved it from the minute she laid eyes on it, but I knew she would never spoil herself like that, so I saved up my pocket money and bought it for her for Christmas. I'll never forget her face when she opened it. We had just finished dishing out the presents from under the tree and she noticed one left that had been sketchily wrapped with newspaper and duct tape. She pulled it out and saw 'Mom'. She opened it and her face filled with joy. I think that was the happiest I ever saw her," Nkechi said, a tear welling up in the corner of her eye. "I know I'll get to talk to her at Halloween and all, but it's still hard." She wiped her eyes.

"That's beautiful, Nkechi. And of course it's hard. I still miss my dad all the time, despite what my mom told me about him. Hey, if you want, I could try this spell I've been working on. It should restore it to its original pristine state and then you can actually wear it again. I broke my mom's vase at home and have been trying to restore it before she wakes up. I've almost done it."

"Yeah, sure, give it a go," Nkechi said approvingly with a smile. She handed it back to Kosum in the hope she could indeed make it as good as new.

"Reverse this scarf's unholy fate. Turn back time to its original state."

Before their eyes, the scarf came to life. It floated in the centre of the room as the strands began to magically weave the moth holes closed, and a blanket of mustard yellow flushed back into the dulled grey scarf. It floated back into Kosum's hands, and she passed it to a smiling Nkechi.

"Wow, Kosum, that was amazing! Thank you so much,"

she said, wrapping it around her neck.

"I can't believe it actually worked. My mom's vase is still in pieces in a box."

"Jeez, you could've mentioned that before," Nkechi said before they both laughed.

"C'mon, we really need to be making better progress than this. So far, you've been keeping almost everything. My mom loves you, but not enough for some of this crap to come with you," Kosum joked. "And, like, do you really need all this old school stuff? Also, how many extracurricular clubs were you in? I thought I was a geek just for being in mathletes," Kosum said, noticing all of the awards for different school activities.

"Mathletes? Damn, you were a geek. You just lost a lot of your street cred," Nkechi laughed. "But yeah, I can probably bin most of this stuff. I'm keeping any certificates, though!"

"I wouldn't expect anything less. You can stick them on the fridge," Kosum teased.

"I'll hold you to that."

Kosum's phone buzzed in her pocket. She grabbed it and saw it was Ana calling.

"I should probably take this, it's Ana." Kosum answered the call while Nkechi continued to sort through her stuff, finally letting go of some of the items that probably should've been thrown away years ago.

Nkechi heard Ana's voice. She sounded excited and nervous at the same time.

"Kosum, come over quick, it's about your mother."

"What is it, Ana?"

"Just come – I'll explain when you get here."

Kosum ended the call and turned to Nkechi. "Will you

come with me?" she asked shakily.

"Of course, let's go."

CHAPTER 2

Across the Pond

Kosum and Nkechi burst through the infirmary doors as if they were a part of a prison escape.

"Ana! What is it?" Kosum shouted, spotting Ana sitting beside her mother's restful body.

"It's okay, Kosum. It's somewhat good news. After the meetin' yesterday one of the witches came to me with an idea for your mom. She told me about the Heart of Hecate. The young witch had a small vile of its essence and we administered it to Kwanjai. Her hand briefly squeezed the blanket, and her eyelids twitched like she was tryin' to free herself of her coma. Though it wasn't enough to bring her back, I think if we can track down some more, it'll awaken her for good."

"Oh wow! Let's go get some more! Who sells it?" Kosum asked.

"Well, she said she got it from Blair," Ana said awkwardly, glancing away.

"Blair? But Blair knows about Mom. Why wouldn't she have said anything before now?" Kosum questioned, looking a little surprised and agitated. After all, they were good friends.

"I don't know, Kosum," Ana sighed.

"And you're sure it was our Blair?" Nkechi asked, in the hope that maybe there was some miscommunication.

"As sure as the day is long, darlin'. Maybe you gurls should pay her a visit?"

"Oh, don't worry, we will. I'll be going over there right now!" Kosum said, clenching her fists. She was so angry the solution had been right under their noses all this time.

Subconsciously, Kosum's telekinetic abilities ignited in tune with her anger. Equipment and potion ingredients all around the room began to levitate a few feet off the ground.

Nkechi saw the panicked look on Ana's face and turned to Kosum, gently placing her hands on her shoulders.

"Look, I don't know why she didn't tell us, but I'm sure she had a good reason. You just need to keep a level head. We're not going to solve anything by going in while you're still riled up."

"Yeah, sweetheart. Take the rest of the evenin' to cool off and head over there in the mornin'," Ana added.

"Fine," Kosum growled. "I suppose we do need to finish boxing up your stuff, anyway," she said calmly, causing all the inanimate objects to gently float back to their original positions.

"Yeah, and I'll even start actually throwing some things away," Nkechi chuckled, making Kosum crack a smile.

The two girls went back to Nkechi's and finished packing her things. It helped to take Kosum's mind off Blair for a little while, but once the task was complete and Nkechi's final boxes had been driven over to the penthouse, Kosum could feel herself slowly getting angry again.

Nkechi noticed the obvious change in Kosum's attitude and offered her one of her sleep remedies. Nkechi had started using them again since the Charlie situation, as sleep was once again something that didn't come easily to her. Kosum reluctantly agreed, and they both swiftly fell asleep.

Yet neither of theirs were peaceful dreams as their own horrible nightmares played out. Nkechi's were about Charlie, and Kosum's were about seeing her mother's grave and feeling she was already too late to save her.

The next morning, Kosum had woken up earlier than she had ever done before. (To be fair that wasn't overly incredible considering her previous record was 8:30 a.m.). Kosum never cared all that much about being late for class – she knew she was smart enough to catch up.

Nothing had ever given Kosum reason to be up and alert like this before.

She ungently shook Nkechi awake and asked her to be ready as soon as possible so that they could get on the road before rush hour. A tired Nkechi knew how much it meant to Kosum and so sloshed a toothbrush about her mouth and got dressed in record time, using a roll-on deodorant in place of a shower.

Managing to miss the New York rush hour, the girls made quick work of their drive. They pulled into the long dirt track that led to Blair's drive, just as they had done so many times before for Nkechi's training. But this time Kosum's driving was even more reckless than usual. She drifted across the driveway and hopped out of the car as if she was the main character in a spy thriller.

Blair's two daughters came out of the house to greet

Kosum at the base of the porch stairs, but she pushed past them and stormed up to the front door. The daughters weren't impressed and Nkechi gave them an awkward look of understanding to excuse Kosum's behaviour.

Blair reached the door to see Kosum's screwed up, flushed face.

"Kosum, what can I do for you?" Blair asked, obviously still unaware of what Kosum knew.

"What you can do for me is tell me why you're hiding something that could potentially save my mom's life?" Kosum barked, her hands firmly planted on either side of the doorframe. Kosum wasn't leaving without answers, and if they weren't ones she liked, she might be leaving with blood on her hands.

"What on earth are you talking about, Kosum?" Blair asked, tilting her confused gaze to Nkechi who now stood behind Kosum.

"Don't look at her, look at me! One of the witches gave us this herb for my mom. It started to work but we need more, and she said she got it from you. So why haven't you mentioned that you had this and that it could help her?"

"Kosum, I'm sorry but I don't know what you're talking about. I told you when I first heard about your mother's state that I searched every potion I had, and we even tried some, but you know nothing worked. Who is this witch and what herb exactly did they say they got from me?" Blair asked, standing her ground.

"It was—" Kosum began before completely forgetting the name of the herb. She clicked her fingers repeatedly, angrily, trying to jog her memory.

"Nkechi, do you remember what it was called?" Blair prompted.

"Erm, I think she said the something of Hecate?" Nkechi proposed, hoping that Blair might recognise it enough to know what they were talking about.

Blair's face changed at the sound of Hecate, which didn't go unnoticed by Kosum.

"The Heart of Hecate… I'm so sorry, Kosum, that witch is indeed right, that herb might just do the trick. But you must know I wasn't trying to hide anything from you. I genuinely forgot. You see, it's not easy to come by. The last vial I sold was years ago. Obviously the witch you encountered must've been the buyer," Blair confessed.

"Well, where did you get it from, then?" Kosum demanded rudely.

Blair knew Kosum's anger came from a place of love and desperation, so chose not to react to it.

"Oh, it was years ago," she said. "I was travelling the world in search for new and rare potion ingredients. I found it in England. I visited a pair of young potion brewers, somewhere in the North – Yorkshire perhaps – and I purchased it from them."

"Could you be any less specific?" Kosum groaned.

Nkechi nudged her and gave her side eye for being rude. Blair was a humble host, but she'd surely only take so much misplaced aggression.

"It was a young witch and warlock. I believe the boy's name was Alexander but I can't be sure. I'm sorry, Kosum, that's all I can remember."

By that point Kosum could see by Blair's wide, doe-like

eyes she was sincere.

"Thank you. And I'm sorry I barged in like this," Kosum replied, sheepishly looking back at Blair's twin daughters whom she had so rudely pushed past.

"It's okay, Kosum, you're emotional about your mother. It's to be expected, and you thought that I was adding to the pain you're feeling. Though now I hope that if you ever feel that way about me again, you'll first give me the chance to explain myself before jumping to conclusions. Besides, you could always pick up the phone and call. I'm a hedge witch, not a cavewoman." She smiled, lovingly cupping Kosum's cheek as a single tear flowed down it.

"Deal," Kosum sniffed, trying to keep her emotions in check.

"I guess we better be booking some flights," Nkechi commented.

"Yeah, c'mon, we should go. Thanks for the lead, Blair."

"No worries, my sweet. I shall call you if I remember anything else."

"Thank you."

Blair walked the girls back to their car and waved them goodbye as they began the next leg of their journey to save Kwanjai.

Nkechi and Kosum had spent the last t two weeks searching the northern towns of England in the hope they might find a warlock by the name of Alexander. It seemed like their search was failing for the most part as in each place they visited, a local witch simply sent them to the neighbouring town.

Nkechi was beginning to tire – they hadn't had much in the way of a break since they arrived – but Kosum needed the next recommendation to be the right one. She needed Alexander to be there.

"Kosum, we've been here for two weeks and we still haven't got any real leads. Please, can we just take a break?" Nkechi pleaded, as they traipsed the streets of yet another town in Yorkshire.

"We have so made progress. We've narrowed it down to the next town over," Kosum defended, walking at a faster pace than Nkechi.

"Have we, though? How do we know any of these people have been telling the truth?" Nkechi couldn't help but feel like they were on a wild goose chase.

Kosum stopped in her tracks and turned to back to Nkechi.

"The truth is, I don't know if any of them are telling the truth. But I have no choice other than to believe them, because if not, then my mom might be in a coma for ever and I can't accept that as her fate."

Of course, Kosum knew that Nkechi was just being realistic, but Kosum didn't have the luxury of logical thinking.

"I understand, and I'm sorry. You know I want nothing more than to save your mom, too. But that doesn't change the fact that we're both exhausted. We *need* a break. Please can we just stay at a B&B tonight and regroup? We can head back out tomorrow morning after a goodnight's sleep. Deal?"

"Yeah, okay."

Kosum took a seat upon a nearby bench while Nkechi

scrolled through her phone to find them a B&B. Kosum took a deep breath of fresh, English countryside air and soon realised her nostrils were filled with the scent of manure from the local farms. She gagged a little but slowly became used to it. She looked around at the stunning centuries-old buildings surrounding her, and for the first time since arriving admired the beauty on offer.

I wish Mom could see this, she thought to herself.

Nkechi, after a few minutes of Googling managed to find a suitable nearby B&B. The Fork and Scythe was a cosy little tavern-cum-bed and breakfast in the centre of the village, built hundreds of years ago in large, irregular-shaped sandstone blocks.

"Hey, I found a place to stay," Nkechi said, offering her hand to pull Kosum up off the bench.

"Okay," she answered, taking Nkechi's hand with a smile. Nkechi showed Kosum the quaint B&B and the one room left available. Kosum took the phone and booked it. It wasn't quite up to Kosum's standards but she didn't want to waste any more time.

They arrived after a twenty-minute walk. Their room was small to say the least. Though everything was small compared to American sizing. It was only for one night, and Nkechi was more than used to living in cramped conditions. Kosum, on the other hand, would surely have to adjust, though she was far too distracted with their goal to worry about the accommodation.

The room had a sooty fireplace and two single beds a foot apart. The girls hopped onto the beds which smacked their asses with force as they hit the world's hardest mattresses.

"Oh my god, these beds are amazing," Kosum said sarcastically, sprawling herself all over the bed on the left side of the room which may as well have been a stone slab.

"Ha-ha, I know they're crap, but it's just for one night. Now, c'mon, let's go get a drink. We're legal here, ya know!" Nkechi exclaimed, pushing Kosum playfully.

"Yeah, I know. You go get a table and drinks – I'll be down in a minute."

"What should I get you?"

"A fruity cocktail," Kosum winked.

"Something tells me this isn't the kind of place that would do fruity cocktails," Nkechi chuckled, "but I'll see what I can do."

Nkechi ventured down into the pub which was awash with British lads holding a pint in each hand.

Meanwhile, Kosum sat on her bed in silence as she tried to mentally catch up with reality. She had been so persistent over the past two weeks that she hadn't ever stopped to process what was actually happening. She had been a woman on a mission, and yet she couldn't help but think she was failing that mission. Kosum pulled out a folded-up photo from her Gucci purse. She unfolded it to reveal a picture of her mother and stared deeply into her face. Her hands lay limp over her legs with the photo displayed in her open palms as she gently stroked her mother's face with her thumb.

"I'm sorry, Mom. I can't believe this is happening. Sometimes I even forget you're lying there, and then I feel even worse when I remember. But I promise, Mom, I promise I'm gonna get you out of this." Kosum kissed the picture and lovingly stared at it for another moment before returning it to her purse. She dried her eyes with the cuff of her long-sleeved, skin-tight gym top and headed down to meet Nkechi.

By now, even more lads had flooded into the pub. Apparently, there was a local 'footy' match on tv according to the barmaid. The pub was dimly lit, full of dark oak furniture, and was carpeted, which only confused the girls.

Nkechi waved Kosum over to the booth where she sat; a half-battered booth she had managed to secure after outpacing two, potbellied, balding middle-aged men.

Kosum questioned what drink Nkechi had bought for her, staring at the groovy, brown glass bottle.

Nkechi saw her wince.

"It's strawberry and lime cider. I think that's as fruity as you're gonna get here, to be honest."

"I guess it'll do," Kosum sighed, before bravely taking a sip. "Huh, that's actually pretty good. What did you get?"

"Well, I asked for a beer and the barmaid asked me which one. I didn't recognise any of them, so I just said surprise me."

"Is it good?" Kosum prompted.

"Yeah, it's great, but I still don't know what it's called."

Kosum smirked.

"Anyway, have you spoken to Nicole recently? You probably talk to her more than I do these days."

"Yeah, briefly. She's okay, I just can't wait to see her in person again and give her a big hug," Kosum confessed.

"It will be nice to see her and my auntie again. Though I wish it was under better circumstances than starting a war with the voodoo king."

"Hey, we're not starting the war, we're finishing it. He started the war when he killed your dad all those years ago.

And quite frankly I've got a lot of pent-up aggression that I can't wait to take out on kicking that guy's ass," Kosum asserted, grasping her bottle and taking another swig.

"I guess you're right," Nkechi mumbled, staring at the beer that she had sandwiched between her palms. Her fingers wrapped around it, and as the condensation began to drench her hands she finally let go and snapped out of her daydream.

"Nkechi, are you all right?"

"Huh?" Nkechi replied, as her exhausted, sunken eyes turned to face Kosum.

"You've been through a lot this year and you haven't really talked much about what happened with Charlie. You know it's not your fault what happened, right?"

"I know. It's just, how do you go from loving someone to hating someone that quickly? I know I should hate him but I just, I don't know how to," she sighed, anxiously re-clutching her pint glass.

"Nkechi, I know it's hard and complicated, but you are allowed to mourn him. For the best part of a year, you were falling in love with him, and we all thought he loved you, too. You don't need to feel guilty about missing him. You're entitled to feel however you feel," Kosum smiled, taking Nkechi's hand and holding it in her own.

"Thanks, Kosum."

"And when you are ready to move on, me and Nicole will be your wing women." Kosum chuckled, trying to lighten the mood.

Nkechi smiled, forgetting about her emotional torment for a split second.

As the girls moved onto their second round, they were

soon interrupted by the two men Nkechi had beaten to the booth earlier. They had clearly drunk too much and were brazen with their opinions.

"Hey, Jeff, mate, what do you say we buy these *birds* a couple of drinks and they can share *our* booth?" the grotesque man spoke before glugging half of his pint.

"Sounds good to me, Carl," the friend responded, licking his lips like a lion eyeing up its prey.

"Thanks, but no thanks," Kosum asserted. "We were here first, and we don't feel like sharing. Sorry." She shrugged, grimacing.

Nkechi could already see the kind of men they were – entitled and predatory. She kept her fists clenched beneath the table, frustrated.

Clearly unimpressed by Kosum's nonchalant attitude to their advances, Carl said, "You know, ladies, this pub is well-known for being haunted and I just wouldn't feel right leaving you two all alone and defenceless." His voice sounded intimidating. He then confidently took a swig of his beer before wiping his mouth with the back of his hand and once again licking his lips, this time looking Nkechi in the eye as he did so.

Nkechi was growing tired of their antics, and Carl was beginning to rile her.

"Like she said, we're not looking to share our booth. And let me assure you, I'd feel more protected if I were sitting next to a Teletubby than one of you assholes," Nkechi scalded.

"Nice British-themed burn," Kosum whispered to Nkechi.

"Good thing I like 'em feisty, aye, Jeff? Nothing gets me going more than when they fight back," Carl spoke as he slid into the booth, close enough for Nkechi to feel his grossly hot, drunken breath on her face. Carl placed his hand on Nkechi's leg as Jeff mirrored his actions on the opposite side of the booth with Kosum.

"I think you boys better fuck off!" Kosum roared as she used her telekinesis to knock Carl's beer into his lap.

Carl jumped up releasing Nkechi's thigh from his grip.

"What the fuck!"

"It must have been one of these bitches, Carl," Jeff concluded, being the omniscient detective he was.

"*Us*? But we didn't move a muscle," Kosum commented innocently.

"It must have been the *ghosts*," Nkechi added with a sly smile.

The two men's faces began to screw up in anger; they knew Kosum and Nkechi were to blame somehow, even if they couldn't prove it. Carl was foaming at the mouth as he went to lift his arm, readying to hit one of them. Nkechi slipped into his mind faster than she had ever done with anyone before. It was much easier to do as he was so drunk. It was like overcoming a baby's mind. Now in the driver's seat, she manipulated Carl's arm and smacked Jeff in the face.

"Jesus, Carl. What the fuck are you doing?" Jeff shouted, holding his now blood-filled nose.

Through Carl's body, Nkechi replied with another punch and then another. Then Jeff finally started hitting back.

"Okay, Nkechi, that's enough!" Kosum stated, pushing Nkechi in the shoulder.

Nkechi left Carl's mind, where he then found himself, mid fight, being dragged out by some of the younger lads that had been watching football on the television. They were surprisingly courteous to Nkechi and Kosum.

One of them wore a Sheffield United shirt, the other was shirtless. They nodded a smile to the girls as they dragged the two embarrassed men out of the tavern.

At least not all men are ignorant dicks, Kosum thought as she politely smiled back at the lads removing Carl and Jeff.

"Jeff, stop. It was them two bitches, they did something to me," Carl shouted, kicking and screaming.

"Fuck off, Carl, you started it, you prick!"

"Don't let the door hit you on the way out," Nkechi said under her breath.

"Hey, are you all right? You really went for those guys," Kosum asked, shocked that Nkechi had possessed the man without a second thought.

"They deserved it, didn't they? Besides, I thought they were gonna hit us," Nkechi said, refusing to excuse her actions.

"Well, yeah, you're right. Just wanted to make sure that you were okay."

"I'm fine. I just feel sorry for all the girls who don't have magic. I mean, how many girls have had to sit here and take shit from gross guys like that?" Nkechi commented, shuddering in disgust.

"I guess we're the lucky ones, in some convoluted way." Kosum joined Nkechi's glum outlook, until a lady approached their table.

"Hey there. I saw what you did. Cool powers.," said the twenty something woman, seemingly coming from nowhere, with a glass of wine in hand.

"What do you mean?" Kosum asked, side eyeing Nkechi

subtly to get her attention.

"Your magic," she whispered, her free hand cupping the side of her mouth. "It was pretty impressive what you did to those guys." She stopped for a moment as she looked at Nkechi and Kosum's concerned faces. "Oh!" she exclaimed, playfully slapping her forehead. "I'm a witch, too," she whispered cupping her hand to her face once again. "God, where are my manners? My name's Ava. What are your names?" Ava asked in a thick Yorkshire accent. She smiled as she waited for their reply, innocently tucking her long, curly, mousey-blonde hair behind her ear.

She was a tall woman with full, rosy cheeks and a curvaceous body. She wore a tight dress with confidence and had a smile that could melt anyone's heart.

"Hi, Ava. I'm Kosum and this is Nkechi. We're from New York. We're trying to track down a warlock in the neighbouring town," Kosum explained.

"Alderdale?"

"Yes, that's the one," Nkechi confirmed.

"I actually live in Alderdale. I'm just here for a Tinder date but they haven't shown up. They always say they're open-minded about the fact I'm trans online, but as soon it comes to meeting in person, they chicken out," she moaned though didn't appear to be too upset.

"Aw, sorry to hear you got stood up. Trust me when I say I know what it feels like to deal with shitty guys," Nkechi commented.

"Yeah, I guess idiots live in all corners of the world, huh?" she cackled. "Anyway, enough moping over guys. Who is it you're looking for?" she asked, her electric blue eyes almost glowing at them.

"Someone called Alexander," Kosum answered. "That's all we know.".

"Well, bloody hell, love, you've just hit the jackpot. There's only one warlock named Alexander in Alderdale and Alex is my best mate. We own a bakery together." She laughed at the coincidence. "Wait, what do you need him for? He's not in trouble, is he?" she added, worried.

"No, no. We actually need his help. My mom is in a coma back home, and apparently he has the only thing that might save her – the Heart of Hecate," Kosum explained.

"Hmm, it doesn't ring a bell, but Alex has always been the academic one so I'm sure he'll know exactly what it is. Listen, I'm staying here tonight, originally for more *selfish* reasons," she winked. "But I'll happily take you to him tomorrow, if you want?"

"That would be great! Thank you, Ava," Kosum beamed.

"Do you wanna join us for a drink?" Nkechi invited, creating a space beside her.

"Sure." Ava returned the smile and slid into the booth, next to Nkechi, with much more grace than Carl, though she did nearly spill her wine.

"So, when did you and Alex first meet?" Kosum asked.

"Er, when we we're like eleven. We went to high school and then to sixth form together. We've kinda just always been besties. We studied catering, and then after a few years of working for crappy chefs, we scraped enough money together to buy an old shop and renovate it into what is now – the best bakery in town."

"Wow, that's a much better meet cute than ours, huh,

Nkechi?" Kosum joked lovingly, the past now behind them.

"Ooh, go on, love, you've gotta let me in on the juicy goss now. How'd ya meet?" Ava asked, bringing her large glass of wine to her lips as her eyes squinted, ready to soak up the gossip.

"Honestly, it's too long a story –it would take all night," Nkechi explained.

"Hey, I've got all night. I certainly won't be watching that shite on the telly," Ava laughed, raising her glass to the ongoing football match.

"Okay. Well, it all started on the first day of freshman year…"

The three of them drank and told each other funny stories until last orders, then staggered arm in arm to their rooms. Their giggling and hiccups could be heard throughout the B&B.

"Night, girls," Ava hiccupped, closing her door for the night.

"Night," Nkechi and Kosum called back before drunkenly fumbling their room key into the door. They just about manged to turn it and stumbled onto their lumpy mattresses before passing out for the night.

The next morning, Nkechi and Kosum awoke to a heavy knocking on their door:

"Wakey, wakey, eggs and bakey. I'll be downstairs having a full English. I'll save you guys a seat." Ava's voice vibrated through the door and smacked the girls right in their hungover brains.

"Jesus, how can she be this chirpy? What time is it?" Kosum murmured, her eyes still glued shut.

Nkechi's eyes hurt as she looked at the bright display on her phone. "It's ten, and breakfast finishes at eleven, so we should probably get moving."

"Oh my god, Nkechi, I can't tell if I'm hungry or if I'm gonna hurl," Kosum cried, trying to lift her head off the pillow.

"I guess the only way to find out is to try and eat something. C'mon, let's get ready."

Twenty minutes later, the pair made it down to the restaurant where breakfast was being served. Ava was sitting with a full English comprised of two sausages, three slices of bacon, two fried eggs, mushrooms, tomatoes, hashbrowns, beans and, best of all, a side order of toast *and* fried bread.

"What's that?" Kosum drooled, staring at Ava's half-eaten meal.

"English fried food!" Nkechi exclaimed, also drooling. "Oh my god, Kosum, it's amazing. Charlie made it fo—" Nkechi stopped when she realised who she was talking about. Although Kosum had made it clear she was allowed to have good memories of Charlie, Nkechi didn't want to lie to herself anymore. Especially knowing in hindsight that the night they spent together had just been a ruse to steal her blood.

"Who's Charlie?" Ava asked, with a mouthful of food.

Kosum gave Ava a sharp look in the hope she would understand not to pursue the conversation and change the subject. She did.

"Hey, why don't you two head over to the drink stand over

there and I'll order another two of these plates for you," Ava smiled.

"Thanks," Kosum accepted gratefully as she took Nkechi over to get some juice and a latte.

"Oh, will you make me a cuppa whilst ya there please, cock?" Ava shouted across the restaurant, which would have been more embarrassing had the restaurant not been almost empty.

Kosum turned with a smile and waved at Ava, as if she had any idea of what she had just asked for.

"What's a cuppa and why are we cocks?" she whispered to Nkechi.

Nkechi giggled. "I'll explain – I've picked up quite a bit of British slang since we've been here."

The girls successfully returned with a tray of juices, lattes and a 'cuppa' for Ava after Nkechi had translated. Their plates arrived and they ravaged the food as if they hadn't been fed since they left New York. Kosum ate so fast that halfway through, she thought she might bring it back up.

"Damn, that was good!" Kosum admitted, leaving a clean plate. "Though, I'm defo gonna need a detox when we get back to the States. I mean, Brits think *our* food is greasy," she joked.

"Ahh, we make an equally as greasy breakfast to be fair. Right, back to business. I've messaged Alex and he's out doing some bits and bobs today, but he said we can meet him at our usual club tonight. It's called Sinners Only."

"Oh, is it a club for witches or something?" Nkechi's head popped up like a meerkat.

"No, ya muppet, it's a gay club," Ava laughed.

"Oh, I guess that makes sense," Nkechi chuckled. "I've never been to a gay club before."

"Me neither," Kosum added, looking a little more timid than usual. Kosum was comfortable in her sexuality now, but she still hadn't really mingled with any other queer people, other than Nicole of course. They had done much *mingling*.

"Bloody hell, girls, you haven't lived yet, then. Don't worry, me and Alex will show you a good time. I'm so excited for you guys to meet him. He's just the best. He really helped me through my transition in school; he's just always been my little inspirational, proud gay boy," Ava rejoiced.

"He sounds great. And I can see how much you love him," Nkechi smiled.

"Yeah…" She smiled for a second in admiration of her friend. "Right, enough soppy shite, let's go! I can show you around town while we kill time," Ava suggested, linking arms with Nkechi and Kosum.

They spent the rest of the day exploring Alderdale, home to some of England's oldest buildings and, in true British summer fashion, they were drenched by rain during the afternoon. It was all in good fun though, something Kosum was in much need of.

After being treated to dinner by Ava at the swankiest restaurant in town, the three of them headed into the centre where Ava led them to Sinners Only. It was one of only two gay bars in the area. The other attracted older gays who wanted to reclaim their glory days. Some of them were genuinely cute older men with inspiring stories, while others were usually married and just looking for a gullible twink to fool around with.

From the outside, the club didn't stand out. It looked just like every other building on the street, , but once you passed the bouncers and cloakroom, it became a gay utopia. There was a huge dance floor with booths along each side and a stage at the back of the room. It was already heaving with people and the strobe lighting revealed faces intermittently.

Ava gave the girls a rundown of the kinds of gays in the club.

"Right d'ya see them there?" Ava shouted, pointing to a couple of skinny guys in cropped tank tops. "They're the harmless twinks; they'll just be shouting 'yas queen' all night. The worst they will do is tell you about their sugar daddy who won't come out for them. "Now those over there," she said, looking over at three beefy guys with beards and flannel shirts, "they're ya bears. Some are muscly, others are a bit podgy, like me," she winked. "But they tend to be gentle giants.

"Those girls over there," she stated, pointing at a couple of drunken girls wooing and singing along to Madonna, "are the straight best friends – like you, Nkechi."

Nkechi wasn't sure if that was an insult, especially when Kosum laughed.

"Now, beware of the leather daddies and the pups. They're usually fine, but whatever you do, if they ask you to touch something, don't, cos ya don't know where it's been. Actually, that last bit goes for anyone. And as for the lesbians, from what you've told me, you guys probably know more about them than I do," she said winking at Kosum. "Now, let's get smashed."

"Wait, what about Alex?" Kosum asked, feeling slightly timid now after Ava's *Mean Girls* style clique run down.

"Oh, don't worry, he's not here yet. You'll know when he is though, *trust* me," Ava shouted with a wink over the deafening music as she squeezed her way through to the crowded bar.

Ava bought a round of drinks and rejoined Nkechi and Kosum. The atmosphere grew in intensity as even more LGBTQ+ youth flooded the dance floor. Smoke machines began to pour out, covering the floor in a murky silver which popped every colour of the rainbow when a strobe light hit it. They quickly downed a couple of vodka and cokes and were dancing around, trying their best not to slosh a drink on someone's shoes. That would've been a surefire way to either piss someone off *or* become their new best friend.

Ava noticed, as the crowd started to veer closer to the stage, that the main event was about to start.

"Ooh, it's showtime! C'mon, girls, grab my hand!" Ava screamed over the heavy baseline.

Nkechi and Kosum held hands as Ava charged her way through the human wall of screeching, excitable twinks, and found them a spot at the front of the stage.

"Best seats in the house. Am I right?"

"Yeah! But what's the show?" Nkechi screamed to be heard.

"It's a drag show!" Ava replied, and with that the entire room went dark as a voice came through the speakers.

"Everybody, are you ready? Let me hear you scream! Sinners Only proudly presents Yorkshire's finest drag act, the Kitty Kat Dolls – Amber Whiskers, Pussy Galore and the Lioness," the voice belted, growing louder with every syllable.

Three, seven-foot drag queens appeared on stage with a spotlight beaming down on each of them. Ginger-haired Amber was curvy, dressed in a sparkly, dark green gown, standing front and centre. To her left was Pussy, a busty blonde donning a silver number with a thigh-high slit up one side. To her right was the Lioness. She had brown hair and dark caramel skin and wore a blue equally as sparkly dress which clung to her slim, supermodel frame. The three giant queens remained still in their fierce poses until the music hit.

What You Waiting For? by Gwen Stefani came on and Amber began singing to the gentle opening bars of the song in perfect pitch. Then the beat kicked in. Each of their dresses tore away as they spun, revealing sexy, sleek, star-spangled bodysuit versions of their dresses. As they began lip syncing, they hit every syllable perfectly while performing splits, tricks and death drops in a carefully choreographed routine. It was gay heaven. The girls felt tired just watching their energised act.

Although the entire group was amazing, it was clear that Amber was the 'Beyonce' of the trio. The first song flew by leaving the fans screaming in awe and, after a few more dance numbers, lip syncs and comedy performances, the show finally came to a close.

Nkechi and Kosum had become so enraptured by the performers that they had almost forgotten why they were there.

"That was amazing! Are there clubs like this back home?" Nkechi asked, looking to Kosum.

"I don't know, but there better be!" she replied, still shouting as she was temporarily deafened by the noise.

The queens had decided to mingle in the club after the performance, making the most of the attention and free drinks from fans. Twinks everywhere were losing their minds trying to get a selfie.

Suddenly, Amber spotted Ava sticking out like a sore thumb in the sea of short gays and headed straight for her.

"Ava!" Amber shouted, running over to give her a hug. "So, who are these two, then?" she asked, waving her finger in Nkechi and Kosum's direction.

"These are the New York girls I told you about," Ava answered, leaving Nkechi and Kosum confused as to how she knew a drag queen and, more importantly, why she had told the drag queen about them.

"Ooh, are they now? Bloody hell, they don't look very 'appy, do they?".

"Shit, that's my fault, they ain't got a clue who you are. Girls, this is Amber Whiskers, otherwise known as Alex Cavendish," Ava explained.

"Oh!" Nkechi and Kosum replied in tandem, wiping the confused look off their faces.

"That was an incredible show, by the way!" Nkechi complimented, once the shock had worn off.

"Awe, thanks, chuck."

Nkechi just smiled as she assumed it was another Northern term of endearment.

"Now then, I'm aware you need my assistance, but that'll have to wait until morning because I'm already tipsy and I plan on getting pissed out me head. So, what do you say, girls? Indulge a big-titted, ginger drag queen in a sequined green leotard and get drunk with us?"

Kosum and Nkechi looked at one another seeming to communicate through eye contact and turning back to Alex.

"Fuck it, let's get wasted!" Kosum shouted. *One more night can't hurt,* she thought to herself. After all, they had finally found the source of what they needed – hadn't they?

"Or, as the Brits say, let's get shitfaced!" Nkechi screamed, having been drunk for a while already.

The four of them threw back shot after shot and danced until they couldn't any longer and, in true British fashion, ended up at a kebab shop in the early hours of the morning, before throwing up in a taxi on the way to Alex's house.

CHAPTER 3

The Heart of Hecate

The next morning, Nkechi and Kosum woke with killer hangovers once more. At least this time they were on a much comfier bed. They'd slept together in Ava's room while Ava bunked in with Alex. Ava told the girls to take a shower and get dressed then she'd take them to hers and Alex's bakery, Sweet Tooth, where Alex had already been for the past hour preparing to open up.

Once ready, Nkechi and Kosum were driven to the bakery by Ava in her soccer-mom-style suburban SUV. Ava loved having a bigger car. Though she certainly didn't need the seven seats as she had no kids, she always thought it would be handy in a car chase scenario. Her 4x4 would be able to plough through traffic. Of course, she'd never had an opportunity to do that. It was just a fantasy of hers. After all, Ava and Alex's lives were nowhere near as crazy as Nkechi and Kosum's. The biggest drama in their lives currently was deciding whether to open the bakery for a fifth day a week. Though there wasn't much in the way of a decision to make as neither of them really wanted to. One of the perks to being your own boss is deciding to only work a four-day week.

"Here we are, Sweet Tooth. Ain't she gorgeous?" Ava smiled as she pulled into a parking space, providing the perfect view of the fancy lit-up sign and red and white striped awning which covered the entrance.

They hopped out and Nkechi and Kosum were instantly drawn to the windows as they saw the amazing display of cakes and pastries.

"Wow, I can't believe you guys own this place," Kosum said in amazement.

"It looks beautiful," Nkechi salivated as she gawped at the delicious-looking display.

"Yeah well, we went in on this place together when it was nothing but a rotten carcass of a building. I'm pretty sure kids were using it for drugs and stuff. It took a lot of TLC, but three years later and it's the most popular bakery in town. And we also sell potion-brewing ingredients to the local witches. Alex's cousin works out front, she's also a witch and if a customer uses the special code, we know they're here for potion supplies rather than cakes."

"So, what are the magic words?" Kosum asked, humouring her.

"Abracadabra," Ava answered, chuckling to herself.

"Seriously?" Nkechi questioned.

"Yup, sometimes the most obvious place to hide is the best one. Anyway, c'mon, let's get inside. Alex should be in the back."

As they walked through the front of the shop, Nkechi's stomach growled and Ava heard.

"Oh, hey, I forgot you girls haven't eaten since last night. Help yourself to some pastries," Ava smiled as she waved her hand to the glass cabinet full of breakfast pastries.

There was everything from croissants to *pain au chocolat* to

Danish custard pastries. Nkechi helped herself to a plateful, taking almost one of each kind. Kosum, on the other hand, was back into work mode and wasn't hungry. As much fun as it had been indulging in the last two nights, it was time to actually make headway in sourcing the herb she needed.

Ava led them into the kitchen, the back wall full of ovens. There was a U-shaped marble counter which ran along the remaining walls and a humongous island made of the same material in the room's centre.

"Hi, guys, now that we're all finally sober, we can talk properly. So, you said you need something for your mum, right?" Alex asked, looking to Kosum as he washed the flour off his hands.

"Yeah, a hedge witch we know back home said that she bought it from you a few years back. The Heart of Hecate, she said it was called. Do you have any?"

"Oh, now that's gonna be a hard one. I've been putting off sourcing some more of that herb for a while because, well, it's a pain in the arse to get," Alex replied, scratching his head in thought.

"Why? Where do you get it from?" Nkechi asked, intrigued as she continued to stuff pastries into her mouth. "These are really good, by the way," she added, smiling with a mouth full of food, flakes of puff pastry covering her lips.

"The Heart of Hecate is a flower that only exists in one place on Earth and only grows during a lunar eclipse – otherwise known as a blood moon, if you're feeling particularly mystical," Alex explained.

"Well, when's the next blood moon?" Kosum asked hastily.

"Oh, I have a moon app on my phone, I'll check," Ava

interjected. "Say's here that the next lunar eclipse is... oh, forty days away. Sorry, Kosum."

"I can't wait that long. She might not survive that long. What am I going to do?" Kosum began to panic, and her breathing became shallow. As she played out the scenario of her mother dying over and over in her mind, her panic only grew, causing her to sink to the ground and gasp for air.

"Oh, my god, I think she's having a panic attack!" Nkechi shouted as she shoved her plate of pastries onto the counter and ran to her aid.

"Ava, you help Nkechi while I try to think of another way," Alex said as he placed his palms on the counter, racking his brain for a swifter solution.

"Kosum, look at me, you're having a panic attack. It's going to be okay." Ava spoke clearly to make sure a panicked Kosum could understand her. She got onto her knees and held Kosum by the shoulders. "I need you to breathe for me, Kosum. Just focus on my eyes, okay, and only listen to my voice. I want you to breathe in through your nose and count to five then breathe out doing the same."

Kosum attempted to do as Ava said but she kept spluttering through her breaths, unable to hold it for the full count.

"Okay, I'm going to count for you. Ready?"

Kosum nodded hastily, still feeling breathless.

Ava completed the breathing exercise alongside Kosum, counting for her and holding her hands to help calm her. Finally after a few times of Ava counting, Kosum managed to catch her breath.

"Hey, you're going to be okay. I promise we'll find a way to get you the herb; you're not leaving England without it.

Now, just keep breathing deeply and try to focus on happy thoughts until you feel calm enough to get up."

Kosum nodded with a look of thanks before closing her eyes and gently letting her head lean against the cupboard door behind her.

"Wow, that was amazing," Nkechi praised.

"Thanks, it's just what I used to do whenever I had them," Ava explained.

"Well, thank you for helping her." Nkechi smiled appreciatively.

"No problem, us witches gotta have each other's backs."

"I've got it!" Alex shouted from the other side of the kitchen island.

A few moments later, Kosum managed to get back on her feet to hear Alex's plan.

"So, it is a powerful spell, but between the four of us, I'm sure we can do it."

"What do we have to do?" Nkechi asked, as Kosum was still a little shaken up to fully engage in conversation.

"We're going to create our own blood moon!" he exclaimed. "We'll go tonight at sunset."

"Thank you," Kosum just about managed.

"You're welcome. I can only imagine what you're going through. My mum's like my best friend—"

Ava feigned a cough to cut Alex off.

"Oh, my god, I said *like*. Obviously, you're my best friend. That better?" He looked at Ava before rolling his eyes in jest.

Ava flitted her gaze elsewhere.

"Anyway, my point is that I'm sure we'd all feel the same way if we were in your boat right now. And on that note, I think this calls for some relaxing baking. Besides, we need to kill time somehow."

"Baking?" Kosum questioned.

"Yeah, it's a great way to relax," Ava added.

"But my nails are really cute, and I don't want to get dough in them," Kosum moaned, swiftly recovering from her panic attack and back to her usual self.

Nkechi laughed at Kosum's excuse, before looking down at her own nails, which weren't as manicured as Kosum's. *Maybe I should treat myself to a manicure at the end of summer?* Nkechi thought to herself.

"You can use your telekinesis instead," Nkechi pointed out.

"Exactly. Right, come on. Ava and Kosum, you stay on that side, Nkechi you come over here with me. And don't worry, the time will fly by, trust me," Alex announced rather ominously.

"Let's do some decorating, that's much more fun than the actual baking part," Ava said as she passed Kosum a piping bag full of buttercream.

"Okay, making things look beautiful I can do," Kosum laughed.

As they began frosting cupcakes, on the other side of the room Nkechi and Alex were knuckle deep in some doughnut dough which had just finished proving.

"So, Ava filled me in on your life story last night. Sounds like you're quite the witch, taking on a satanist and a crazy boyfriend." Alex tried his best to compliment Nkechi.

Nkechi laughed modestly. "Yeah, it's certainly not how I saw my freshman year of college going."

"I bet! How are you dealing with everything? Not that you have to tell me anything, of course. It's just that sometimes I find that telling someone I don't know is easier than telling a best friend."

"I'm okay," Nkechi mumbled.

"Now that was the most unconvincing okay I think I've ever heard," Alex chuckled, gently nudging his shoulder against hers.

Nkechi smirked to herself as she too knew she was lying.

"It's just a weird situation. How do you get over someone you loved but are now supposed to hate?"

"Well, I'm not gonna pretend that I know everything because I definitely don't, but I do know a thing or two about heartbreak. I think that maybe you should try to separate the two Charlie's and say goodbye to the boy you loved. But whatever you do, don't use magic!" Alex said sternly. "I've tried it so that others like you don't have to."

"Why, what happened?" Nkechi asked as they began to roll out the doughnuts, or in Nkechi's case, beat up the doughnuts. It would seem that one thing Nkechi hadn't picked up from her mother was her cooking skills.

"I dated a closeted guy once and I was really falling for him. I obviously knew he wasn't out yet and I was okay with that. Until I found out why he wasn't out. He had a wife and kid. Now, I'm all for discovering who you are, no matter how late in life, but have the common decency and respect to do that without lying and hurting others. Anyway, I was so angry and hurt that I just wanted the pain to go away as soon as possible. So, me and Ava performed a spell for me to forget our whole relationship. But what I didn't realise is that

I am the person I am today because of the things I've gone through in life. Experiences like that, no matter how shitty they are, shape you. I became a different person without those memories and not a particularly nice one to be around. The worst part was that I had no idea why I was being that way. Luckily, Ava saw sense and reversed the spell, and of course it hurt like hell to have all those memories rush back and to get over him again but feeling that was much better than whatever life I was living where I forgot about him."

"That's crazy. But to be honest, you don't really have to worry about that with me – I've already had memories taken and returned once before and I don't intend on ever letting anyone change them again. But I think you're right about the other thing – I should do something that brings me closure. I should say goodbye to the kind Charlie I knew."

"Bloody hell, kid, you have been through a lot," Alex joked, lightening the mood.

"Yeah, but haven't we all?" she said, still pounding the dough.

"Okay, I'm gonna need you to stop taking all that aggression out on my poor doughnuts. You've somehow made them square."

They both laughed as Alex held up Nkechi's doughnut. It was truly a baking monstrosity.

"Hey, it worked, though. I do feel much more relaxed now," she said, mid laughter.

Alex swiftly fixed all the doughnuts that Nkechi had disfigured. Nkechi looked over and smiled at Kosum, and it was only then that she saw through the window daylight beginning to fade.

Nkechi looked confused.

"What's wrong, Nkechi?" asked Kosum.

"The sun, it's setting already. I could swear we've been here less than thirty minutes."

"I told you time would *fly* by," Alex commented, smiling as he placed the shaped doughnuts on a tray and back into the prover.

"But how?" Nkechi asked.

"This kitchen is enchanted – it exists outside of Earth's time. That means that if I woke up late one morning and had to make hundreds of cakes, I could do it easily by making time go slower outside. And it also means that if I have too much time to kill, like today, I can do the opposite and make hours out there feel like thirty mere minutes in here." Alex explained in layman's terms.

"Okay, that hurts my brain," Kosum said as she tried to wrap her head around the idea.

"So, how powerful are you?" Nkechi asked, impressed by the magic at play.

"Probably not as powerful as you, but I am older, and over time I guess a warlock just picks up a thing or two," Alex answered modestly.

"What he really means is we kept making up spells and rituals until one actually worked," Ava laughed. "He just likes to be theatrical," she teased.

"Oh, my god, I was trying to sound cool for once." Alex feigned annoyance.

Nkechi and Kosum giggled at the bickering pair as it was like looking into a mirror of the future. Nkechi and Kosum would love to have a business together one day, while still managing to remain best friends, like Ava and Alex clearly were.

"Should we be getting ready now?" Kosum asked, a gentle nudge to remind them of the task at hand.

"Yes, sorry, let's get going. You guys head to the car – we can drive the first part of the way – and I'll bring the supplies."

Five minutes later everyone reconvened in Ava's car. Alex hopped in the front passenger seat with a lap full of so-called spell equipment. There was a palm-sized piece of moonstone, a jar, an athame, and a deliciously indulgent, red velvet cake.

"Hey, what's the cake for?" Kosum questioned as she pulled herself up and poked her head through the middle of the two front seats like a child.

"Well, we need to offer Hecate a gift in return for her help, so let's hope she likes our baking, aye, Ava?" Alex strapped his belt across himself being careful not knock the cake.

"Er yeah, here's hoping," Ava nervously smiled, having never had so much resting on her baking skills before. She stuck the car in gear and set off.

Alderdale was a small town and soon they reached the outskirts where the road slowly turned into a gravely dirt track. Eventually they came to the end of the track, where they would have to venture the rest of the way on foot.

They got out of the car and Alex took charge carrying the rucksack full of the supplies for their spell while Ava carried the cake box. As they began their trek through the woods, it was almost pitch-black, though luckily a clear sky meant the rising moon garnered some natural light. They lit the trail before them with their phone torches to ensure they weren't going around in circles, especially as Alex was navigating this expedition solely from his faded memory of the trip.

Alex led them deeper into the woods until the trees became so large that the intertwined branches weaved in and out of one another to create a natural roof, obscuring the moon. Nkechi and Kosum were beginning to get wary of their surroundings. Every whistle of wind and rustling of a bush made them jump, which was ironic considering the powerful witches that they were.

"What was that?" Kosum jumped, after hearing a rather loud bone-crunching sound.

"I'm not sure but stay close. There are things in these woods that you don't want to come face to face with," Alex answered ominously.

"Like what?" Kosum asked, curious of what dangers she should prepare herself for.

"Well, werewolves for a start," he replied rather calmy, as if they were low down on the list of likely creatures to kill you.

"Werewolves?" Kosum questioned, rather sceptically.

"Yeah, they might not exist in NYC but here in England we're exposed to much older magic."

"Yeah but werewolves, really? What's next? A yeti?" Nkechi asked, still not buying in to the idea either.

"He's not joking, ya know. My Auntie Kath was eaten by a yeti," Ava said, corroborating Alex's story.

"Is that supposed to be another weird British joke we don't get?" Kosum asked, as she accidentally shone her torch in Ava's face.

"Ow!" she shouted, before raising her arm to cover eyes. "And no, why would that be a joke? Though it happened when she was in the Himalayan Mountains so we should be safe here."

"Shit, sorry, and sorry about your aunt," Kosum apologised, feeling like an idiot.

"Oh, don't be, we all hated Auntie Kath anyway; she was a right bitch," Ava said, breaking into an infectious laughter.

They continued to traipse their way through the ever-thickening forest. The floor was smothered in deep moss which they sank into a little every time they stepped, taking extra effort to move through it.

An hour had passed, and to the girls it seemed as though they hadn't gained much ground at all.

"How much further is it?" Kosum asked, her feet becoming tired, not to mention her eyes as she struggled to stay awake. Even after two weeks of being in the UK, Kosum had never gotten over the jet lag and was in a time zone all of her own. Though the time-travelling bakery certainly hadn't helped to reset her natural clock.

"Er, not much further. We should be coming up on a river soon and then we follow that downstream to a waterfall, and behind that is a cave. That will be our destination," Alex answered, hoping that he had indeed been going the right way thus far.

A few minutes later, Alex heard the rushing of the river and called out to the girls to follow him as he picked up the pace and started to run in its direction. He could just about see a clearing up ahead where the trees didn't inhabit every square inch, as they had done up until that point. The girls tried to follow in his tracks, but he was like a whippet in full sprint.

"Oi! Slow down, ya plonker!" Ava called out to him,

puffing air as she tried to keep up.

Alex always loved running; he did it most mornings before work. Ava was not a runner; she hated it. A brisk walk was more her speed, literally.

Alex turned back and shouted, "Shut up and catch ya arses up!" As he did so he didn't notice the approaching cliff. Before he could turn his gaze back to see what was happening, he fell straight off the edge.

"Shit! Alex!" Ava screamed as she saw his silhouette drop below ground level.

Kosum had been the closest to him and now ran faster than she had ever done before. She slid to the edge of the cliff where he was still freefalling. She reached her hands out and caught him with her telekinesis, his body inches away from being torn apart by the river rapids below. She levitated him back over the cliffside to safe ground, before plopping him onto the floor and dropping to her knees in exhaustion.

"Jesus Christ, Alex, you fucking numpty! Watch where you're going. You almost died!" Ava shouted, dishing out a bit of tough love.

"Yeah, sorry. I got a little carried away there, huh?" Hysteria at his near-death experience made him giggle. "Thanks, Kosum."

"No… probs…" she panted, still on her knees.

"Well, at least we're here. See, I said not much further," he smirked.

"Ya know, I didn't think I'd ever meet a crazier pair than me and Kosum, but I think you guys just topped us," Nkechi joked.

"You're not kidding," Ava chuckled.

"So, how are we getting down there to the river, then?" Kosum asked as she pointed down to the riverbank a hundred feet down.

"Can't you—" Nkechi began to ask Kosum.

"No, I cannot levitate us all down there, especially not after that. I'm drained."

"Don't worry, I've got this one covered, guys," Ava said, rubbing her hands together to warm them up before walking to the edge of the cliff.

"How?" Nkechi asked.

"I can orb us down there."

"You can what us down there?" Kosum interjected.

"Orb. It's my natural power, like teleporting," she explained.

"You mean to say we could have teleported here this whole time?" Kosum asked, with a slight crazed twitch in one eye.

"No, it doesn't work like that. I need to be able to see where I'm going."

"Hmm, OK, I guess I'll let you off, then," Kosum teased.

"Everybody, hold hands and I'll get us down there," Ava announced to the group.

The four of them joined hands and Ava closed her eyes, having now seen their destination. Ava's body began to turn into a spiral of what looked like fireflies and, in turn, so did the bodies of the others. The tiny white orbs of light gently descended in a swarm down the cliff and over the river to the safety of the riverbank on the other side. They then materialized back into the four of them. Most of the ground around them was made of slate which was slippery from the river spray.

"Woah, that felt euphoric," Nkechi said, trying not to slip.

"Yeah, that was amazing. Why don't you do that all the time?" Kosum added.

"Well, it's not exactly something you can do with mortals around," Ava pointed out.

"Okay yeah, that's a fair point," Nkechi chuckled, before slipping. She stretched out her hand and Kosum grabbed it, holding her up before her head smacked onto the rock below. For a second, a memory flashed in front Nkechi's eyes. It was last Christmas when she, Kosum and Charlie went ice-skating and how she'd been like *Bambi* on ice.

"You okay?" Kosum asked.

"Yeah, fine," Nkechi answered, putting on a brave smile. This was about saving Kosum's mom; she couldn't make it about her and how she felt about Charlie.

"If you're both all right, follow me, it's not far now," Alex said as he spotted the waterfall in the distance.

They arrived at the foot of the waterfall. There was a ledge being beaten down upon by the constant heavy flow of water. Nkechi positioned her hand to bend the path of the water so that they could slip through to the cave entrance behind. Only when they had all made it to the other side did Nkechi release the water from her grip and allow it to seal the cave behind them once more.

"Now, from what I remember, the Heart of Hecate can only be grown under the blood moon, meaning that we need to find the spot in the cave where it opens to the sky. I think it's in this general direction, so just keep your eyes peeled," Alex explained as they edged further into the damp, musky-smelling cave.

"Great, more walking," Kosum groaned.

"Come on, Kosum, we're almost there," Nkechi smiled, with a friendly pat on the shoulder.

"Yeah, I know. Sorry, I'm just exhausted. I don't want you to think I'm ungrateful though, I do really appreciate what you're all doing for me.".

"Hey, don't sweat—"

"Ah!" Kosum screamed, as a flock of bats came futtering down from the cave ceiling. Everyone ducked, immediately covering their heads as hundreds of bats flew deeper into the cave.

"Oh, my god, that was like some horror movie shit."

"I suppose they're vampires, then?" Nkechi joked.

"Don't be silly, real vampires don't turn into bats. Besides, British bats are tiny. It's the ogres you should be really scared of," Alex corrected.

"What, like *Shrek*?" Kosum sniggered.

"Girl, you wish *Shrek* was as bad as they came. No, imagine a ten-foot, overweight neanderthal-like beast who could pop your head like a grape."

"What the actual fuck? I thought England was supposed to be the tame version of the US, not have werewolves, vampires, ogres and God knows what other crazy shit!" Kosum exclaimed.

"Well, the mortal side is pretty normal, but there are more species of magical creatures out here than breeds of dog," Alex said nonchalantly.

"Then why don't any humans see them?" Nkechi chimed in.

"Because in the last two hundred years, humans developed

their weapons of war exponentially and magical creatures realised that if there was to be an all-out war, they'd lose. So, now they all live in deep pockets of wilderness in the UK. The carnivores usually live off deer and the odd dog and their owner who venture a little too close. Some humans do still see magical creatures, but no one in this day and age believes them, other than the diehard conspiracy theorists. I mean, look at the Loch Ness Monster, she gets spotted all the time, but no one can prove it. Though, it would be pretty funny to blow one of their minds and tell them that they're right about everything."

"You know, with all due respect, I really can't wait to go home," Kosum said, only half in jest.

"Speaking of which, we should probably follow the direction in which the bats went," Ava proposed.

"Why?" Nkechi asked.

"Because they obviously know a way out of here that we don't, which is probably the place we need to do our spell, ya know, under the blood moon," Ava explained.

"Good thinking, Ava. Let's go," Alex said, before once again taking the lead and lighting the way with his phone.

After twenty more minutes of walking through the cave, twisting, crouching and contorting their bodies to fit through the various shapes, they finally reached a small area open to the clear night sky.

"We're here!" Alex called out, as the girls finished squeezing themselves through the last tiny gap.

"Don't jinx it! The last time you said something like that you almost fell to ya death, remember?"

"Pfft, I dunno what you're talking about. I totally had that situation under control."

"God, these Brits sure do love their sarcasm, huh?" Kosum whispered to Nkechi.

"Yeah, it's a bit excessive," she muttered under her breath.

The cave opening was almost a perfect circle and about ten metres wide. However, the gap above them was only about half a metre wide, meaning that they'd only have one chance at the spell as the moon would surely pass over the gap in a matter of minutes.

Below it, was a large, smooth boulder with a flattened top coated in burgundy-coloured moss.

"This is where it'll grow from," Alex said, pointing to the mossy rock. "We'll have to be quick to harvest it. Even if all goes well, the flower will die as quickly as it blossoms. So, at the point it reaches its peak, we need to cut it and get it out from under the blood moon. Do you want to do that bit Kosum? For your mum?"

"Honestly, I'm not sure I want that pressure. Would someone else mind doing it?"

Nkechi volunteered without a second thought. "I'll do it, Kosum. Don't worry."

"Thanks, Nkechi."

"For the record, I totally would have done it too," Ava jumped in playfully, keeping the mood light.

"Thanks, Ava," Kosum chuckled.

"Okay, enough cutesy shit, let's get ready. We've only got one shot at this," Alex reminded them, gathering the group's attention. "I hope no one's squeamish because we have to use our blood to create the blood moon, though I suppose the clue was in the name, right?" He awkwardly chuckled.

"We've been through worse," Nkechi answered on behalf of herself and Kosum.

"I'm sure we can rustle up some healing potion when we get back," Ava smiled.

"Great, let's begin."

Alex placed the red velvet cake on one side of the large rock and placed the piece of moonstone on the other, the patch of moss between them, before taking the final object from his bag – the athame. They each took a turn slicing their palms, readying themselves for the spell to begin. Alex gave one last look at the girls to confirm they were ready. With a nod from each, and the moon taking its place directly above them, he began the spell.

"Oh, great Hecate, protector of witches, heed our call upon this night. Forgive our impatience as we humbly ask to harvest your magical flora to heal a fellow witch. We call upon your power to bring forth the blood moon. Take this cake as our offering and allow the moon to mimic our moonstone as we coat it in our blood."

The cake vanished before their eyes and a heavy wind circled around them – they were indeed feeling the presence of Hecate.

"Now!" Alex signalled to the girls. All four of them held out their wounded palms and squeezed droplets of blood over the moonstone. As each droplet plummeted onto the stone, a patch of the bright white moon was tainted red. Once the stone was fully coated in a powerful mix of their blood, the full lunar eclipse was formed. Almost instantaneously a small green seedling began to sprout from within the moss-covered rock. They watched closely as, under the blood moon's rays, the seedling quickly blossomed into a large, beautiful flower with long, pointed purple petals and a pompom-like yellow centre.

Once the flower had fully bloomed, Alex told Nkechi to snip it. She reached out with the athame to cut the flower, but from the roots up it was already beginning to wilt. Nkechi had to swiftly raise her hand in order to cut higher up the stem before it could be corrupted. She sliced it and pulled it into her chest. She closed her eyes in the madness of the moment, but as she reopened them and unfolded her hands, she saw a beautiful flower full of life.

"You did it!" Alex beamed.

"Yeah, well done, Nkechi!" Ava cheered.

"Thank you," Kosum smiled, as she became teary-eyed. For a second, she could relax now she had the means to save her mother, and they could finally leave that strange forest.

CHAPTER 4

A Whisper for Help

Once Alex had securely stored the Heart of Hecate in a jar in his bag, they began their perilous journey back to the car.

"So, how much oil does this little flower make?" Kosum asked, as they slowly made their way to the cave entrance.

"More than enough for your mum. As soon as we get back, I'll get to work on extracting the oil," Alex answered encouragingly.

"Oh, that's great! Thanks again, guys," Kosum smiled, as they reached the waterfall.

As before, Nkechi deflected the water off course so that they could pass through the narrow platform and back to the safety of dry land.

"I suppose that wasn't too bad, after all," Ava said, speaking too soon as all four of them began to feel a rumbling beneath their feet.

"Earthquake!" Nkechi and Kosum shouted.

"Wait, no," Alex said calmly, stopping the girls as they darted around for a safe space to lay low. "It's extremely rare to get earthquakes here."

"Then what is it?" Kosum asked, before the crashing of the waterfall began to get louder.

Alex turned to face the gorge at the base of the waterfall

and out jumped an ogre, causing water to splash in every direction. It must've been living in a part of the cave they hadn't ventured.

It was even bigger and scarier than Alex's description. It was at least twelve feet tall, with a deep scar that crossed the entirety of its face – a face that already looked like a deformed creature. It was hairless, wearing nothing but a patch of cloth covering its genitals.

Holding an old, uprooted tree trunk in one hand, it menacingly batted the trunk into its other hand before roaring at them. The four of them turned on their heels and ran. Ava called out for them to link hands so she could orb them back up to the top of the cliff. The ogre was hot on their trail though, and as each heavy foot hit the ground, it caused a ripple that lifted them up.

It began swinging the tree trunk as far as its long burly arms could reach. It was quickly gaining on them, and it took one large swing for Alex's head. The four of them managed to grab one another's hands just in time for Ava to do her thing and transform them into a flurry of orbs.

The tree trunk dispersed the orbs of light as they flew up to the cliff. The firefly-looking cluster materialized,. though the dispersing had left them all with a pounding headache. At least they had escaped.

Or so they thought.

Nkechi and Kosum took a second to widen their eyes and rub their foreheads before turning to Alex. He was looking a little light-headed, pale in the face and swaying slightly. They hoped he could still remember the way back despite the ringing in his head. Ava seemed rather unscathed by the transition; she was a pro at orbing and so a little knock off course wasn't enough to affect her.

They began to follow Alex when suddenly a thunderingly loud thud came from behind them and, chunks of dirt flew past their faces. The ogre had cleared the hundred-foot cliff with ease in just one jump and was right behind them once more.

"Run!" Ava screamed, the first to notice the ogre. Ogres were rather dim creatures but highly emotional and held a grudge. It wouldn't give up that easily.

"What the fuck, Alex! You didn't say that they were fucking ninjas, too!" Kosum shouted as they all raced through the forest.

As they ventured deeper into the wooded area, they hoped the closeness of the trees would create too tight a gap for the ogre to follow their path. But to their surprise, once again the ogre ran through just as quickly as them, easily knocking the trees down with a nudge of his shoulders.

"Can you throw him off course?" Nkechi shouted to Kosum as they ran for their lives.

"No, he's huge! Can't you use the trees or something?" she asked Nkechi.

"No, he's huge!" she retorted, which probably would've made them laugh if they weren't so close to becoming the ogre's midnight feast.

"What about you, Alex? You've not even told us your power yet!" Kosum called out as he continued to lead their sprint.

"I'm a conjurer," he admitted, panting. "I can conjure pretty much any inanimate object."

"Well, what are you waiting for, then? Conjure something to kick this guy's ass!"

"Okay! Okay… Kosum, can you throw me?" he asked, without context.

"What?"

"*Can you?*"

"I – yeah, sure."

"Okay, well get ready to do it when I tell you." Alex, still running, held one hand out and waved his other sideways as he ran. As his hand glided across the air, a large sword appeared behind it. "Hey, Nkechi can you light this bad boy on fire?"

"Okay," Nkechi replied, with a snap of her fingers. The sword began sparking before quickly becoming engulfed in flames.

"Now, Kosum, throw me straight at it," Alex called back to her.

"Damn, you're crazy, man. Here goes nothing."

They all ground to a halt and Kosum, using her telekinesis, swiftly launched Alex through the air in the direction of the ogre, who was still barrelling towards them. Alex positioned himself perfectly as he glided just above the ogre's head. He took his flaming sword and, as gracefully as one can, sliced the ogre's head clean off. Being the true performer he was, Alex landed perfectly while the others got covered in a congealed ogre blood.

"Ew!" Ava laughed at the ridiculous situation they found themselves in.

"What the fuck even is this place?" a blood-soaked Kosum moaned.

"Don't worry, we'll get you guys cleaned up," Alex said rather smugly as he had managed to avoid the literal blood bath.

Ava didn't think that was fair so flicked the blood from her hand onto his face.

Alex gagged. "Oh, my god, you absolute bitch, Ava!" Alex shouted, causing all of them to belly laugh.

"Maybe next time warn us there's gonna be an ogre," Kosum moaned, as they all began to walk back to the car.

"I swear, it wasn't there last time."

"Right, c'mon, you lot, let's get back home. I need a cuppa," Ava said, hurrying them along before any other magical creatures fancied their chances.

"Yeah, let's go. Though, I think I'm gonna need something stronger than a 'cuppa'," Nkechi chuckled.

By the time they made it back to Alex and Ava's apartment, it was three in the morning. Nkechi and Kosum had asked Alex if he needed any help extracting the oil but he kindly turned them down as he confessed that it would be easier for him to focus alone. Kosum was a little antsy to leave her mother's fate in someone else's hands but Nkechi calmed her thoughts as she reminded Kosum of everything Alex had done to help them so far. Instead they engaged in a quick nightcap before happily dropping straight back onto the spare double bed, exhausted from their adventure. Alex, on the other hand, didn't waste any time, keen to extract the oil from the flower. Every passing moment risked it becoming damaged which would dramatically affect its healing abilities. He didn't bother telling Kosum that though as he didn't want her to worry any more than she already was.

Ava tried to stay up with him in the kitchen as he got to work, but she too soon gave in to sleep and drifted off on a stool beside the breakfast bar.

Alex spent the following few hours draining the flower of every last drop of oil. His set-up resembled that of a high school science lab. The flower was submerged in a beaker filled with a clear solution. The beaker sat upon an open flame, and once boiled, the liquid would climb a small plastic tube that carried it into a fresh vial. It only produced one hundred millilitres but that was more than sufficient as Alex was sure Kwanjai would only require about ten.

Alex separated the liquid into two miniscule glass bottles with a cork cap firmly wedged in both, one for himself and one for the girls to take with them. He considered it a fair trade.

As Alex finished clearing everything away, morning broke through the window in the form of warm beams of summer sun. He was more than ready to join the girls in slumber, but as he contemplated climbing beneath the comfort of his duvet, the rest of the apartment woke up.

"Hey, you been at it all night?" Ava asked as she slowly peeled her face off the breakfast bar and wiped drool from her cheek.

"Yup," Alex answered, with a droopy thumbs up as he struggled to keep his eyes from clamping shut.

"Hey, guys," Nkechi smiled.

As she and Kosum entered the kitchen, they were met

with two groans and weak hand waves.

"That was a long night, huh?" Ava chuckled.

"You can say that aga—" Alex stopped, yawning.

"So… did everything go to plan with the extraction?" Kosum asked, unable to wait any longer.

"It went perfectly, Kosum. Your mum is going to be all right. Here's your Heart of Hecate oil," he said, holding up the glass bottle of oil which was lilac flecked with golden yellow.

"Thank you so much. We don't need all of this though; you guys keep some!" Kosum exclaimed, feeling it was the least she could do to repay them.

"Way ahead of ya there, girl," Alex smiled, holding up his identical bottle of the viscous liquid. "Listen, as much as I've loved having you" – he began to yawn again – "I really need some sleep. I imagine you'll be wanting to get the next flight home, so I'm sure Ava will give you a ride to the airport. And if you're ever in Yorkshire again, hit us up!"

"Thanks, Alex. I don't know what I would've done without your help." Kosum smiled, wrapping her arms around him and squeezing tightly.

"Yeah, you've been amazing," Nkechi added, as she joined in to make it a group hug.

"Don't sweat it," he brushed off, as they swallowed him in a hug.

After that, Alex finally headed off for a well-deserved rest, leaving Ava to be hostess for a few more hours.

"Pancakes, anyone?" Ava proposed, at which the girls nodded enthusiastically.

Ava swiftly whipped up some fluffy American-style

pancakes to make the girls feel at home. She stacked them up on the breakfast bar with two plates and a vat of maple syrup and sat back as the girls tucked in like feral animals. It had indeed been a long night.

Ava loved feeding people; it was one of her motherly instincts. Though she was still quite young and very much single, she'd always seen herself as a mother, and hoped that one day she'd become one.

"Ya know, girls, I've had so much fun in the last two days. I mean we partied, twice, and went on a quest to find a magical flower where we were almost murdered by an ogre. It was exhilarating. Thanks for spicing things up a bit while you've been here." Ava smiled as she took a pancake from the stack before they were all gone.

"We've had fun too, haven't we, Nkechi?" Kosum said, nudging Nkechi who was still face deep in her pancakes.

"Er yeah, it's been great," she smiled, coming up for air, a chunk of pancake popping out of her syrupy mouth. As Nkechi swallowed and looked around the kitchen, she believed what she had just agreed to even more. The simple things like eating breakfast with other people was something Nkechi had missed. It reminded her of when she would sit and chat to Cece each morning. Nkechi was looking forward to living with Kosum when they returned. Not that it would be for long though, as they'd soon have to embark on their next adventure in New Orleans.

"You'll have to come visit us sometime," Nkechi said, her mouth now empty.

"You mean it?" Ava asked nervously, an emotion they hadn't witnessed until now.

"Yeah, of course," Kosum added.

"Thanks, guys. It's nice to make some likeminded friends. Most people say I'm a bit too much, which I get, but it kinda sucks, ya know?"

"Trust us when we say we know how you feel. I was always the shy one no one would even approach until I met Kosum. And, well, Kosum was a raging bitch until she met me!" Nkechi jokingly jabbed at Kosum, causing Ava to hold back from laughing as she waited for Kosum to confirm it was okay.

Kosum rolled her eyes. "Yeah, I wish I could disagree, but she's kinda right."

"Kinda?" Nkechi teased.

"Okay, don't push it," Kosum chuckled, which finally confirmed to Ava that she could, too.

After they had finished their breakfast, Nkechi helped Ava tidy the mess while Kosum searched for the next flights back to New York.

"There's one in three hours which has seats left. If we set off now, we can still make it," Kosum said to the girls as they washed the dishes.

"Are you sure you don't mind taking us?" Nkechi asked.

"Course I don't. C'mon, I'll finish these later," she confirmed, flicking her hands free of the soapy water.

They gathered their things and Ava dropped them off at the airport. As they said their goodbyes, they reminded Ava that she could call anytime. As far as Nkechi and Kosum were concerned, Alex and Ava were their people now; they were friends, the first Nkechi and Kosum had made as a pair. They never mingled with any of their classmates and, after Charlie, a part of them was too scared to put their trust in a new member to join their group. Now they had two more, albeit halfway across the world.

But magic has a way of making the world feel like a smaller place. You're only ever a spell away, if you know the right one.

Nkechi had slept for the majority of the flight back home and now woke groggily with an hour left of their journey. Kosum sat beside her but in her own little first-class cubicle and was staring into space. She'd been doing just that the entire time Nkechi slept.

"Hey, you all right?" Nkechi asked, peering over the divider and waking Kosum from her daydream.

"Yeah, yeah. I'm good," she replied, unconvincingly.

"Are you sure? You seem quiet. And if ever I had to describe you to someone, quiet is not a word I'd use! What's up?"

"Don't get me wrong, I'm really happy and grateful that we got the oil and everything, but there's still a part of me that's scared in case it doesn't work," she answered, swirling the melting ice in her glass – all that remained of her diet coke.

"I understand, but it *will* work, I'm sure of it," Nkechi reassured, though she of course didn't know.

"Yeah, you're right. I need to think positive and just stop moping about things that I can't change. Sorry if I've been super selfish lately, I was just so—"

"Hey, your mom's in a coma. I think that gives you a little leeway to focus on yourself for a while.".

They were finally on the right track, and Nkechi didn't want Kosum to start feeling guilty. She needed her hopeful and free of regret, ready to take on the next Herculean task on their summer mystical to-do list: defeating the voodoo king.

"Thanks, Nkechi. You always know how to cheer a girl up. I just can't wait to get home and see her."

"I know, me too; she's been like a mother figure to me this past year. Plus, she keeps you in check," Nkechi laughed.

"Hey!" Kosum playfully moaned, poking Nkechi in the side.

"If you want, we can postpone going to New Orleans for a few more days so you can spend some time with your mom."

"No, honestly, it's okay. Anuli and Nkechi have been waiting long enough for our help. As soon as my mom's awake, we can set off."

"Okay, great. But you can still change your mind."

Kosum smiled appreciatively. "I know."

"Hey, I just remembered, it'll be Nicole's birthday while we're there over the summer. Maybe, if it's safe, we can throw her a party. Or you two could do something more intimate and get some *alone* time," Nkechi suggested, with an exaggerative wink.

Kosum laughed before realising that she'd have to buy Nicole a present – when would she have the time for that?

"What should I get her? You'll have to help me."

"Oh, don't worry, she's not really big into gifts. She's more of an it's-the-thought-that-counts girl."

"Oh, so the complete opposite of me then," Kosum joked, causing them both to chuckle.

"Hey, they say opposites attract, right? Besides, it could

be worse. Look at my track record for dating. I wouldn't even know how to categorise the men I attract."

"Well, I can certainly think of a few: smoking-hot, smart, psychotic, murderous. Should I go on?" she teased. "Too soon?" she added, noting Nkechi's unimpressed face.

"Definitely," Nkechi said feigning seriousness before giving in to laughter.

"Yeah, you've definitely been through the ringer for a first relationship. But hey, at the end of summer – provided we're both still alive that is – I'll jet us off to a fancy island where the sexiest guys wait on you hand and foot."

"Well, let's just see how the next few weeks play out first, shall we. But thanks for the offer."

"Would you like any drinks, ladies?" the first-class flight attendant asked, a notepad in hand.

"Yes, we'll have two flutes of champagne, please," Kosum smiled, answering for the both of them.

"Can I see your ID?"

Kosum took a fifty dollar bill out of her purse and waved it around suggestively. Unfortunately for Kosum the flight attendant wasn't the kind to accept bribes. Instead Kosum whispered a little makeshift spell under her breath as she pulled out her ID.

Let these printed numbers change in her mind, from 2006 to 1999.

The flight attendant looked at the ID and happily gave it back to Kosum. "Right away, ma'am."

"Nice spell. Are we celebrating?" Nkechi asked.

"Well, it's like you said, we've got what we needed and mom's going to be fine, so we're celebrating a successful trip," Kosum said in a much chipper tone than she had when Nkechi first woke up.

"Here we are, ladies," the flight attendant announced as she carefully handed them a bubbling flute each.

They both thanked her and toasted their successful trip and Kwanjai's recovery.

An hour after their plane landed the girls were back in familiar territory, the skyscrapers and concrete streets a welcome metaphorical hug. As much as Nkechi and Kosum enjoyed exploring the country roads of Yorkshire, it was safe to say that they were city girls at heart. Even though Nkechi hadn't been born in the city, she didn't realise how much she'd missed it. There was something about honking taxis and air pollution that felt homely to them.

They arrived at Ana's infirmary, having sent her a message on their way to tell her the good news and to ensure she would be present upon their arrival.

They walked into the room to see Ana sat by Kwanjai's bedside awaiting the girls' return.

"Kosum! Nkechi!" Ana exclaimed as she leapt up to engage in a group hug. Ana was thrilled to see the girls safe and sound; she'd spent the last three weeks worrying. Ana knew that Kwanjai would never forgive her if she let anything happen to them.

Ana exhaled a sigh of relief as she held them safely in her arms. "I've missed you, gurls."

"We missed you, too." The girls smiled as they slowly

pulled out of the hug.

"Right, yes, let's get to work. Where's the oil?" Ana asked, remembering the reason that they had been apart for so long.

"Here," Kosum said, holding out the vial of liquid in her hand.

"Wow, that should be more than enough! What'd ya have to do to get that?" Ana asked, intrigued.

"Oh, we just had to trek through some enchanted woods, find a cave behind a waterfall, cast a group spell to create a lunar eclipse and chop the head off an ogre." Nkechi smiled nonchalantly having now come to terms with just how crazy everything in their life sounded.

"Ogre? Jesus, gurls! I gotta say to ya, job well done. I thought that lunar eclipse wasn't on my calendar. Sounds like you guys pulled off some real feats of magic. Your mom would be proud, Kosum, and I'm sure yours too, Nkechi darlin'."

"Thanks." They smiled appreciatively.

"Anyhow, let me get this mixed up with a few essentials to give your mom's immune system a boost when she wakes up. The Heart of Hecate should bring her out of the coma but she'll still be drained," Ana said, turning to her brewing station.

Kosum walked over to sit by her mother's side. Seeing her unconscious again lead her to ask:

"When will she wake up? How long will it take to work?"

Ana stopped and turned around to answer.

"Well, there's no real way of knowing, but I'm hopeful that it'll only be twenty-four hours, or so."

"Okay, good," Kosum said, allowing her tense shoulders to relax a little as she placed her mother's limp hand in her own.

"Nkechi darlin', could you grab me some peppermint from over there, please? Oh, and some sage, too." Ana chose Nkechi as she noticed that Kosum's gaze and mind were fixed on her mother.

"Sure."

Nkechi brought Ana the final ingredients, and Ana put a little of everything into a sandstone mortar and began to grind with her matching pestle. Ana's bicep flexed slightly as she pummelled the mixture together. After a few minutes of intense mixing, the dry ingredients had combined with the Hecate essence to form a liquid once more.

Ana walked over to Kwanjai and gently opened her mouth. She poured the remedy down Kwanjai's throat and closed her mouth before gently massaging her neck to help it go down.

There was no immediate reaction, and Ana could see the slight disappointment on Kosum's face.

"Gurls, you better head home and get some rest. We've done everything we can. I'll keep an eye on her and call you the second she wakes up."

"Thanks, Ana," Nkechi smiled as she gently guided Kosum's hand away from her mother's.

"Yeah, thanks." Kosum half smiled as she got up.

Ana saw the girls out and, as they left, Kwanjai's index finger twitched and a whisper left her lips.

A whisper for Kosum.

Two days went by without so much as a syllable from Kwanjai

except the whisper no one had heard.

Kosum was becoming worried that the cure hadn't worked. Nkechi, on the other hand, had worries of her own. Of course, she cared for Kwanjai, but she'd heard news from Anuli that things were escalating quickly. Nkechi would do anything to help Kosum and Kwanjai but now there was nothing more they *could* do.

Nkechi couldn't postpone going back to New Orleans any longer; she needed to tell Kosum she was leaving immediately. She just hoped Kosum would understand her decision.

Kosum spent every second by her mother's side. Nkechi had kept her supplied with snacks, but it wasn't sustainable. Kosum was still sat there holding her mother's hand and scrolling through her phone in the other, as Nkechi made her way to the infirmary to tell Kosum of her decision.

Nkechi knocked on the infirmary door and Kosum called her in.

"Hey, how've you been?" Nkechi asked, knowing it was a silly question.

"Ya know, just the usual."

"Yeah, I know." Nkechi sighed as the guilt of what she was about to say ate away at her.

She walked over to sit beside Kosum and finally uttered, "I'm sorry, Kosum, I don't know how to tell you this but I'm going… tonight."

"Going where?" Kosum raised an eyebrow in confusion.

"New Orleans." Nkechi sighed again.

"You're leaving me?" Kosum asked with annoyingly cute puppy dog eyes.

"Well, yeah. But listen, Kosum," Nkechi began as she

crouched in front of her and grasped her hand, "I love you and your mom. But there's nothing more I can do here. She just needs time, something that Anuli and Nicole are running out of. Things back in New Orleans are getting worse; they need me. So, I'm gonna get a flight out later. I understand that you want to stay here, and you can join us whenever your mom is better, but I need to go now. I'm sorry."

"I understand," Kosum muttered as her eyes glazed over with sadness.

"I'll see you soon though, okay?" Nkechi smiled.

"Yeah, of course."

They hugged one another before Nkechi slipped back out of the room and prepared for the trip.

Once Kosum was left alone with her thoughts, she looked at her mother's sleeping face and wondered whether she was where she needed to be. She loved her mother, but she also loved Nkechi and Nicole. Nkechi had been the only constant in Kosum's life in the past year and maybe it was time Kosum returned the favour.

As Nkechi headed to her gate, the last call for her flight came through the airport speakers. She handed the flight attendant her ticket and, as she did so, an obnoxiously loud voice shouted, "Nkechi! Wait!"

Nkechi turned to see Kosum running towards her.

Once she stopped, her hands dropped to her knees and her back arched over as she panted for breath.

"Kosum! What's wrong?" a worried Nkechi asked.

"I'm" – Kosum gasped for some more air – "I'm… coming with you."

"But—"

"No buts. You were right, there's nothing more I can do right now. And though it pains me to leave her, I know she's in safe hands. Besides, you're my bestie. How could I let you go fight the big bad voodoo king without me by your side? You've stuck by me these last few weeks, even when I've been insufferable. And now it's my turn. I promised I'd be there and that's what I'm gonna do. Plus, even though you're like crazy powerful and all, I guarantee at some point you'll need me to rescue your ass." Kosum smiled sassily.

"Thanks, Kosum," Nkechi chuckled.

The two of them boarded another plane and began the second leg of their supernatural summer journey.

CHAPTER 5

Entering the War Zone

After their plane landed, an exhausted Nkechi and Kosum were glad to be in New Orleans. Granted, the circumstances of their visit weren't ideal, but Nkechi was happy to be back in her home state, and Kosum was excited to see her beloved Nicole once again.

Kosum had booked a taxi to take them to Anuli's house, which had now also somewhat become the base of operations for the resistance against the voodoo king.

With tensions higher than ever and the local streets practically a war zone, there was no way Anuli and Nicole could spare the time to pick them up, hence the taxi. The voodoo king had spies everywhere and if he learned that they'd left the town unprotected, he wouldn't waste any time in going after the more vulnerable members of the community.

The voodoo king was a predator, except at least the majority of natural predators killed for food, no, he was much worse. He was like a hunter, killing for sport and showmanship as a way of demonstrating his power. All he cared about was strengthening his hold on the earth – every inch of soil under his control was another win in his eyes – and he wouldn't be content until the world was his.

Kosum spotted a man in the airport's arrivals area, holding

a sign with their names inscribed across it. He had on a pair of extremely tinted sunglasses and wore a suit. The man greeted them rather briefly, only asking their names to confirm they were the girls he was paid to drive. He abruptly turned on his heel and waved for them to follow.

The girls left the terminal and headed straight into the thick, hot New Orleans air. The humidity almost choked Kosum, while Nkechi breathed it in like a sweet nectar.

They pulled their luggage along as the taxi driver led them to his car.

"Not exactly five-star service," Kosum whispered to Nkechi, unimpressed she had to lug her own bags. Had they not been in public, a quick flick of the wrist and they'd float behind her.

"Where did you find this guy?" Nkechi whispered back.

"He was an independent – I thought I'd be nice and support a small local business."

"Wow, you're really going all out on this whole being a better person thing, huh?"

"Yes, I really am." Kosum smiled exaggeratively.

"You're regretting it already, aren't you?" Nkechi sniggered.

"No. Maybe. To be honest, I'll just take it as a win if he doesn't turn out to be a creep. I think we've stomached enough of them already this summer."

"Yeah, here's hoping," Nkechi answered with a quick raise of her eyebrows.

Nkechi and Kosum got into the back of the car, and the driver set off. An awkward silence filled the air as the prepaid taxi man already had the address and therefore no reason or apparent desire to engage in conversation.

Quickly becoming bored, Kosum leaned forward and asked, "Hey, can we have some music on, please?"

He simply rolled up the tinted glass divider in reply, and they remained in silence.

"Well, that was rude," Nkechi commented.

"Hey!" Kosum said, raising her voice as she knocked on the divider window. "I'll be leaving you a bad review if you don't open this right now."

There was still no reply. The divider didn't budge an inch and not a single decibel of music came from the back seat speakers.

"Hey, c'mon, just leave it, he's clearly ignorant. We can survive a car ride without music; we've survived much worse," Nkechi said, pulling Kosum back into her seat.

"True. And I suppose I could talk to you or whatever," Kosum teased.

Nkechi playfully nudged her in the arm in retaliation.

Ten minutes into their journey, Nkechi was snoring with her head against the window and Kosum was staring at her phone, just in case any news came from Ana. Alas, none did. Her notifications remained silent apart from the odd annoying pop-up that she couldn't figure out how to unsubscribe from. It once again buzzed in her palm and she glared at the screen to see another pointless notification. She'd tried to keep her hopes up, but the constant teasing was beginning to frustrate her.

"Ugh!" she groaned, angrily stuffing her phone into her pocket.

The commotion caused Nkechi to wake from her power nap.

"What's wrong?" Nkechi asked as she stretched and yawned.

"Nothing. Are we nearly there yet?" Kosum knew she'd feel a little better the second she saw Nicole again.

"Er, I'll have a look," Nkechi answered, rubbing her eyes and peering out of her window. "I dunno."

"What do you mean? I thought you remembered the way, or at least you seemed to last time."

"Yeah, you're right. And I think we're going the wrong way."

Nkechi softly knocked on the divider window. The driver unsurprisingly didn't respond but he did suddenly speed up, throwing Nkechi back into her seat.

"Okay, this guy is a total dick!" A ruffled Nkechi groaned.

"Hey!" Kosum shouted once again, aggressively banging on the plexiglass.

"Kosum, I don't think he's gonna answer us. And I don't think he's a real taxi driver. Pull the window down," Nkechi demanded hastily.

Kosum waved her hand over the screen using her telekinesis. The man turned and flicked his wrist through the little window, expelling a plume of green mist.

Kosum spluttered for a moment and looked back to Nkechi in confusion as the mist dissipated. That's when she noticed that Nkechi's seatbelt had come to life.

"Nkec—" Kosum tried to speak but her seatbelt also became animated as it pulled her back into the chair. With the buckle of the belt swathed in the same green mist, it approximated to the head of a snake.

The belts swiftly wrapped themselves around the girls'

necks, with the 'head' dancing around in front of them, taunting them as they choked. The buckles began to hiss and launch themselves at the girls' faces, forcing them to dodge the attacks while they gasped for air. They grasped the belts, trying to free their necks of the serpent-like creatures, but it was no use. It was as if the belts were enchanted with the power of a giant python.

"Nkechi, possess him!" Kosum croaked.

"It's not easy… when you're being half… choked to death," Nkechi stuttered back.

Kosum stretched out her hand and used her telekinetic abilities to ease the belt from around Nkechi's neck slightly. She wouldn't be able to keep it up for long though as the belt around her own neck served as quite the distraction.

With Nkechi now having a little breathing room, she wasted no time in delving into the man's psyche. As she reached the depths of the driver's mind, Nkechi could feel that something was off. It wasn't the same dark stickiness she had felt in the professor's mind, but there was definitely something equally as evil.

As Nkechi fought her way to his main control system, she was shocked to see that the astral form of someone else had already beaten her to the punch. It was a large man wearing thick robes and he stood with a staff in hand.

The voodoo king, Nkechi realised.

He turned to reveal his scarred face and snake-like pupils to Nkechi, throwing a sickening grin in her direction. With the flick of his finger, he sent Nkechi's astral form back into her own body with ease.

It made perfect sense that the voodoo king was behind the

man's odd behaviour; it was likely that one of his spies had found out about their arrival and this poor taxi driver was being controlled like a pawn. It also explained the powerful magic at play inside the car. Bringing an inanimate object to life wasn't easy, and even a witch didn't see such magic on a regular basis.

Nkechi had never had to fight a fellow voodoo witch, let alone a voodoo king. He had the same, if not more, abilities than Nkechi, and he was clearly more powerful and experienced in the art of voodoo than her.

What didn't make sense to Nkechi was the voodoo king's whereabouts. How was he managing to keep in possession of the taxi driver over such a vast distance, and for so long? Nkechi had only ever accomplished it with someone in the same room. Even in her 'God mode' as Kosum described it, Nkechi wasn't sure she could possess someone over such a distance.

Nkechi didn't have time to ponder such questions though, as her astral form bounced back into her own body. She had to figure out another way to save them both.

Nkechi gasped one last breath just before Kosum's telekinesis failed and the belt once again tightened around Nkechi's neck.

"What happened?" Kosum squeaked, her hands clawing at the constricting belt.

"I think... I just met the voodoo king," Nkechi spluttered back.

"That's him?"

"No, he's possessed him," Nkechi explained with another gasp for air as she managed to pull the belt away for a split second.

"Well," Kosum coughed, "what do we do?"

Nkechi racked her brain for a solution. She didn't have long to come up with a new plan before her brain became starved of oxygen.

Thankfully, Nkechi had a eureka moment.

"Kosum, I have a crazy idea!"

"What?"

"Force down the accelerator and make us crash. Then just before we do, bubble us in a forcefield."

"You're right, that is crazy!"

"Can you do it or not?"

Kosum saved her energy and nodded. She saw the taxi driver's leg and forced it down harshly onto the accelerator, causing them to gain speed fast. The voodoo king's puppet looked confused but then he turned to Kosum and realised what was happening.

The second he took his eyes off the road, Kosum, having now built up enough speed, switched her focus from the gas pedal to the steering wheel, flicking her wrist at it. She quickly then bubbled herself and Nkechi in a forcefield of translucent, blue telekinetic energy as the car swerved and crashed into a tree. The speed at which they hit the dense tree caused it to split the hood and front seats down the middle. Thanks to Kosum's forcefield, the back seats remained untouched, and with the driver now unconscious, the animation curse on the belts ended, enabling the girls to breathe again with ease.

They climbed out of the car and pulled the man from the wreckage. They knew he wasn't acting of his own volition and so checked to make sure he was still breathing before anonymously calling an ambulance.

"I can't believe that worked," Kosum sighed in exhaustion.

"Me neither," Nkechi muttered, also breathless.

"But it was your plan!" Kosum moaned.

"Look, let's just count ourselves lucky and agree to walk the rest of the way," Nkechi proposed.

"How long will that take?"

"Forty-five minutes," Nkechi mumbled, hoping Kosum wouldn't hear and moan.

Kosum did hear and moaned, as Nkechi expected.

"Gross, but I suppose we don't really have a choice, do we?"

"No. Now, come on, let's go. The quicker we get there, the quicker I can collapse onto a bed."

They grabbed their bags and started the long, tiresome walk home. Kosum's energy was so spent, she couldn't decide whether it took more effort to levitate her bags or drag them, so she did neither and Nkechi took the brunt of the weight for a while.

Meanwhile, across town in an old, abandoned warehouse-cum-base of operations, the voodoo king's astral form was hurtled back into his body without warning. He awoke and gasped for air, holding his chest, having felt the effects of the crash upon the man he'd possessed. He composed himself and stood up. It would seem that perhaps the voodoo king wasn't as powerful as he led Nkechi to believe.

He stood in the centre of a large circle, around which

were littered his followers and top voodoo practitioners who were still unconscious from the exertion of energy. They had been bolstering his powers, including the ability to possess someone over such a vast distance.

The voodoo king had clearly underestimated the girls, thinking that it would be easy to take them off the playing board. It spoke volumes about his general arrogance.

All those years ago when he originally overthrew Nkechi's mother, he assumed that he would rule easily with an iron first, and for a few years he did just that. But seeing Nkechi last year lit a fire under the citizens who began to revolt. What started as a small spark within Anuli and Nicole, soon roared into a full-on resistance. The majority of sensical citizens joined in, but those too scared, or foolish enough to succumb to the voodoo king's beliefs, defected to his original hometown for 'protection'.

To stop any of his followers from defecting, the voodoo king twisted the Resistance's heroic acts to appear as terrorism, when in reality they were fighting a very just cause – one for freedom and peace.

Over the past few months, battles had slowly broken out in the streets. With everyone in both towns either opposed to the voodoo king's beliefs or sympathisers, there was no need for the fighters to be discreet when using their magic.

With Anuli acting as the unofficial leader of the Resistance, her home became the operational headquarters for all plans of attack. Her own, and many other of the neighbouring houses, were filled to the brim with vulnerable members of the community. The healthy adults of the town who hadn't already defected through lack of hope, were often the ones on the front line fighting in the streets to keep the voodoo king's goons at a safe distance. And although they were losing as many battles as they were winning, Anuli and Nicole remained hopeful, as they knew once Nkechi and Kosum arrived, they stood a fighting chance of winning the war.

They'd told the town all about Nkechi and Kosum's battles with crazed children and a satanic witch, as well as how they thwarted Charlie's plan. It meant that the girls had become famous amongst the town and many of the citizens had faith in the girls being the final nail in the voodoo king's coffin.

One by one, the practitioners around the voodoo king also awoke as he no longer needed their support. His inner circle was made up of the strongest and most loyal followers.

One of the voodoo king's many proclivities was his chauvinism. He saw women as nothing but servants to cook, clean and appease him and his men.

The voodoo king was angry.

"How? How did they do that? I had them choking in the back of a car and yet still they escaped!" he growled. "You," he said, pointing at one of the seemingly more timid, younger men. "You've always been the weakest link, and you'll pay for your insolence! Feed him to the damned, they'll need to build up strength for the end plan."

The voodoo king's head practitioner, Gaudence, snapped his fingers and the young man was dragged by two other practitioners, kicking and screaming. The poor soul pleaded for them to let him go, but they knew if they did they'd only suffer the same fate, and so they continued to drag him by the arms across the floor to the pit.

The pit was a hole in the ground floor of the warehouse

that dropped several metres down. The pit was something the voodoo king had installed when he took over the warehouse and it was built for the sole purpose of keeping wild creatures from escaping.

After a quick struggle, they managed to push him down into the ten-metre-deep hole. His body hit the bottom of the concrete pit with enough intensity to break every bone in his body. Still, he wasn't dead, not yet. He was very much alive enough to feel what happened next.

One of the men at the entrance to the hole shone his phone's torch down to look at the horror show. The phone shone over the prisoner's broken and contorted body for a split second before he was dragged away, out of sight, by the beasts that lay within.

As Nkechi and Kosum got closer to the heart of Nkechi's hometown, the effects of the ongoing war were clear to see. Most of the streets were deserted, with the homes around them crumbling. It was like a post-apocalyptic world contained within one small town; a world with a raging war that no one outside the county lines knew existed.

Nkechi had known that the situation was bad, but she could've never imagined it to this degree.

Finally, the girls arrived at Anuli's house which, along with the neighbouring ones, seemed unscathed by the war. This was thanks to their efforts thus far.

Before Nkechi could muster up the energy to climb the porch steps and knock on the door, Nicole spotted them through the lounge window. She raced to the door, flung it open, and launched herself towards Nkechi and Kosum, arms wide open as she enveloped them both.

"I've missed you guys so much!" Nicole exclaimed as she squeezed them in her arms.

"Missed you, too," Nkechi muttered in reply, still lacking enough energy to show their full excitement.

"Nicole!" Kosum replied, squeezing Nicole as tightly as she could. Seeing her beaming face gave Kosum a little burst of energy.

As Nicole pulled herself out of the group hug, it was then that she noticed just how fatigued and beaten they looked.

"What happened to you guys?"

"We'll explain inside," Nkechi muttered, gasping for a drink. Walking in the hot New Orleans sun had taken its toll on them.

"Yeah, of course, let's get you guys inside. I'll carry the bags in."

"Thanks," Kosum smiled, sneaking a quick kiss as Nicole took the bags from her.

Nkechi and Kosum entered the house, dropped onto the sofa, and let out an audible sigh of relief as their feet finally rested.

"Mom! They're here!" Nicole shouted down the basement stairs.

"Coming!" Anuli called back.

While they waited for Anuli, Nicole grabbed them a couple of ice-cold glasses of lemonade, but Kosum asked if she had anything stronger. Nicole waltzed over to her mother's liquor cabinet and quickly snuck a glug of vodka into Kosum's lemonade. Nkechi rolled her eyes but then the second Nicole held the bottle out as an offer for Nkechi to have some too, she smiled and nodded. Nicole chuckled and topped Nkechi's glass up with the spirit.

"Thanks," Nkechi smiled while unsubtly staring at Nicole's hair. Her once perfectly styled, short blonde afro was now long and unkempt and the colour had grown out, showing her jet-black roots.

"What?" Nicole sassed, noticing Nkechi's gaze fixed on her hair.

"Nothing, it's just your hair is, erm, a bit—"

"A bit what?" Nicole cut her off with a sassily raised eyebrow and pursed lips. "I know it's crazy but it's kinda hard to keep on top of it in the middle of a war, ya know? And besides, you're one to talk – when's the last time you did anything with this?" Nicole asked, rubbing Nkechi's dry curls between her fingers.

"Well, it hasn't exactly been leisurely walks in the park for me lately, either," Nkechi replied, squinting her eyes at Nicole sarcastically.

"Oh, please. You never were good at doing your hair," Nicole laughed. "Don't worry, cuz, we can all have a nice selfcare night when this is over."

"I hope I'm included in this," Kosum chimed in.

"Of course," Nicole winked suavely. "You'll be front and centre, learning how to take care of Nkechi's mane because *she* certainly doesn't care."

"Hey, I'm still sat right here."

They all laughed just as Anuli finally joined the three of them. Anuli's deep brown eyes lit up as she saw them laughing together, and her full lips smiled as she greeted them.

"Ah, it's good to see my girls laughing, especially when there isn't much to laugh about these days. Come here," Anuli commanded with open arms.

Nkechi and Kosum slowly got back on their feet and hugged Anuli, their faces squished into her bosom, almost suffocating them. Anuli noticed their fatigue and instructed them to sit back on the sofa. She nestled herself between them so that they could give her a debrief on their perilous journey thus far.

"Long story short, I preordered a taxi and the driver turned out to be crazy and tried to kill us," Kosum said casually, not having the energy to go into the usual dramatics that she would when storytelling.

"I think you're missing out the key part where it wasn't actually the poor driver who was crazy – the voodoo king was possessing him. Though I don't know how he managed to do so without being anywhere near us," Nkechi pondered aloud.

"Yes, well, we have reason to believe he's using his followers and fellow practitioners to bolster his powers, almost using them like batteries," Anuli said.

"And what happens when the batteries run out?" Kosum asked.

"I don't know."

"I doubt it's hard to imagine," Nkechi said, becoming even more disgusted with a man she hadn't even met. She'd surely make him regret it the day they did.

"Yes, it is, but they made their choice. We offered everyone freedom yet they chose to live under his rule," Anuli said, rather coldly dismissing the fact that some complied out of utter fear.

"Auntie, I'm so sorry. I feel like I kickstarted this rebellion for you. I never meant for it to cause so much death and destruction. Until now, I haven't even been around to help the fight." Nkechi sighed.

Kosum dropped her gaze to the ground as she knew that it was only because of her own quest to save her mother that Nkechi hadn't been here sooner.

"Nonsense, my dear," came the deep croaky voice of a man from the basement.

Nkechi turned to see a man and a woman, around her auntie's age, ascending the final steps into the living area. The man was rather short with a small beer belly and a thinning, grey afro. The woman, his wife, was slimmer than Anuli but still curvaceous and was slightly taller than her husband. Her eyes were a stunning crystal blue, unlike anyone else's in the room. Her skin was also much lighter than everyone else's (other than Kosum's).

Nkechi looked confused and turned to Anuli with a raised eyebrow, signalling some insight was needed.

"Nkechi, this is Adame and Evélia. They are my closest allies in this fight. They knew your mother too, way back when."

"It's a pleasure to meet you." Nkechi stood to shake their hands.

"No, no, child, the pleasure is all ours. And don't for a second think that any of this is your fault. This is a long overdue battle. All you did was inspire us to finally take action. It's what your mother would have wanted. Besides, now you're here to aid us in our battle, we'll be sure to prevail.

Anuli informed us of the incredible feats you accomplished back in New York, and we are honoured to have you fight alongside us. Your mother would be proud." Adame smiled, before kissing his fingers and briefly pointing them at the ceiling.

"Yes, well said, my love. I suppose you do get things right every now and then," Evélia teased, tucking her long wavy hair behind her ear.

"Thank you, both." Nkechi beamed. Hearing such words from people who actually knew her mother meant a lot. Of course, Anuli praised her, and that was nice too, but Anuli was family – there's an unspoken rule of supporting one another. It's a different feeling when a stranger does it.

"Right, well, why don't you girls get some rest? You look like you need it, then we can talk strategy in the morning," Anuli proposed.

"Yeah, that sounds great, thank you." Nkechi couldn't wait to lay down and rest.

"Though, I must admit, it won't be as cosy as your last stay here, girls. We're a bit cramped at the moment, what with some of the local girls taking up the spare rooms. Nkechi, you can bunk in with me and, Kosum, you may share Nicole's room," Anuli said casually, signifying her approval of their relationship.

"No problem," Nkechi replied.

Meanwhile, Kosum grinned as she glanced in Nicole's direction. Nicole blushed slightly as she caught Kosum's gaze, both knowing that they had some lost time to make up for.

"Right, well good night, everyone," Kosum said, suddenly with a bit more bounce in her step.

"Night," everyone replied, almost in tandem. For a brief second, to Nkechi it felt like some quirky dysfunctional family unit, something that she had always longed for. She loved her mother and enjoyed her childhood with her, and she loved Kosum and was glad to have her, but Nkechi always dreamed of having it all in one place – everyone she loved in one place, even just for a fleeting moment. It would seem that this was the closest she'd get. She was sure that her mother was there too, in spirit.

Nicole lugged the girls' bags upstairs while they slothfully followed on behind. Nkechi retired to her aunt's room and unpacked her things into a couple of small drawers Anuli had emptied for her. She then snuggled up onto the airbed on the floor besides Anuli's bed. It was by no means comfortable, but Nkechi's bed in her old apartment wasn't much better, so for Nkechi it was relatively easy to drift off to sleep.

It was the staying asleep that Nkechi was finding hard. Since Charlie, Nkechi's sleeping pattern had become like that of a toddler, thus even a hundred mattresses wouldn't give her the amazing night's sleep she so desperately desired.

A few doors down in the box room, Nicole and Kosum were getting reacquainted. Nicole had unfortunately been downgraded to the box bedroom. Nicole didn't mind, though. It was all for a good cause – so that they could fit more bunkbeds in the other rooms for the local, vulnerable young girls. Nicole's new room was still big enough for a small double bed, even if it did touch three of the four walls.

Kosum didn't waste any time in unpacking as there were more pressing matters – making love with Nicole. Instead, she threw her bags to the floor and they launched themselves onto the bed and exchanged kisses.

"I've missed you so much," they said to one another in between quick kissing breaks before once again becoming entwined. They were so excited to be beside one another again that the foreplay was kept to a minimum; they couldn't wait to feel an other-worldly orgasm. Kosum dropped her lips onto Nicole's breasts, teasing her nipples with her flickering tongue, before sliding it down the rest of her stomach until she reached the perfect point. Nicole was thrashing about on the bed with pleasure, her hands stretched out, gripping the edge of the mattress as Kosum worked her magic.

Their session of lovemaking continued for another hour as they took turns in pleasuring one another, almost to the point of fulfilment, only to tease and prolong their lovemaking a little longer. Finally, they both collapsed onto their backs on the bed. They were exhausted and breathless.

Once she'd caught her breath, Nicole turned onto her side to face Kosum.

"So, how are you? I assume your mom's okay now that you're here?" Nicole asked, noting that they hadn't yet spent any time catching up on news.

"Well, we've given her the Heart of Hecate herb; there's not much else we can do other than wait. But Ana's there and she'll let me know the second she wakes up," Kosum said optimistically.

"Oh, I'm sorry, I didn't realise she was still—"

"It's okay, it's not like you haven't had your own shit going on. Speaking of which, why didn't you tell me how bad things had got here?" Kosum asked, still feeling guilty for delaying Nkechi's arrival.

"Because I knew what you were going through, and I didn't want you to feel pressured to come sooner," she answered, caressing Kosum's cheek.

"I get that, and you're sweet for trying to protect me, but I'm your girlfriend and I'm here to listen to all of your problems. I don't want you to go through anything alone, regardless of how you think it might make me feel. If this is going to work, especially with the distance thing, then we need to be completely honest with each other. So, next time you wanna talk to unload, cry or whatever, please call me. I'd hate for you to feel like you can't do that," Kosum said, placing her hand on top of Nicole's.

"Thank you, I'm really glad you're here." Nicole smiled.

"Me too. Now, come here," Kosum said, opening her arms wide.

Nicole snuggled into Kosum and they both fell into a blissful sleep. For a few precious hours they forgot all about the raging war they would wake up to.

CHAPTER 6

From One Nightmare to Another

During the night, Nkechi only stirred once, when Anuli had gone up to bed, though that didn't mean her night had been peaceful. Nkechi's face winced in her sleep while her subconscious self was plagued by nightmares of Charlie. It played out as some sick and twisted version of their relationship together, sped up. Flashes of their fake meet-cute, adorable dates and tender kisses slowly rotted and warped into those final moments, where he was nothing like the Charlie she had known, the Charlie she had loved.

Unfortunately for Nkechi, since the ordeal it had become a recurring dream. She hadn't told anyone about it, not even Kosum, despite knowing that her friend sympathised with her mixed feelings towards Charlie.

Alas, Nkechi saw this as something she would have to work through on her own. But of course that would have to wait until the more pressing matters in her life had been dealt with – like defeating the voodoo king.

It was still the early hours of the morning, and Anuli hadn't long fallen asleep before she and Nkechi were suddenly awoken by the sound of a house alarm. Though it wasn't theirs, the whole house began to wake in a panic. Anuli threw Nkechi a pair of jeans and told her to follow her as she got dressed.

"What's going on?" Nkechi asked, still yawning.

Anuli whispered, "The alarm – there's one in each house that's housing any young or vulnerable members of the community. It sounds like it's coming from next door, where the elders are."

"What, the voodoo king's here? Now?" Nkechi asked, quickly scaring herself awake.

"No, it'll be his henchmen, no doubt. Now that he knows you're back home and more powerful than he probably first realised, he won't risk venturing out this far. Though be careful, Nkechi, his men are just as well trained in the voodoo arts as you or me," Anuli warned.

She then banged on Nicole and Kosum's bedroom door, shouting at them to get up and watch over the girls while she and Nkechi went next door to check on the situation.

A startled Kosum and Nicole mumbled in reply as they scrambled to get dressed.

Anuli and Nkechi left home and headed through a side gate to the neighbouring garden, entering the house through the back door. As they grew close, they began to hear screams and bangs coming from the second floor.

"Quick, this way," Anuli said in haste, waving Nkechi to follow her.

"Isn't there any of our guys in there to watch over the elders?" Nkechi asked in a hushed tone as she ran on behind her.

"Yes, dear, but by the sounds of it, they're not winning."

They reached the back door. Anuli became silent and prompted Nkechi to do the same, turning to her and putting her finger to her lips.

Anuli, using a spare key, opened the back door to the kitchen. The two of them slipped in without making a sound. The kitchen had an island at its centre, the other side of which opened up to a hallway. Anuli glanced over and could see a corpse by the stairs. Her jaw clenched, her fists tightening at the sight. Nkechi couldn't help but notice her twitching eyes and the biting of her lip, clearly trying to stop herself from screaming in anger.

Anuli grabbed a knife from the wooden block beside her. Nkechi didn't. It was one thing for Nkechi to fight with magic, but she didn't like the idea of using such a primitive weapon; it felt more barbaric in a way. However, that didn't mean Nkechi wasn't prepared to do whatever it took to stop the voodoo king's men, even if meant taking a life to save one of their own.

They walked down the hallway, their gaze firmly on the staircase to their right. The muffled screams and clanging they had heard outside had come to an eerie end. They stayed close to the wall and slowly poked their heads out to see the upstairs landing, looking for any intruders. As they edged closer to the staircase, another alarm began to sound.

Anuli's eyes widened in shock. "Damn, that's our house."

"I'm sure Nicole and Kosum will handle it. We're already here now; we need finish what we came here to do," Nkechi whispered, reminding her auntie of the horrific screams that they had originally heard.

"You're right. Okay, I'm gonna go up and—" Before Anuli could finish, a herd of muscular young men came barrelling down the stairs. They pushed Anuli to the ground causing her to bang her head on a doorframe on the way down, rendering her unconscious. Nkechi summoned a gust of wind to blast them back into the wall behind them, buying her a little time to react. But it wasn't long enough to check on Anuli, as the four perpetrators quickly dusted themselves off and got back on their feet.

The first two came for Nkechi, but before they could reach her, she whispered, "*Écraser*," and waved her hand in the direction of one of the henchmen's ankles. With his next step, his ankle crushed on impact, crippling him to the floor. The second man swung a punch towards Nkechi's face. Luckily, she evaded it by the skin of her teeth and directed another gust of wind straight into his stomach, winding him and sending him flying a few metres back down the hallway. The remaining two men watched his lump of a body fly past them and slam into the front door.

One of the two remaining fighters grabbed the knife Anuli had dropped and charged at Nkechi. Her eyes glazed over, and just milliseconds later she'd slipped into his mind. She could see his point of view and managed to freeze his muscles in place, just in time, the blade mere inches away from Nkechi's chest.

Now that she was out of immediate danger, she turned the man's hand holding the knife towards himself and plunged it into him. She quickly relinquished control of his mind. The feeling of the knife in her hands, even through the control of another body, made her uneasy, though it was a necessity that war had thrust upon her. The thug gasped for breath before falling to his knees in agony, blood pouring out of his chest like an open faucet.

Learning from his comrades' mistakes, the final attacker didn't rush in but instead smashed a glass vial on the ground by his feet. It turned into a plume of green smoke which surrounded him and, once cleared, revealed a shield made of pure energy to protect him.

What the hell is that? Nkechi thought to herself, before attempting to break it with a ball of fire. As the fiery globe hit the shield, the flames dispersed across it with no visible damage done. The fire dissipated to reveal the man's gaze fixed upon Nkechi. She didn't have a clue what he was trying to do, but the look alone was disturbing.

He started to utter the phrase, "*Ne vois aucun mal*," reciting the words while maintaining eye contact with Nkechi.

It was only when she tried to avert her gaze, did she realise she couldn't. She tried her best to steer her vision away, but it was no use, she was locked in place until whatever spell he was casting was over.

As she watched him continue to utter his cursed words, he seemed to slowly fade out of her vision until he was completely invisible. Nkechi could finally look where she wished, but no matter where she looked, she couldn't see him. She spun round in a circle to try to survey the area, only to then be sucker punched in the face by an invisible force.

Nkechi fell to the ground, dazed by the surprise impact which had seemingly come from thin air. She tried to get up, but as she rose to her knees, she felt a boot kicking her in the stomach with such force, it slid her across the floor and into kitchen.

Nkechi still couldn't see the man and was in too much pain to stand. She began to panic and cried out for Anuli while holding her stomach, in the hope she would wake up and come to her aid.

Anuli's eyes fluttered open, hearing the desperate sound of her niece's voice. Her head was pounding, and she was struggling to see straight, but even with her impaired vision, she spotted the man standing over Nkechi.

She unwedged the kitchen knife from the dead man's chest before sneaking up behind the final culprit and driving it between his shoulder blades. His back arched forward in shock and he yelled in pain and anger. Anuli took a step back for a second to watch as he squirmed, trying to reach behind himself to pull it out. Anuli smiled for a moment, knowing she'd placed it just out of reach.

Unable to remove the knife, he turned to face Anuli, grinding his teeth in pain, his mouth beginning to froth. He took a step towards her, and she threw her clenched fist into the middle of his face, breaking his nose and knocking him to the ground beside Nkechi. He fell backwards, landing on the knife and pushing it even deeper into his back. He lay there, choking on the blood that filled his throat, until finally he was silent, gone.

"Christ, that hurt," Anuli moaned, caressing her grazed knuckles.

Nkechi was still on the floor and hadn't seen the ordeal, too crippled by pain to notice. Despite the man lying beside her, she still couldn't see him.

"Are you okay, my sweet?" Anuli asked as she helped Nkechi back to her feet.

"No. I couldn't see him and I don't know why. I can't see *any* of them anymore for that matter. What's going on?" Nkechi looked into the hallway, filled with bodies she couldn't see.

Anuli tutted as she realised what they had done to Nkechi.

"He used the 'See No Evil' curse," she breathed. "It means the victim is blind to any threats and attackers, hence why you can't see any of them. Come here." She guided Nkechi to the kitchen sink and placed her head face down into the basin, telling her to keep her eyes open. Nkechi shuffled her head enough to nod before Anuli turned on the tap. She cupped her hands to gather water and lifted it to Nkechi's eyes while repeating the phrase, "*Purifier la malédiction.*" She washed Nkechi's eyes a few more times while continuing to recite the counter-curse. It was uncomfortable for Nkechi, and her body twinged in pain, but she knew it was necessary. If she wasn't cleared of the curse, she'd continue to be blind to all enemies in the future including the voodoo king.

Her hands gripped either side of the basin as she tried her best to keep her eyes open. After the fifth recitation, Anuli gently lifted Nkechi's head and passed her a dish towel to dry off with. Nkechi dabbed her face and slowly opened her eyes, now bloodshot, the red outweighing the white.

Anuli walked Nkechi back to the bodies of the men.

"Can you see them now?"

"Yes. I see him, I see all of them," she confirmed, though it did take a little squinting for them to become clear. "Thanks, Auntie."

"You're welcome, dear. Now, we need to see what happened up there," she said, gulping down the anxious saliva lingering in her mouth.

As they ventured up the staircase, the eerie silence played on Anuli's mind. She hoped for the best but knew to expect the worst. Nkechi slowly followed. As Anuli took the last step, she saw that the door to one of the communal bedrooms was open. Her stomach dropped as she feared her horrid thoughts were true.

She walked over to the open door, clinging to the wall, and took a deep breath before bravely peering around the corner. What she saw only confirmed her worst fears. The frail and defenceless elders, once respected staples of the community, were now lifeless, battered and bloodied, sprawled across the room. Anuli covered her trembling jaw with her hand and burst into tears. She had lots of words she wanted to scream in that moment, but she was in too much shock to utter a single one. Instead, she stood contemplating how any of this was fair. They were innocent; they had no part in this war. Their deaths were a pointless act of violence and spite.

No matter what happened now, Anuli was adamant that the voodoo king would not be allowed to survive this war.

Nkechi tried her best to console her distraught aunt but they both knew there wasn't much anyone could say or do to make the pain feel any less excruciating.

Nkechi decided to leave her to grieve while she reassessed the situation downstairs. The four intruders lay there, only one still drawing breath – the one whose ankle had been crushed by Nkechi. He sat crying, cradling his limp foot and, as he looked up, he noticed Nkechi. He became filled with fear, shaking as he caressed his broken ankle.

She stood over him as she contemplated what to do. Nkechi could easily kill him there and then. Or she could break his other ankle or, come to think of it, his entire leg. As Nkechi continued to ponder her next actions she heard footsteps coming from the kitchen. She turned and readied herself for another fight before, thankfully, spotting that the sound came from Nicole and Kosum.

"Nkechi! The girls are gone, all of them!" Kosum blurted out as soon as she saw her.

"How? What happened?"

"Well, Kosum was possessed by two of them and they tried turning her powers on me. There were just too many for me to fight off alone, especially while also trying to keep Kosum away without actually hurting her," Nicole explained.

"It's not something that I'd like to experience again," Kosum commented. "We're sorry we couldn't help the girls, Nkechi."

"It's okay, we'll work everything out." She turned to Nicole. "You should probably go see your mom, but prepare yourself, it's not good up there."

Nicole sighed before anxiously ascending the stairs to console her mother.

"So, what do we do now?" Kosum asked.

Nkechi had an idea what to do with the lone survivor. "You're coming with us," Nkechi said ominously, looking down at him. "Kosum, can you help me drag this guy out the back?"

"C'mon, Nkechi, by now you should know I can do far better than that. Why drag him when I can do this?" She levitated him off the ground and began walking, the man floating behind her.

"You know, of all the powers I have, I really hate that I don't have that one," Nkechi called, making Kosum snigger.

Nkechi caught up with Kosum in the back garden just in

time to see her sling the guy into a fence.

"Now what?" Kosum whispered to Nkechi.

"We interrogate him," she answered casually. She turned to the man. "Tell us where they're taking the girls!" she demanded.

The man didn't dignify her with a response. Though he was clearly scared, Nkechi suspected he was even more fearful of what the voodoo king might do to him if he gave up precious information.

Still, she persisted.

"What do you want with them?"

There was no reply.

"Okay, well if you're not going to give the information freely, then maybe Kosum here can prise it out of you," Nkechi said nonchalantly, like a mob boss.

Kosum looked slightly off put by Nkechi's comment and pulled her to the side.

"Nkechi, what are you doing?"

"Relax, we're not going to kill him, but we need to make him believe that we will do whatever it takes," Nkechi explained, trying to calm Kosum's nerves.

"Just start bending his fingers back until he talks," she whispered with her hand covering the side of her mouth from the man's sight.

"What if he doesn't?"

"He will. He has to!"

"Okay," Kosum replied nervously.

Kosum began to slowly bend back the man's fingers with her mind, while Nkechi told him to start talking or Kosum would snap them off. As the pain increased, the man's face began to screw up in discomfort which, as Kosum applied more pressure, quickly turned into a groan and then a scream.

"Tell us what we want to know!" Nkechi shouted over his screaming.

"No!" he yelled back.

"Nkechi, if I keep going, they're gonna snap."

"Good," Nkechi uttered, feeling no sympathy for the man. "Where are they?" she shouted again.

"I'm… not telling you!" He struggled to answer through the pain.

"Kosum, keep going," Nkechi said menacingly. This wasn't like her but after seeing what happened to the elders, she couldn't allow the same thing to repeat itself with the kidnapped girls.

Kosum felt weird. It was one thing to fight back and even kill in self-defence, but this was wrong.

"No," Kosum answered, releasing his fingers.

The man sighed in relief as he brought his tortured hands to his lips.

"Kosum! Why did you stop? We almost had him."

"Nkechi, he wasn't going to give the information up. This isn't like you. Maybe Blair was right, maybe the power has gone to your head," Kosum barked, wearing a look of disgust.

"In case you've forgotten, we're in the middle of a war, Kosum. This isn't New York where we were fighting innocent brainwashed kids. These are soldiers – soldiers who serve the man who killed my parents; soldiers who have just killed innocent elders and kidnapped young girls; soldiers who wouldn't show us any mercy if the roles were reversed."

"But we're *not* soldiers, we're teenagers. And yes, you're

right, they probably wouldn't show us any mercy, but that's what's supposed to separate us from them."

Kosum's reasoning only riled Nkechi even more. Nkechi would've done anything to help Kosum and now she felt like her one true friend wasn't willing to do the same for her.

"You would've done *anything* to save your mom, and even if it had got a little dark, I would've been right there beside you through it. But now that *I* need to save what remnants of the broken family I have left, you're not willing to do the same. Maybe you should've just stayed in Manhattan," Nkechi spat angrily.

But the emotion was misdirected. In truth, Nkechi was angry at so many things; Charlie, the voodoo king, and Blair's comment that she might become a different person with all the power that she possessed. And now she was angry at herself for screaming in the face of the only true friend she had.

"Fuck you, Nkechi." Kosum stalked off back to Anuli's house. Kosum wasn't one for hanging around where she wasn't wanted, so if Nkechi didn't want her there, then maybe she should just pack up and leave.

Nkechi stood alone, the goon sat on the dirt beside her, hating herself. The self-pity would have to wait though, as now Nkechi needed to figure out another way to extract the information they needed.

As Nkechi contemplated her next move, Nicole and Anuli came out from the kitchen. Anuli's eyes were red and puffy, but finally dry.

"Hi, Auntie," Nkechi greeted, sounding defeated.

"Hello, dear." Anuli noticed the man, who'd almost passed out, behind Nkechi.

"What are you doing with him?" she asked, spitting on the ground in disgust at the sight of the man.

"Well, we were interrogating him, but he didn't give anything up. And now me and Kosum have fallen out," Nkechi explained, saddened.

"I have ways of making him talk," Anuli said ominously.

"We already tried torturing him; he still wouldn't budge," Nkechi, upon hearing the words leave her own mouth, realised how right Kosum was. Nkechi wasn't a torturer. She believed, not that long ago, that most disputes could be resolved by talking rather than resorting to violence. Was she a bad person? Or was she just adapting to the new, higher-stakes environment they were now in?

"I'm not talking about physical pain," Anuli explained, "I'm talking about memory possession. When possessing someone, there is a way that you can access their memories as well as their central nervous system for their body. We don't tend to do it, because unlike a usual possession, routing through someone's memories can often damage the mind. However, in an extreme case such as this one, when I don't particularly care what happens to the victim, I'm more than willing to give it a try."

"How do we even do that?" Nicole asked, slightly worried by her mother's disregard for the man's life.

"Well, the voodoo king has probably reinforced the psyche of his soldiers in case of such attacks, thus it will take all three of us to use our full concentration to break through and extract what we need," Anuli explained.

"Now then, Nkechi, help me drag him into our kitchen. Nicole, you go find Kosum – we'll need her to watch over us while we're unconscious."

"Okay." Nicole obeyed her mother's wishes and walked back to the house in search of Kosum.

Nkechi helped her auntie drag the man back to the kitchen where they propped him up against one of the cupboards. He was still visibly in pain as he held his damaged fingers to his chest and stretched out the leg which had the shattered ankle.

Nkechi felt guilty, not for the man's pain as he most definitely deserved it, but for how she had spoken to Kosum. Kosum was right, Nkechi was being more brutal than normal, and it wasn't something Nkechi was proud of. Yet it was definitely something the pair of them would have to become more accustomed to, at least until the war was over.

Upstairs, Nicole had just discovered Kosum sulkily packing her clothes into her suitcase.

"What are you doing?" she asked in confusion.

"Oh, hey. I'm packing," Kosum muttered numbly.

"Yeah, I can see that. I meant, why?"

"Me and Nkechi had an argument. She made it *very* clear that I should go back home." Kosum rambled, frustrated and hurt.

"Oh. So that means you're just going to leave then, does it?"

"Well, yeah."

"Kosum, you had an argument. You say things you don't mean when you have arguments, it's normal. And I'm quite sure that Nkechi probably already regrets it. You're best friends – best friends who have gone through a lot of shit that normal besties don't. Give each other a bit of time and I'm sure you'll work it out. Right now we need you, *I* need you. Oh, and if you thought you were gonna sneak off home without telling me, then Nkechi wouldn't be the only one you'd be arguing with," she said as she sassily folded her arms.

"I guess you're right. And of course I wasn't going to leave without telling you." Kosum smiled.

Nicole reached her hands out to Kosum. She pulled her up from the floor and kissed her. "See, now that is definitely worth sticking around for, right?"

"Yes, indeed it is," Kosum answered with a grin.

They headed back down to meet Nkechi and Anuli in the kitchen. Kosum had agreed to help and hoped in time she and Nkechi would be on good terms again. But that time wasn't now and she actively avoided eye contact.

"Now then, Nkechi and Nicole, I need you to hold my hands so we can possess him together. Only then will we be strong enough to break through the voodoo king's mental protection.

"Once we've gained possession, we need to split up and sift through his most recent memories to find what we need. I'll look for what they're planning to do with the girls; Nkechi, you look for where they are taking them, and, Nicole, you try to find the voodoo king's whereabouts," Anuli instructed.

"Okay," the girls answered.

"And what am I supposed to do?" Kosum asked.

"Watch over us. Like when we restored Nkechi's memories last year, this is once again a dangerous spell. It is always the case when interfering with another's mind. Initially it will look like we're about to have a seizure, but that's normal. Give us a minute or two to break through the mental barriers and we should calm down. But if it takes too long, then wake us up. If not, we might not be able to save ourselves," she explained.

"Awesome. So like, no pressure, then," Kosum muttered under her breath.

Nicole heard her and gave a reassuring smile.

Anuli, Nkechi and Nicole stood in a line, Nkechi in the middle, and held hands. Their eyes began to glaze over simultaneously, which from Kosum's perspective looked rather creepy.

As they delved into the man's mind, their entire bodies began to shake and convulse as their astral forms fought to pass the barriers placed in his psyche. Kosum watched anxiously as she tried her best to time them, but Anuli's instructions had been vague as to when exactly they should be awoken and what might happen to them if she didn't.

Kosum had been meticulously watching the second hand on the clock, and as it ticked another thirty seconds, the seizures began to slow before finally stopping. It signalled that they had successfully bypassed the walls in his mind.

Yet they weren't out of the woods. Kosum was faced with another dilemma: the man's body had begun to fit. His eyes rolled back and his eyelids flickered like a flame in the wind. As each second of memory-probing went by, the man's quaking became more vigorous. Kosum had no idea what to do – Anuli hadn't mentioned the possibility of *him* having a seizure. For all Kosum knew, if he died with them still routing around in his brain, they could perish along with him.

Kosum eye's bounced between the man and the clock, using the same two-minute rule Anuli had given as a limit. It was all Kosum had to go on. As the clock ticked past the second minute, the man's symptoms worsened rapidly. His seizure became crazed, limbs flailing. Even his broken ankle came to life. He began foaming at the mouth, at which point Kosum decided to pull the metaphorical plug.

Fuck this, I can't risk it any longer, she thought as she started to gently try to awaken them. She called their names and tried to shake them awake, but it wasn't working. Kosum's eyes darted about the kitchen, looking for any means to wake them. Then she noticed the kitchen tap. She turned it on, and used her telekinesis to guide the stream of water into a large globule over Nkechi's head. She then released it, drenching Nkechi in the cold water and jolting her out of her trance.

Her hands unclamped from Nicole and Anuli's in a knee jerk reaction which then also awakened them from the possession.

Nkechi's wet hair flopped over her face and she put her forearm under it to flip the hefty locks back over her head. Kosum had to hide the slight snigger trying to escape her lips.

Now, in the safety of their own earthly vessels, they watched as the man continued to spasm and foam until suddenly everything stopped. His body went limp, his head dropped, and his eyes drained of any signs of life. His mind had been fried, and he was no more.

"Is he…?" Nicole pondered aloud.

"Yes. I said it was a dangerous spell. I guess he was just too weak to survive." Anuli spoke coldly, not really having much empathy for the cold-blooded murderer cluttering up her kitchen. "Good job pulling us out when you did, Kosum."

Nkechi rolled her eyes, knowing it wasn't a coincidence that she was the one who got soaked.

"So, did you guys get what you needed?" Kosum asked.

"I couldn't get anything about the voodoo king's location, unfortunately," Nicole said, looking disappointed with herself.

Kosum put her arm around her. "Don't worry, we'll find him, I'm sure of it," she reassured, pecking Nicole on the cheek.

"I'm afraid I didn't come up with much information, either. I just saw a memory of them talking in vague terms about adding them to 'the herd'. Whatever that is, it doesn't sound good, and I think the details were above his pay grade," Anuli shared. "What about you, Nkechi? Please tell me you got something we can use," Anuli asked, looking hopeful.

Nkechi wiped some more of the water off her face.

"I did get something… I found the girls' location."

CHAPTER 7

All's Fair in Love and War

After Nkechi revealed the location of the kidnapped girls, Anuli called for an emergency meeting. Everyone gathered downstairs in the basement-cum-war room.

Having only just arrived the night before, Nkechi and Kosum hadn't been privy to it yet. They entered the dimly lit room, a single lightbulb dangling from a wire the only thing keeping them alight. There was a small window in the top right-hand corner that would normally offer a glimpse of the garden. Butas it was still the early hours of the morning, it remained a pitch-black square. There was a large table in the centre of the room which came up to Nkechi's waist. On top was a map of the local area sandwiched beneath a piece of glass. There was a pot of different coloured marker pens that correlated to a little key drawn in the corner of the map. Areas coloured green were considered safe zones and under control of the Resistance; anywhere red was the voodoo king's territory, and orange denoted a current battleground.

In light of recent events, it all seemed rather pointless. Anuli's house was in the green zone, but still the voodoo king's men had manged to infiltrate the area with ease.

As they all gathered around the table, Nicole made sure to plant herself between Nkechi and Kosum, the tension between the pair awkward. Anuli, Adame and Evélia joined the table and were accompanied by one other – a young man, about the same age as the girls. He was handsome, rather muscular, and he certainly caught Nkechi's eye. She couldn't help it; it was a kneejerk reaction. His cheekbones were almost as prominent as the bulging pectorals discernible beneath his tight shirt. He had deep brown skin and piercingly blue eyes, much like Evélia's, and cornrows running along his head, with an inch of hair hanging down the nape of his neck.

Nkechi sensed a familiarity about him, something that drew her to him. None of that mattered though, as Nkechi knew she wasn't ready for anyone else. After all, she still had Charlie plaguing her dreams. The eye candy was more than welcome though as most of the time it felt like a bit of a girls' only club, which of course was fine for Nicole and Kosum but not so much for her.

Anuli addressed the table passionately, a fury in her eyes as she slammed her hands down and informed the others of the missing girls' whereabouts.

"So, what's the plan?" the handsome stranger asked.

"You and Nkechi will track down the girls, while Kosum and Nicole show the traitors what happens when they step foot in our home," Anuli answered.

"Mom, what do you mean?" Nicole asked.

"I want you girls to take the bodies to the town square and put them on show. Let it be a message to the voodoo king and his men," Anuli said coldly.

"Anuli, that's a little extreme, no?" Evélia questioned.

"No. If they wish to act like vermin then that is how they shall be treated. And do you know what you do to scare vermin off?"

No one had time or the gall to answer.

"You show them what happens to them if they don't leave."

Jesus, what is with everyone? Kosum thought to herself as her eyes coyly darted about the room. *I understand the stakes are high, but this is weird. And I never thought I'd be the one to be the voice of reason.* She wasn't used to being the quiet one, but equally she felt she didn't have the right to tell them how to fight their war. Besides, after what happened with Nkechi, she saw it best to bite her tongue, even if that did go against every fibre of her being.

"But the town square is in the orange zone," Nkechi stated, a little worried.

Adame interjected. "Well, we haven't heard any reports of fighting there in the last few days, and it's highly unlikely that they will strike again so soon, especially when they are clearly wanting to use the girls for something important."

"Precisely. Besides Nicole and Kosum can handle themselves. Right, girls?" Anuli added.

"Yes, Mom. We'll go dispose of the bodies," Nicole said, feeling that she couldn't disobey her mother. "C'mon, Kosum, let's go."

As Kosum left the table guided by Nicole's hand, she took one last glance to see Nkechi watching her leave. Nkechi's eyes looked full of guilt, but Kosum's glance in return was still an icy one.

"You know, I can go it alone. I have my elixirs, I'll be fine," the handsome stranger said. His tone suggested to Nkechi that he didn't want her with him.

"Hush, Parfait. Don't be so rude. You should be honoured

to have Nkechi fighting alongside you," Evélia said, smacking the back of his head.

"Argh, Jesus, Mother. Fine! I'll take her," he said, rolling his eyes, which warranted another clip across the back of his head, this time by his father, Adame.

"Don't speak to your mother like that! Sorry for his insolence, Nkechi. He doesn't always think before he speaks," Adame apologised, embarrassed by his son.

"Oh, it's fine," Nkechi said awkwardly. She could feel Parfait's eyes burning into her and his jaw grinding like a flour mill, so she didn't want to wind him up more.

"So, it's settled – you *two* will go and find the girls, then once you've located them, assess whether you need backup. Nicole and Kosum should be done by then and I will ask them to meet you if needed," Anuli instructed.

Nkechi smiled and nodded, while Parfait screwed up his face, clearly unhappy with the outcome.

Nkechi was bewildered, not knowing what she had done to offend him. After all, they'd only met a few minutes ago.

As they left the basement, Parfait stormed past, pushing her shoulder as he did so.

Nkechi waited until they were out of earshot before confronting him.

"Hey! What's your problem, man?"

"Don't worry ya pretty little head about it, uh," he grunted, continuing to walk moodily towards a car parked in the driveway next door.

Nkechi caught up with him and tugged at his arm to turn him around.

"Dude, I dunno what your problem is – I don't even know

you – but we have to work together, so can you at least give me the time of day instead of grunting at me?"

He rolled his eyes and turned around, muttering, "Whatever, princess."

That really wound Nkechi up. "What did you just say?"

"Sorry, *warrior* princess. That better?" he retorted sarcastically, without turning to look at her.

Nkechi sprinted in front of him and stopped him in his tracks, firmly placing her hand against his chest.

"No, no it's really no better. Tell me what your problem is right now, or I'm gonna torch your tyres," she said, conjuring a fireball in her hand, with a smile. Nkechi saw the car up ahead. It was a huge white Jeep with black alloys. It looked to be well maintained – he clearly cared a lot about it.

"All right, all right, jeez. Just don't hurt the car, she's precious," he moaned.

Jesus Christ, Nkechi thought.

"Look, my parents seem to think that you're our saviour who will destroy the voodoo king, and that it doesn't really matter what the rest of us do, so long as you're here. But, let me reassure you, you're not my saviour and I could easily do this mission without you," he said brushing past her once again and hopping into the driver's seat.

What he had said was a lot for Nkechi to digest. She had no idea she had been revered so much. She didn't really know how to respond, so she kept quiet and got into the passenger seat, and they pulled away.

Nicole and Kosum were pushing a wheelbarrow with two hefty bodies to the town square, taking it in turns as they went.

"You know, this isn't exactly what I had in mind for our next trip out as a couple," Nicole commented.

"Oh, so you didn't want to be wheeling two dead guys across town?" Kosum teased, trying to lighten the mood as she walked along the road, wheelbarrow in hand.

"I *mean* it was definitely an option, but I was hoping for more of a wine and dine kinda date, maybe some cinema, bowling, or literally anything other than what we're doing right now," Nicole chuckled.

"Well, I'm just happy to spend time with you, even if it is in Grim Reaper style," Kosum said. Unable to take her eyes off Nicole, she didn't see the rock in the road which almost knocked the wheelbarrow over.

Nicole belly laughed. "Smooth. But seriously, once this is all over, I'm taking you on a proper date."

"Hey, you'll have no complaints from me about that! Can we take a break for a minute? I think I pulled a muscle because of that stupid rock," Kosum said, having already come to a halt as she placed a hand on her back for support.

"Come over here for a second," Nicole waved, walking on ahead of her.

"What is it?"

"You'll see," she answered, vaguely.

Kosum followed Nicole as she walked further down the road. She hadn't noticed the road had been slowly increasing in height as the ground fell away around them. They were venturing onto a bridge. Kosum was struggling to keep up, but thankfully Nicole came to a stop as she leaned against the bridge's railing and looked out.

Kosum caught up with her, but before she could speak, she parked her body next to Nicole and caught a glimpse of the beautiful sunrise. It was the perfect view – the sun rose over a valley of trees in the distance.

"Wow," Kosum uttered.

"Yep, pretty cool, huh?"

"I'll say," Kosum replied, gazing out at the picturesque scenery.

Standing there reminded them of the first time they had kissed, back on the bridge with all the pesky flies. Nicole slid her hand along the rail to join Kosum's. They turned to face each other and kissed. One side of their faces was cast in the early morning sunshine while the other half was in shadow, creating a beautiful silhouette.

"You know, you and Nkechi shou—"

"Shh." Kosum placed a finger on Nicole's lips. "I know Nkechi and I need to talk, but right now I'm not thinking about her." Kosum pulled Nicole's chin close to hers and their lips met again.

Nicole was surprised by Kosum's new attitude, but it was welcome. They embraced a little longer, making the most of their moment in the sun, before reluctantly getting back to work, this time Nicole driving the wheelbarrow.

Back in Parfait's Jeep, Nkechi had remained quiet during the journey, but she knew they couldn't sit in silence forever.

"Hey, what do those do?" Nkechi asked, pointing to his belt filled with different coloured vials.

He rolled his eyes as if she should've known. "They're my elixirs. Each has a different purpose. Some give me powers – making me stronger or invisible, or they can heal me. Others are negative affecting elixirs for the enemy."

"Oh, that's cool," Nkechi said, trying to appease him.

"Yeah, I know," he grunted.

My god! He is so annoying! Nkechi thought, while her lips screwed up and her teeth ground together.

"So, what else can you do?" Nkechi asked, in the hope they might at least find some magical common ground.

"Nothing. I'm a practitioner, not a warlock, so that's about it. Sorry if I'm not magic enough for ya!" He snapped at her once again, rolling his eyes.

"What's the difference?" Nkechi asked, naively.

"Jesus! And my parents think that you're gonna be our saviour! Do you even know voodoo?" he scoffed.

"Yes, I do! But unfortunately, unlike you, both of my parents are dead. And when my mom *was* alive, she had to focus on teaching me to defend myself and provide a roof over our heads, instead of teaching me the ins and outs of voodoo politics," Nkechi ranted.

"All right, all right, easy." He sighed. "Fine, if I have to, I'll explain. You are a witch; I am a practitioner. I can create elixirs, which I do very well, and I can take part in rituals, but unlike witches I cannot create spells or possess people."

"Oh, I didn't know that. So, what's the difference between you and me? Why aren't you a witch?" Nkechi asked.

"Over time, within the voodoo community men became

less dominant with their magic until they pretty much stopped using it. The women did most of the casting, and took charge in major rituals. That's why the voodoo king is so powerful – he's centuries' years old, when men also had great voodoo power. And it seems he's shared his gifts, or at least some of them, with his most trusted men."

"I see. Why didn't anyone mention this earlier?"

"Because they probably thought the same as me – that your mother had told you this stuff when you were growing up," Parfait explained, finally relaxing a little.

Nkechi felt slightly disappointed. She questioned whether her mother had taught her such things and she had just forgotten or wasn't as good as student as she believed herself to be. Either way, it was beginning to dawn on her that she might have as much to learn about her mother's heritage as she did her father's.

"Hey, we're almost there. We should probably do the last leg of the journey on foot. If they see us in this thing, they'll definitely be on to us," he said to Nkechi, who was a little sidetracked by her thoughts.

"Nkechi?" Parfait prompted, lightly snapping his fingers to get her attention.

"Yeah, sorry. That's a good idea," Nkechi said, breaking herself out the trance.

"Look, you're clearly not in the right head space for a fight and I don't need another liability out there in the battlefield, so just sit this one out, will you?"

"No, I'll be fine. Besides, I'm no quitter. And I *won't* be a liability, thank you!"

"Ugh, if you insist," Parfait muttered, rolling his eyes before he pulled up a couple of blocks out from the destination. He made sure his belt, and the inside pockets of his leather jacket were fully stocked with his elixirs before setting off to finish the rest of their journey on foot.

Nicole and Kosum had finally reached the centre of town. They were both growing tired and so decided to take a handle each of the wheelbarrow to share the weight. As they struggled down the road, their phones rang simultaneously. They dropped the wheelbarrow to answer.

On Kosum's screen was Ana's caller ID, while Anuli's appeared on Nicole's. Kosum swiped her thumb across the screen to answer, eager for news of her mother.

"Ana?" Kosum belted down the phone.

"Hello." It was her mother's voice, albeit a weaker and quieter version of it.

"Mom! Is that really you? Are you okay? Where's Ana?" she asked frantically.

"Yes, my dear, it's really me. I'm okay, and Ana is right here beside me," Kwanjai muttered, sounding weak. "She's told me the great lengths you went through for me. Thank you, my love."

"You don't have to thank me, Mom. I'd have done anything," she said, realising she had just confirmed exactly what Nkechi had said a few hours earlier. "Do you want me to come home?" Kosum happily offered.

"No, no," Kwanjai croaked, "Nkechi needs you. I'll still be here when you get back, don't worry about that. You need to be there for Nkechi, like she was for you. You're like sisters," Kwanjai said, confirming in Kosum's mind that she indeed needed to make up with Nkechi.

"Okay. But promise that you will call me if anything happens."

"I give you my word." Kwanjai spoke softly, smiling to herself.

"I love you. Goodbye for now."

"Goodbye, sweetheart."

Once the call had ended, Kwanjai turned to Ana who was sitting on the bed beside her.

"Ana, I need your help with something."

"Anything," Ana smiled.

Kosum slid the phone back into her pocket and turned to Nicole, a beaming smile on her face. Nicole, having strolled off to answer her own call, wasn't privy to the conversation Kosum had just had.

"What's got you so smiley?" Nicole asked.

"My mom's awake and she's okay!"

"Oh, my god, Kosum, that's amazing!" Nicole said, grabbing her girlfriend and pulling her in for a warm hug.

"Thanks," Kosum whispered over her shoulder as they embraced. "Wait, what was your call about?" she asked as they released each other from their loving grasp.

"It was my mom – she told me the address Nkechi and Parfait are heading to and asked us to meet them there once we've dealt with this," Nicole answered.

"Parfait… So, that's the name of the hunk at the meeting."

"Yep, but he's a knuckle head."

"A knuckle head Nkechi could get under?"

"Ew, Kosum! She's still my cousin. And I thought you said she wasn't ready for anyone, that she's not over Charlie yet.".

"Chill, I'm not saying they should get married. But I think a little friends-with-benefits might help her get over Charlie."

"I really hope you won't have that attitude if I die," Nicole commented, folding her arms.

"That's *so* different – unless you're a sociopathic murderer and haven't told me," Kosum teased.

"Okay, you got me there. But still, maybe we should just stay out of Nkechi's love life – let her figure things out for herself," Nicole suggested.

"Ugh, fine, I'll try. But I'm not promising anything." Kosum submitted, though with a mischievous smile.

Kosum already felt more like her usual self after hearing her mother's voice. She felt like a weight had been lifted, which meant she could finally put her all into stopping the voodoo king with Nkechi.

Now they just needed to make up.

Grabbing Kosum by the waist, Nicole pulled her close before planting a kiss on her lips. They could have quite easily taken their passionate kiss much further, though the fact they were surrounded by dead bodies was a slight metaphorical cockblock.

"Right c'mon, we need to get these guys hoisted up there and then meet Nkechi," Nicole reminded, reluctantly pulling herself away from a very horny Kosum.

"Okay, but it'll be quicker if I do it," Kosum said before one by one levitating the bodies onto two balconies of buildings within the town square.

Once the bodies were on show for all their enemies to

see, Nicole and Kosum began running across town to meet Nkechi and Parfait.

Nkechi and Parfait warily kept an eye out for any of the voodoo king's men while they continued their journey on foot. Now that they had entered the red zone, they had to be extra careful.

They eventually reached their destination after ten minutes of walking in silence. The old factory building stood before them, ten storeys tall. It had clearly been abandoned for many years before the voodoo king's recent residence there. Most of the windows were smashed and boarded up, with the remaining few smeared with substances Nkechi didn't want to hazard a guess at. She reluctantly hugged the wall of the building, Parfait following behind, trying their best not to be spotted. The only advantage they had was the element of surprise.

As they continued to shuffle along the perimeter of the building, they came across a side door. It was unguarded and seemingly unalarmed – maybe the voodoo king was becoming negligent, or perhaps it was just to lure them in.

Nkechi tried opening the door, but it was locked, so she gave it a nudge with her shoulder. The same result undoubtedly occurred although now she also had an achy shoulder. She could've easily blasted the whole door off with a magical gust of wind, but that would draw too much attention.

"Can you?" she prompted, reluctantly glancing at Parfait and then back at the door.

"Sure," he smiled smugly. He pulled a purple elixir from his belt, popped the cork off and glugged it all at once. His eyes glowed the same purple hue before returning to their natural electric blue. He cracked his neck on each side, showboating a little, before grasping the handle. With a small but powerful nudge, the door opened.

"Wow, all those muscles and you still needed a strength-bolstering elixir," Nkechi commented sassily.

"I'm sorry, did you open the door? No, so zip it," he quipped with equal sass.

Once inside, there was a long, bleak hallway ahead of them – the kind you'd expect to see in a horror movie. It was dimly lit and there were damp patches floor to ceiling. Parfait took the lead and slowly walked down the vacant corridor.

Many footsteps later and they reached a wall that split the corridor in two directions. They looked at each other to see if either of them had any indication of which direction to take.

Nkechi suggested. "Should we split up?"

"Have you never seen a scary movie?" Parfait retorted.

"Look, I know it's dangerous, but I'm pretty sure we can handle ourselves. You wanted to come alone, remember?"

"Well, that was before we got here. Now there are two of us, we should stick together. Besides, we're black, we're always the first to die in scary movies."

"Ya know, I don't think that rule applies when everyone involved is black, look around… do you see any white 'final' girls? No."

"Hey, guys," Kosum whispered from behind them, causing Parfait to jump.

Nkechi sniggered at his expense.

"I wasn't scared," he commented, puffing out his chest.

"No, of course not," Kosum smirked.

"I mean… now there's someone who's not black," Parfait muttered under his breath, though still loud enough for Nkechi to hear.

"Excuse you! Kosum is gay *and* Asian – she'd have a much worse chance in a scary movie, dumbass!" Nkechi said, exhausted by his presence.

"Er, what did we just walk into?" Nicole asked, sensing the awkward tension in the air.

"Nothing, we were just deciding which way to go," Nkechi huffed.

"Yeah, and now that there's more of us, I'd be okay with splitting up," Parfait stated.

Jesus Christ, of course now it's a fine idea, Nkechi internally moaned.

"Great!" she said. "Kosum, you're with me," she demanded, pulling Kosum's hand and dragging her down the right-hand corridor.

"Oh, okay, 'bye," Kosum called to Nicole as she was quickly pulled out of sight.

"I guess it's me and you then," Nicole said to Parfait with an awkward smile.

"Yup," he replied in a flat voice.

Nkechi and Kosum had been walking in an awkward silence for a few minutes, neither of them really knowing how to start the conversation they both knew they needed to have. Nkechi had had enough and stopped walking to turn to Kosum.

Kosum took a deep breath and turned to face her best friend, a little anxious to hear what she was about to say.

"I'm sorry. You were right, I have become less morally sound, and I definitely shouldn't have asked you to torture that guy.

"I hate us not speaking, even if it has only been a few hours. You're my best friend and I didn't mean what I said. I think I was just angry at myself because I knew that you were right." Nkechi spoke from the heart and watched Kosum's face, eagerly, in the hope she'd forgive her.

"I'm sorry, too. You said a lot of things that were true. My mom called earlier, and I got to hear her voice for the first time in a month, something that I thought I might never hear again. It reminded me that, I would've done whatever it took to save her. Nkechi, you're not just my bestie, you're my sister from another mister. You were there for me when I needed you most, and I'm here for you now. And though in the real world what we're doing would be seen as wrong, we don't live in that world. We're living in a warzone, a magical one at that, and unfortunately that does mean we have to adapt. Nkechi, I'm with you, I would do anything to protect you. But please, no more torturing. So, what do you say, besties again?" Kosum proposed with a heavy heart.

"Like we could ever not be besties. I love you, girl!" Nkechi said, pulling her into a tight embrace. "I promise I'll never ask you to snap someone's fingers off again," she muttered into Kosum's ear as they hugged.

Kosum smirked at that.

They let go of one another to see that they both had

tear-soaked faces, before once again chuckling at their 'ugly' crying.

"I love you, too," Kosum smiled, wiping the tears from her face. "It's a good job I didn't have time to put make-up on this morning or it would've been ruined," she chuckled.

"*Please*, I've seen the price of your make-up – for that much, the shit better be fireproof, let alone waterproof," Nkechi teased. "I'm glad your mom is okay," she added once the giggling had died down.

"Thanks, me too. Now, what the hell was all that about earlier? You and Parfait looked like you were either gonna fuck each other up or just fuck each other," Kosum laughed.

"Oh, my god, don't even start! He is the most annoying person I've ever met!"

"Hmm," Kosum hummed, her eyes mischievously darting about.

"What?"

"I think you guys wanna do the second one," Kosum smiled playfully.

"No, I promise you it's the first one, and I already told you, I'm not ready for a new boyfriend, especially not him."

"And *I* already told *you*, you don't need to date him or anyone, just get under him, or over, whatever floats ya boat I suppose," she winked.

Nkechi rolled her eyes. "Shut up," she said, pushing Kosum lightly.

"Okay, okay, c'mon then, let's keep going." Kosum wrapped her arm around Nkechi's shoulder and continued down the eerily dark corridor.

On the other side of the warehouse, Nicole and Parfait were also talking about the possible connection between Nkechi and himself. Nicole had given up trying to convince Kosum otherwise and so thought she'd join in on the playful teasing.

"So, what do you think of Nkechi? Pretty cute, huh?" Nicole prompted.

"I guess, but she's hella annoying." He shrugged indifferently.

"That's my cousin you're talking about, remember?"

"Sorry. She's just not for me," he replied casually.

"What, so pretty, smart an—"

"Shh, I hear something." Parfait put his large hand over her mouth. He had noticed a door up ahead; the noise seemed to be coming from there. It sounded like whimpering – the missing young girls? – with the deeper voices of a few men taunting them.

Nicole pulled his hand off her face.

"Don't do that ever again," she whispered angrily.

"I think the girls are in there," he said, pointing his thumb at the door.

"How do you know?"

"I took a heightened senses elixir when you stopped to go pee in the corner, which is gross by the way. Even I wouldn't do that and I'm a guy."

"First of all, I don't appreciate the lowkey sexism, and secondly, I'm sorry, but believe it or not I've not had time to take a bathroom break today after waking up at the crack of dawn and hauling two dead bodies across town. But hey, good thinking with the heightened senses crap." Nicole reluctantly acknowledged the smart idea.

"Thanks… I guess," he uttered, a little taken back by Nicole's rant. "Look, we need to sneak in and assess the situation."

They moved to the door, opened it and crawled through, managing to hide behind some stacked crates. They peered through the gaps in the crates to see Parfait's suspicions were confirmed. They spotted a cell where the girls were being kept. It was like an oversized rabbit cage, except without the comfy bedding or food and water supply. The cell was nothing more than four iron barred walls and a concrete floor.

Two men dressed in what looked like scavenged tactical gear, were clanging weapons across the bars to intimidate the girls. One of them had a crowbar and the other a hammer – not exactly a professional operation.

"So, how do you wanna play this?" Nicole asked hastily. Hearing the fear in the girls' cries fuelled her own urge to beat up the evil men.

"You take the one on the left and I'll take the one on the right," Parfait suggested, cracking his knuckles.

"Sure, let's go."

They split up and snuck around the remaining crates when Parfait noticed one of them had been opened slightly. He peered in to see multiple vials containing a metallic red, swirling elixir. An inexperienced practitioner wouldn't have a clue what it was but Parfait, knew they exactly what they were capable of. They contained an explosive potion. Who knows what the voodoo king had planned for that many explosives. Parfait knew he'd have to secure it for the Resistance so the voodoo king couldn't use it against them, but first the girls.

He slipped in on the right, smacking the goon's head into the bars of the cell, before engaging in a full-on fist fight. The second guard turned to help, but before he could do so, Nicole popped out from behind him and shouted to grab his attention. The second she got him away from Parfait and focusing on her, she began to whisper: "*Couper.*"

She whispered it over and over and each time she did, a patch of his skin was sliced open by an invisible force. At first the odd cut was just a nuisance, but as he charged to her, she intensified her voice, causing the spell's impact to increase. Great gashes appeared on his legs and even beneath the armoured vest he wore.

He slowed down as his body began to contort in pain. It wasn't long before he was brought to his knees, spasming, almost lifeless and out of breath, blood pouring across his ebony skin. The final few whispers of Nicole's spell caused cuts to appear on his face and then one last slice across his throat. The man's life was swiftly snuffed out as the puddle of blood around him grew by the second.

"Need any help?" Nicole asked, with her arms folded as she watched Parfait make a meal of taking out his guard.

"No, I've got it," he said, wrangling the equally well-built man into a headlock.

"Oh, yeah, it really looks like it," she smirked.

"Shut up!" he groaned, before finally twisting the man's neck with a crunch. "See, I handled it. He must've also had an elixir in his system."

"Awesome. Now, do me a favour and yank that padlock off."

"Sure, in a minute." He hunched over, holding his finger in the air and panting, a little out of breath. He walked over to the cell where the incarcerated girls were finally starting to calm down, now they'd seen some familiar faces. Grasping the padlock in his hands, he pulled at it, but it didn't budge.

"I thought you had a strength elixir in you?"

"I do, and trust me, I'm pulling *really* hard," he grunted, expending most of his energy trying again. It was still no use and as his hands began to hurt, he took a step back with a confused look across his face.

"Well, there must be a key here somewhere. Check the guy's pockets," Nicole suggested.

"Yes, boss." He sarcastically saluted, feeling like he was doing all the hard work.

He found a big loop of keys on the guy's belt. Luckily, there were only a few that looked as though they would fit, so after a couple of tries, he found the one that fitted the lock.

Yet even then, it didn't unlock. The key fitted the internal grooves perfectly, but no matter how hard he tried, Parfait couldn't turn it.

"What the hell is this thing?" he shouted, losing patience and feeling slightly emasculated in front of all the girls. By then a few of them had become comfortable enough to snigger at the situation which only wound him up more.

"It must be a magical lock. Nkechi told me about the time she used one on her apartment back in New York."

"And?" he prompted impatiently, clearly angered by the name of his so called 'saviour.'

"It worked that only her hand could open it. Maybe they placed the same spell on the key. So..." Nicole hinted, looking towards the two corpses.

"Ew, seriously?"

"Afraid so. You hoist him up and I'll use his hand to turn the key. Got it?"

"OK." Parfait hoisted up the heavy man's dead body by the armpits and propped him up against the cell wall.

"Quick, he's heavy and my strength elixir is wearing off."

"Okay, okay," Nicole answered, fumbling the man's fingers around the key. "There," she said, as she turned his limp wrist, and the padlock popped off.

Parfait dumped the body back to the ground with a grunt. "I can't believe it actually worked."

"Well, you can thank Nkechi when you see her," she taunted.

Parfait rolled his eyes and tutted disapprovingly.

They opened the gate and, one by one, the girls left the prison.

"Well, that wasn't so hard," Nicole commented.

"Why would you say that? Seriously, does no one know scary movie rules?" Parfait stressed.

"Oh relax, this is real life, not some fantasy novel."

As Nicole spoke, three more guards appeared, one from each exit of the room, making Nicole wish she'd bit her tongue.

"See!"

"Yeah, okay, I take full responsibility for that one. Girls, get back in the cell while we sort these idiots out," Nicole said. "Ready for round two?"

"I guess so. I'll take these guys on," Parfait answered, pointing at the two smaller men.

"How does it track that I get the giant?" she shouted over her shoulder, as the seven-foot man began walking in her direction.

"Because he's closer to you," he said, now wrestling his guards.

Fuck, she thought.

Knowing she had nowhere to run, Nicole started her cutting spell once more muttering, "*Couper.*" However, it soon became apparent that the brute of a man was unphased by it unlike her previous foe. The minor cuts to his beefy body seemed to merely provoke him as he marched his way over to her. Nicole panicked and froze. When he reached her, he swatted her to the ground with ease. His mammoth hand left a stinging mark across Nicole's cheek.

On the ground, Nicole's vision was a bit hazy, and she struggled to stop herself from falling unconscious. She could just about see that Parfait was also losing as he was down on his knees being kicked in the stomach. It was safe to say they were both losing, and fast.

The tall husky man gripped Nicole by her throat and held her out in front him, her feet squirming, trying to reach the ground. Her hands were latched onto his arms, yanking at them to try to free herself, but it was no use – her physical strength was no match for his. But perhaps she would be a match for his mind.

Though the voodoo king's men had some protection to prevent them from being possessed, Nicole fancied her chances with this guy. Big and tough he might be, but he didn't seem to be much of a thinker.

Nicole faked choking to death in the hope the oaf might

toss her back to the ground. Her plan partially worked as her Oscar-winning performance did lead him to believe she'd died. But instead of releasing her, he threw her over his shoulder and mumbled something about throwing her into a pit.

In that moment, Nicole didn't have time to ponder what the pit might be as the man began to head in Parfait's direction. Already losing his own fight, Parfait certainly didn't need the big not-so-friendly giant joining in.

Nicole's eyes rolled back in her head as she wormed her way into the oaf's mind. Though it wasn't easy, Nicole managed to take control of him. She used his great strength to gently place her body back on the ground before walking over to Parfait. She picked up the two smaller goons by their heads and smashed them together. Nicole wasn't sure if she'd knocked them out or left them braindead, not that it mattered much to her. Nicole had to grow up fast living where she did, watching people die in the streets on a regular basis. To her, this was simply karma.

To finish off the second round of goons, she ran her vessel's body into the wall headfirst, knocking him out, releasing Nicole back into her own body, albeit with a searing headache.

"Nice job," Parfait complemented as he got up off the ground and compressed his now bruised torso. "But what took you so long?"

Nicole looked at him with menace.

"I'm joking, relax," he chuckled.

"Haha, very funny. Now c'mon, let's get out of here. Call Nkechi and tell her we have the girls," Nicole said, furrowing her eyebrows in pain.

"Why can't you ring her?"

"Because I feel like I've been stabbed in the brain, *and* I just saved your ass. So unless you'd like me to tell Nkechi all about that…"

"Ugh, fine!" Parfait pulled out his phone and called Nkechi. It rang for a while until finally someone picked up

Someone who was most definitely not Nkechi.

"Hello?"

CHAPTER 8

The Voodoo King

Nkechi and Kosum had been traipsing their side of the warehouse for what felt like for ever. Each room they came across looked abandoned, with no clues as to where the missing young girls could be.

"I'm so glad your mom's awake, Kosum. What did she say? Is she okay?"

"She's fine. She said I should thank you on her behalf for helping me, and that I should stay here with you until the war is over. She said she'll let me know if she needs me."

"Are you sure you don't want to go back home? I of all people understand how you've been feeling this past month; you thought you might never see your mom again. I get it if you want to be with her… I'd give anything to see my mom again," Nkechi said solemnly.

"Thank you, but my mom is safe, she doesn't need me right now. My sis does." Kosum smiled and lovingly grasped Nkechi's hand in her own.

"Thanks," Nkechi gave one last squeeze of Kosum's hand before letting go. "You know, it's really cute saying I'm like a sister, but that would make you and Nicole related." Nkechi chuckled, ruining the touching moment.

"Ew, Nkechi! Why would you put that thought in my

mind?" Kosum groaned.

"Sorry," she laughed.

"C'mon, we need to get back to work, those poor girls aren't gonna find themselves," Kosum said, trying to refocus.

"Yeah, let's go."

Nkechi and Kosum once again became vigilant as they walked the corridors of their enemy's base. Nkechi noticed a door up ahead with some light pouring beneath its frame. They silently stalked up to the door. Kosum mouthed to Nkechi, holding up three fingers, "On three."

Nkechi nodded before they both began to count, holding their fingers up to each other: *one, two, three.*

They burst through the door and immediately took a defensive stance, Nkechi with globes of fire floating above her palms and Kosum projecting a telekinetic forcefield around them.

"Well, that was anticlimactic," Kosum moaned as she looked around at the vacant room.

"Yeah, it was, wasn't it? Stay alert, there's still something off about this room," Nkechi said, squinting her eyes as she continued to survey it. It was the largest room they'd come across thus far, but also the barest. Even the abandoned rooms they had seen had remnants of the building's past – old machinery and what not – but this one was purposely empty. It had exposed brick walls, and large arched windows on the back wall. The light scattered in through the broken panes causing a few miniature rainbows to hit the grey concrete floor. There was only one thing in the centre of this room: a singular throne belonging to the voodoo king; a poignant reminder that this was a dictatorship and they were fighting for freedom.

"Maybe it's *this* that's giving you the creeps about the room," Kosum said, walking over to the throne and running her fingers along the hand-carved ivory handles.

"Kosum, don't touch it!"

"Why?"

"It could be boobytrapped for a start, and also I'm pretty sure that's real bone," Nkechi commented, having inspected the chair closer.

"What! Like human bone?"

"Probably."

Kosum freaked, gagging at what she'd just stroked her hand across. "That's disgusting!" she screamed.

Nkechi continued to inspect the throne as Kosum shook her hands frantically in the air, as if that would cleanse them.

"Kosum, please stop, you're distracting me. I'm trying to make this out."

"Make what out?"

"This," Nkechi said, pointing towards an inscription at the head of the throne. "It's French."

"Well, what does it say?" Kosum asked.

"Give me a second, my French isn't great. I only know the stuff I use in spells. Wait…" Nkechi squinted to focus on the words. "I think it says, 'ruler of the undead'."

"I thought your buddy, Papa Legba, was in charge of all that death and limbo stuff?"

"There's more than one voodoo deity who deals with life and death. The other is Baron Samedi. If the voodoo king is using magic with the help of Baron Samedi, then this might be a whole lot harder than any of us realised. I don't know what his plans are but messing with the undead sounds pretty dangerous to me."

"Well, as fun as that sounds, I don't fancy sticking around to become his next victim so, how about we move on? Look, there's another door, hopefully that one will lead us to the girls and not another creepy bone-chair room."

"Okay, I'm coming," Nkechi replied, lingering beside the throne for a few seconds longer, deep in thought.

As Nkechi turned to join Kosum, a plume of green smoke appeared from thin air and smacked into the ground before Kosum. She let out a high screech in shock before stepping back and turning to look for Nkechi. They met halfway and stood closely so that they could feel the support of their shoulders brushing one another. The smoke dispersed slowly to reveal the voodoo king.

"*Bonjour*, Nkechi," greeted the smarmy-looking voodoo king. He zhuzhed his short curly grey hair with one hand and twiddled his staff in the other. His robes hit the floor around him whilst also leaving his beefy chest exposed. "Oh, and this must be the now equally infamous Kosum. What brings you to my humble abode, ladies?"

"I think we both know the answer to that," Nkechi retorted.

"Hmm, no. It must have slipped my mind. Do remind me, dear," he grinned, mocking them.

"You killed innocent elders and kidnapped young girls! Is that enough of a memory jog for you?" Kosum snapped.

"Oh yes, of course, how could I have forgotten? That was just a little *pruning* before I make the town mine again." He spoke nonchalantly, which only riled Nkechi more.

"The town was never yours and I assure you, it never will be," Nkechi spat in anger.

"We shall see." He appeared unconcerned by their presence, or at least he didn't want to allow them to think he felt threatened by them. "Anyhow, I couldn't possibly in good faith allow you to take *my* girls. I have plans for them to join my—" He paused, stroking his equally grey beard for a moment. "Well, let's keep it a surprise for now."

"We're not leaving here without them," Nkechi growled.

"That settles it then – *you're* not leaving." With a wave of his hand, the voodoo king summoned ten more plumes of green smoke which surrounded Nkechi and Kosum. Each plume faded to reveal one of the voodoo king's practitioners.

The room was silent for a moment as they stared at Nkechi and Kosum.

"Well, seize them!" he commanded, before turning himself back into puff of smoke and teleporting himself to his throne to watch the carnage unfold.

Nkechi and Kosum turned back-to-back as the circle of goons closed in on them. Kosum threw her hands out in front of her in the shape of claws. She levitated two of the men by their throats. They began to splutter and squirm in the air, their hands scratching at their necks trying to free themselves of the invisible force constricting them.

On the other side of the room, Nkechi was busy trying to figure out a counter curse. Six men were stood in a line before her. Their palms were clamped together as they whispered a curse. Nkechi couldn't tell which it was, but she definitely wasn't ready to have her sight taken away for a second time.

Still clueless of the curse they were busy imposing on her,

Nkechi tried to possess one of the men in a bid to find out. But before Nkechi could even attempt to extract any information, her astral form was bounced back into her own body. The group curse must've been providing them with some sort of hive mind protection against mental attacks.

The only option Nkechi had left was to try to break them up the old-fashioned way with some good old brute force. She cradled her hands by her stomach to summon a gust of wind before blasting the gale towards the men. The mighty gust, which should've easily broken the group apart, simply dispersed across an invisible barrier that surrounded them all. Not a single hair on any of their heads was knocked out of place by the blast of air.

Nkechi became frustrated. She felt useless against whatever they were doing to her, and catching a glimpse of the voodoo king sitting smugly in his throne only wound her up more. She decided to turn around in a bid to try to aid Kosum with her fight instead.

As Nkechi pivoted to Kosum, all became silent. The two men she had been strangling in midair were now back firmly on their feet.

"Kosum?" Nkechi muttered, worried. There was no reply. Nkechi slowly placed her hands upon Kosum's arm to swivel her around.

Kosum turned to face Nkechi, her eyes glazed over and a dull expression on her face. Nkechi's eyes widened as she realised she had been possessed, but before she could move another muscle, a possessed Kosum sent Nkechi flying across the room. Nkechi smacked into the magical barrier still surrounding the six men who were supposedly cursing her.

She turned to see them and wondered, *What the hell kinda curse is this?*

Nkechi got up and dusted herself off, only for Kosum to then place her in the same chokehold as she had used on the two goons earlier. She pinned Nkechi to the wall as she tightened the grip on her throat. With Kosum possessed and Nkechi being strangled, unable to speak, it seemed that the voodoo king was winning.

Although Nkechi was too short of breath to utter any spell, she wasn't prepared to give up. She managed to spark the corner of Kosum's jacket on fire with the snap of her fingers and hoped it would be enough of a distraction for Kosum to lose focus and drop her. Fortunately, it was. As the spark roared to life, the flames began to crawl up Kosum's arm. She flung her jacket off and stamped on it to snuff out the flame, which was all the time Nkechi needed to be released. She dropped to the ground and swiftly jumped back up, ready to fight once more.

Nkechi began walking over to Kosum with a half-baked plan to try to free her mind. She hoped that maybe she'd be stronger than the men possessing Kosum and therefore she'd be able to free her. But with every step she took, Nkechi's muscles began to feel heavier and her chest tighter. Her body slowed until mere seconds later she was frozen in place, paralysed.

A paralysis curse, shit, Nkechi thought.

The six men who had cursed Nkechi seemed to be continuously whispering a group chant. It was clear that this curse was a powerful one and needed to be kept alive, and if the men stopped, so would the immobilisation of Nkechi's body.

The voodoo king had won his first face-to-face battle with Nkechi, albeit with the help of ten of his followers. Alas, all he saw was the win. He sat back in his chair and waved his goons to bring Nkechi to him. Using Kosum's telekinesis, they lifted Nkechi's stiff body and placed her in front of her the voodoo king.

"Well, well, well. And to think I was almost – dare I say it – worried when I heard of your return. It seems that your reputation far outweighs your abilities. You're just as weak and pathetic as the rest of your family. It will make the next step in my plan go all the more smoothly now that you pesky children are out of the way."

The voodoo king's monologue was infuriating Nkechi, but with her lips closed shut and her eyes involuntarily fixed on him, all she could do was groan at his petulance.

"Where are my manners?" he said, waving his hand over Nkechi's face and allowing her lips and eyes to move freely so she could at least respond.

Having had a few seconds of silent thought beforehand, Nkechi decided not to play into his hands with an angry response but instead tried to provoke him as he had her.

"That's all rather hypocritical, isn't it? I'm weak and pathetic yet it took six of your men to stop me. It almost seems to me like you're scared to go head-to-head with me without backup."

The voodoo king scoffed. "Please, Nkechi, don't embarrass yourself. There's no question in anyone's mind who would win that fight."

"Well, at least we agree on that. *I* know I could take down a tired old man any day." Nkechi smiled provokingly.

Nkechi could see the voodoo king's jaw tense as he ground his teeth.

"That's enough from you!" he yelled, clearly disgruntled. He waved his hand over Nkechi's face, rendering her mouth useless once more, before continuing his evil monologue.

"Now then, where was I? Ah, yes. Once I'm done with your underwhelming town, I shall move on to the next, and so on, until the whole country is under my rule. No other nation will dare to challenge me."

The voodoo king had seemingly forgotten to re-freeze Nkechi's eyes, meaning that she could roll them in response to the spiel he was spouting.

God, his voice is irritating. If only they'd blessed me with a deafening curse! Nkechi internally chuckled to herself as she was forced to listen to him.

Noticing Nkechi's nonchalance, the voodoo king decided to try and push her buttons again.

"You know, it was your mother who reawakened this vengeance in me. I spent hundreds of years thinking that perhaps if we just kept to ourselves then we could rebuild a life worth living. But seeing a black baby with an ivory stain across its face reminded me that *they* will always impose themselves into our lives. The matrimony between your parents was unholy and disgusting, and you are merely the byproduct of such filth. No more shall we be seen as the inferior race! It's time that we dark-skinned folk rule this land with an iron fist. Let *them* become slaves; let them feel the inferiority they have drummed into us for years. They've sat in their ivory towers for far too long, and it will be me who causes their downfall. I will burn each building to the ground, and from the rubble make them rebuild a world in my image. The best part is that they won't even see it coming."

He croaked an evil laugh, and if Nkechi hadn't been literally frozen, she'd have probably thrown shade about it.

Though, all joking aside, Nkechi was a little taken aback by the voodoo king's plans. She had assumed that this was all about her mother, but it seemed that her mother had just lit the fire of hatred within him. She also wondered whether the voodoo king really was so ignorant as to think her vitiligo was the direct result of having a black mother and white father.

Nkechi may not have known how she was going to stop the voodoo king, but she knew that she would, and the first part of doing that was freeing herself of this curse.

Her eyes darted about the room, contemplating how she might escape. She looked to the voodoo king as he continued to drone on and thought about possessing him. It was a quick and fleeting thought as she soon remembered what had happened back in the taxi. The voodoo king had been too powerful to release control of the driver's mind, so there was no chance that she'd be able to take control of the king's mind.

Before Nkechi could come up with another plan, her phone began to vibrate in her jeans pocket. She hoped he might not notice but alas he had. A stiff Nkechi was helpless to stop him from burying his hand deep into her pocket and prising out her phone. Nkechi knew he let his hand linger longer than necessary. It would seem that misogyny was just another arrow in his evil arsenal.

"Well then, what do we have here?" he asked, waving

Nkechi's phone around for the whole room to see, though most of his men were unconscious due to Kosum's possession and Nkechi's curse.

"No caller ID? Very mysterious," he grinned, before swiping the screen across to answer it, making sure to hit the speaker button so that Nkechi could hear every word.

"Hello? Nkechi, you there?" Parfait's voice carried through the phone.

Nkechi never thought she'd be happy to hear him but in that moment, she'd take all the help she could get.

The voodoo king answered while smugly looking at Nkechi.

"I'm afraid Nkechi can't come to the phone right now, she's otherwise engaged. I'm sure I can be of service, though. What can I do for you, boy?"

On the other side of the call, Parfait covered the phone's speaker with his hand as he whispered to Nicole, "Hey, it's him… the voodoo king."

"Shit," Nicole spat.

"I think they're in trouble. What do we do?"

"I don't know. We need some sort of distraction so we can surprise them with our attack," Nicole said, though having no idea what that distraction could be.

Parfait paced, trying to think, as he heard the impatient voodoo king's muffled moan through the phone.

"Wait, I've got it!" Parfait said quietly to Nicole. His eye caught a glimpse of the explosive potions he'd noticed earlier.

Parfait placed the phone to his mouth and uncovered the speaker to say, "Nkechi, if you can hear me, I'm coming for you and Kosum. You'll know the signal when it comes, trust me."

Parfait ended the call before the voodoo king could react.

"So, would you care to fill me in on the plan which is going to save my cousin and girlfriend?" Nicole demanded.

"Those crates are filled to the brim with explosive elixir, enough to bring this whole building down."

Parfait's explanation didn't exactly fill Nicole with confidence.

"So, your plan is to blow shit up?" she asked, crossing her arms in defiance.

"Do you have a better one?",

Nicole sighed. "No, I suppose not."

"Great. So, you take the girls and start making your way back and I'll rescue Nkechi and Kosum. Here, take the Jeep. You should all be able to squeeze in," he said, throwing her the keys.

"You're joking, right? You think that I'm just going to leave the lives of my family in your hands?"

"Nicole, the mission was to rescue the girls – we've done that. We can't risk losing them again. Look at them," he added, pointing to the now distressed girls. "You need to get them to safety while I go after Nkechi and Kosum."

"And why can't I be the one to get Nkechi and Kosum? Let me guess, because you're a big strong man?" Nicole sassed getting rather infuriated.

"Jesus Christ. We really don't have time for this bullshit but since you started it… No, it's not because I'm a guy; I'm actually a feminist. It's because I know how to set off the explosives without killing myself. Do you?"

"No…"

"Didn't think so."

Once Parfait had made his point, he could see that the captured girls weren't the only ones looking distressed. Of course Nicole was anxious about leaving, she loved Nkechi and Kosum. Parfait realised that his one-upmanship wasn't making her feel any better so decided to reassure her instead.

"Hey, look, I know you're scared of losing them, but I promise" – he placed a comforting hand on her shoulder – "I won't let anything happen to them. I'll bring them both home safely."

"Okay," Nicole half smiled, appreciating his new approach.

"C'mon, girls, let's get out of here. I'll come straight back with the Jeep once I've dropped the girls home."

Parfait smiled and nodded.

Nicole led the girls safely out of the building while Parfait began to work his magic on the explosives.

He noticed a watch on the wrist of one of the men they had taken out before. Using whatever else he could find and a few supplies from his elixir belt, he rigged a timer to set off one of the volatile vials of elixir which in turn would create a chain reaction, blowing up the entire crate. Parfait set the timer for two minutes and began to run in the direction he remembered seeing Nkechi and Kosum go in.

Back on his throne, the voodoo king wasn't impressed by

Parfait cutting the call.

"Well, that was rude, wasn't it?" he said to Nkechi even though she couldn't reply. "No bother, at least with the rest of your rag tag gang arriving soon, I can kill you all in one go," he grinned.

"Tie them up," he barked to the remaining two henchmen that weren't involved in any of the ongoing spells.

One of the young men replied, confused, "But they're both incapacitated."

"Yes, but cockroaches always find a way of wriggling in and out of where they aren't wanted. Now do it! And don't question my judgment again!"

"Yes, my king." The young man cowered.

Nkechi's stiff body was dragged to meet Kosum's possessed one where they were tied together back-to-back by a thick, scratchy rope.

The second the knot had been completed, Parfait burst through the door. He was panting as his eyes scanned the room for Nkechi and Kosum.

"Ah, perfect. You're here to join your friends," the voodoo king remarked cockily.

"Nope, I'm here to rescue them," Parfait replied, with an equally cocksure manner.

"We'll see about th—"

Before the voodoo king could finish his sentence, a deafening bang rippled through the walls and floor beneath them, causing the building to quake. The voodoo king was knocked to the ground as the ceiling began to crumble upon them. The ensuing carnage broke both spells binding Nkechi and Kosum. Falling debris had taken out the two men possessing Kosum and a hole in the floor beneath them swallowed the men paralysing Nkechi, therefore breaking the hive mind needed for the curse.

Parfait raced over to the girls as their tied-up bodies fell to the ground in unison. Kosum blinked until her vision cleared and she had regained full consciousness.

"Parfait!" she called out.

"I'm coming," he shouted back in reply as he dodged the falling rubble around him.

"Nkechi? Are you okay?" Kosum asked, as she tried to turn her head to face her.

There was no answer as Nkechi's body was still limp. Though the curse may have been broken, it would take a while for her to regain the strength to move freely again.

Parfait knelt beside them as he pulled out a pocketknife to cut them free. Nkechi's body slowly slumped to the ground.

"Is she okay?" Parfait asked.

"They paralysed her, I think she's still stuck," Kosum answered, concerned.

"Okay, I'll carry her. Are you gonna be able to keep up?"

"Yeah. C'mon, let's get out of here."

Parfait scooped Nkechi up into his bulging biceps, cradling her body and allowing her head to rest against his chest.

As they made their way towards the exit, the voodoo king made one last desperate attempt to block their path. But Kosum, without so much as a second of thought, launched him across the room.

They managed to escape a few blocks away where Nicole had returned with the Jeep. Kosum hopped in the front and Parfait sat in the back with Nkechi, who lay across the seats with her head in his lap. His gaze stayed on her for the entire journey home. Though he might've found her annoying, he couldn't deny how beautiful Nkechi was and how easy it was to become lost in that beauty.

They arrived back at Anuli's house where Nicole and Kosum took a moment to embrace and kiss one another.

"Ya know, for a second, I thought I'd lost you back there," Nicole said, holding Kosum close, feeling like she never wanted to let her go again.

"Hey, it's gonna be a lot harder than that to get rid of me," Kosum smiled.

"Shut up! You were ready to abandon me and go back to New York this morning," Nicole countered with a raised eyebrow.

"Yeah, well, look who convinced me to stay." Kosum smiled wider as they drew closer to each other and kissed.

Parfait once again scooped Nkechi into his arms and carried her from the Jeep. She awoke, though still a little dazed.

"Hey, you can put me down, ya know."

"You sure? You're pretty easy to carry around, even without the strength elixir."

Nkechi blushed, nodding, and Parfait placed her back on her two feet.

"Thanks for saving us… I guess," Nkechi teased, nudging her fist into his bicep.

"I'll give you credit, you did have a few more bad guys to deal with than me and Nicole," he admitted.

"Yeah, not to mention the voodoo king himself!"

"Nah, I think I could've taken him."

"Mmm." Nkechi rolled her eyes and tried to hide the smirk sprawled across her face.

"Hey, mock me all you want, but a punch or two from these guys and he'd be out for the count," Parfait said, flexing his arms.

"You are so cringe!" Nkechi made a gagging gesture at him.

They laughed at each other's stupidity before softening to a smile. Without realising it, they had been gazing into each other's eyes for a moment.

Parfait faked a cough to break the silence. It wasn't awkward but it was definitely a little loaded - something neither of them had expected. "Hey, sorry I was a dick this morning. Can we start afresh?"

Nkechi looked up at his cheesy grin and smiled back. "Yeah, sure." She held out her hand. "Hi, I'm Nkechi."

"Nice to meet you, Nkechi. I'm Parfait," he said grasping her soft hand in his.

As they shook hands, a nosey Kosum couldn't help but make a point to Nicole, "See, I told you they liked each other."

"They do look a little cosy, don't they?"

Hearing voices, Anuli opened the front door with a warm welcome.

"Ah, the heroes have retuned," she smiled, holding out her arms. "Now come, let us debrief."

Everyone headed back to the basement-cum-war room where Parfait's parents, Adame and Evélia, were already waiting.

The girls and Parfait explained everything that had happened during their mission.

"So, did you find any information on what their plans are?" Adame asked, rather irrelevantly to the mission at hand.

"No, Pa. Besides, wasn't everything we just said enough?" Parfait answered back, which Adame clearly didn't appreciate as a he scowled at his son.

"Well, it sounds like it was a successful mission, nonetheless," Evélia announced, trying to break the tension between her son and husband.

"Exactly. And we're already getting reports from some of our outposts that the voodoo king's men are retreating," Anuli added, trying to bolster everyone's spirits.

"That's great!" Kosum exclaimed.

"Not necessarily. It's more than likely their forces are retreating so that they can regroup and launch an even bigger attack next time," Adame retorted, sounding angry.

Evélia placed her hands over her husband's, which were firmly gripping the table. She looked at him disapprovingly with her piercing blue eyes.

Nkechi could now see why Parfait had been the way he had with her that morning – his father wasn't exactly the most sympathetic of men.

"Look, you did a great job today and you all deserve some rest. So, go upstairs and relax," Anuli insisted, waving them off.

The girls and Parfait headed back up the stairs.

"What the hell was all that about?" Anuli turned to Adame once she heard the door close. "Why must you be so doom and gloom all the time? Just let them have their victory. They've surely earned it."

"They can have their victory when this war is over. We can't allow ourselves to become complacent. That's what cost us the elders last night and that's what could cost us everything."

"Yes, well. Leave it to us to be more vigilant. Do I need to remind you that they're still teenagers?"

"Well, now they're soldiers."

"Temporarily, maybe. But it's *our* war they're fighting. We should have fought harder over ten years ago when all this began. It is because of *our* weakness, *our* failures that they have to step up, and I'll be damned if I let them lose their humanity in the process. It's Nicole's birthday in a couple of days. They will indulge in a little fun while *we* keep guard, understood?" Anuli announced to the room, though looking pointedly at Adame.

Evélia gracefully nodded while Adame muttered, "Fine," with his arms folded.

Across town, the voodoo king stood in his personal chambers in a building he had claimed as his. He awaited news from his men who searched through the rubble at their base.

He began to pace the room impatiently, angry, mulling over the fact that Nkechi, someone whom he deemed pathetic and inferior, had once again escaped death by his hand. His two handmaidens tried to calm him by sensually placing their delicate hands across his muscular body, but in his anger, even his sexual servants couldn't please him. One of them tried to disrobe him but was swatted to the ground, her efforts having only revealed one half of his naked chest.

Finally, news came in the form of knock on the door.

"Enter," he bellowed, causing the two servants behind him to cower back into the four-poster bed.

Gaudence gracefully entered the room and awaited his master's permission to speak.

"Spit it out! Did you find them? Are they alive?" the voodoo king shouted impatiently.

"Yes, the damned are perfectly fine," Gaudence answered with a bow.

"Good. Starve them for a few days; we'll be needing them very soon."

Following the news, the voodoo king was in a much more excitable mood, and he turned to his two maidens with a wicked smile.

As Gaudence attempted to leave the voodoo king's chambers, he was stopped. He turned back to see the voodoo king pointing to the poor girl who had tried to please him earlier.

In a low guttural voice, he said, "Add her to the pit."

CHAPTER 9

A Birthday to Remeber

A couple of days had passed since the rescue mission, and all had been quiet. Not a single one of the king's henchmen had been spotted about the town. Some of the more naïve in the community believed they were slowly winning the war, while others knew all too well that it was a farce, a ruse to lull them into a false sense of security. They knew that soon the voodoo king and his men would set in motion a retaliation tenfold the size of any of their prior attacks.

Adame was one of these people; Anuli too – she wasn't stupid. She knew that the war was far from over, but she also knew to have hope during such trying times, something that Adame was seemingly forgetting, much to his wife's disappointment. Yet Adame conceded to Anuli and Evélia's wishes and the three of them took on lookout duty in readiness for the raging storm that lay ahead, while the youth got to be just that – youthful.

It was the eve of Nicole's birthday, but before they could fully relax there was still one magical task to be performed. After the debriefing, Kosum had asked Anuli in private if there was some way of protecting herself from being possessed. She didn't want to bring it up in front of Nicole and Nkechi because she felt embarrassed. She always prided herself on being a powerful witch, but so far in the two fights she'd been in, she'd done more damage to her friends than the enemy. The fact that she could be so easily turned into a mindless weapon didn't sit right with Kosum and she wouldn't let it happen again.

Anuli agreed to help Kosum place a protection barrier within her mind, but she told her that she would need Nicole and Nkechi's help to do so. Although Kosum didn't want them to know of how inferior she was feeling, if it was the only way, she had to accept it.

Kosum found Nicole and Nkechi and brought them to the back garden where Anuli was awaiting their arrival.

"Kosum, will you just tell us what's going on?" Nicole asked as she and Nkechi were being dragged through the house by Kosum.

Kosum exhaled deeply as she prepared herself to be vulnerable, something she didn't enjoy.

"Look, it's clear that I'm a liability at the moment – I'm susceptible to possession – and with my powers, they could do some serious damage to you guys. So, you're going to help Anuli place a barrier in my mind to protect me. I didn't wanna tell you because… well, it's embarrassing, and I feel useless," Kosum admitted, her head bowed in shame.

"Kosum, you've got nothing to be embarrassed about," Nicole consoled as she grabbed Kosum's hands in her own.

"Yeah, well, it's not like you or Nkechi have to do this – you guys are already stronger than me."

Overhearing Kosum's comment, Anuli thought it best to explain.

"You are no weaker than they are, my dear, you just aren't

voodoo. When a voodoo witch develops their possession abilities, it's a natural by-product that they receive a certain amount of protection from any incoming mental attacks."

"Kosum, you're one of the strongest people I know! All we're doing is giving you a boost. Now, c'mon, you got this," Nkechi smiled.

"Thanks," Kosum said, smiling faintly. She shook off all self-doubt and turned to Anuli with a determined look on her face. "So, how does this all work anyway?"

"It'll probably feel strange, but I promise I'll try my best to make it painless," Anuli said, not really answering the question or settling Kosum's nerves.

"Okay…" Kosum replied, hoping Anuli would elaborate.

"We'll lay you on the ground and then summon Papa Legba to—"

"Papa Legba?" Kosum interrupted.

"Yes, dear," Anuli replied nonchalantly.

"I thought it was going to be *you* inside my head," Kosum blurted, voicing the worry that was bouncing around her brain.

"No, of course not, my sweet child. To protect someone's mind who is not of voodoo descent requires the blessing of a voodoo deity. We could use Baron Samedi, but he's not exactly the most morally sound of the deities, hence why we are summoning Papa Legba. Besides, with his close connection to Nkechi and my sister, I'm sure he'll happily grant you protection.".

Although Kosum had been listening, she zoned out for the most part as she contemplated whether she really wanted a god inside her mind.

Oh, God, will he see my thoughts? Will he see that I just thought 'oh, God?' Is that offensive? Jesus Christ! OMFG what if he's friends with Jesus? Kosum's inner rambles translated into an uncontrollable twitch in her right eye.

"Kosum, are you okay?" Nkechi prompted as she waved her hands in front of her face.

"Huh? Oh yeah, I'm fine," she muttered, clearly not fine. "So just to clarify, there will be a god inside my brain?"

"Yes," Anuli answered flatly.

"Will he say anything to me?"

"To be honest, I'm not sure. I've never had to perform this spell before – I found it in one of my mother's old grimoires. But like I said, Papa is much more considerate than Baron. The Baron's morals flipflop more than a fish out of water," Anuli added in bid to reassure Kosum, not that it did.

"Or like two 'vers' gay guys," Nicole whispered into Kosum's ear to make her chuckle and try to ease her anxiety.

It worked a little as Kosum smirked before taking one last deep breath and readying herself for the ritual to commence.

Kosum lay down on her back, her body nestling into the grass. She couldn't help but flinch a little as she saw a bug crawling towards her, though with the flutter of her eyes she soon sent it flying telekinetically across the garden. She then turned her gaze to the sky and tried to watch the clouds to distract her mind.

Anuli pulled a small wooden totem, carved to resemble Papa Legba, from her pocket and placed it on Kosum's forehead. Anuli, Nkechi and Nicole then stood in a line at Kosum's feet with Anuli in the centre. Anuli began to recite the words to summon Papa Legba:

"Papa Legba, oh puissant divin, bénis cet enfant avec une protection mentale."

Kosum's body began to lift off the ground. Anuli repeated the words and joined hands with her niece and daughter while signalling them to join in with the chant. As all three of them uttered the words, a gale force wind encircled them. Kosum's gaze didn't know where to land as fear started to creep in, but it was too late to go back, and they soon glazed over, becoming a milky white colour.

Papa Legba had arrived.

As the wind whipped up Nkechi's hair and Anuli's summery dress, they had to stay focused and keep Kosum suspended while Papa did his work.

Inside Kosum's mind she found her astral self walking through her childhood bedroom. At first, she looked around in confusion but then as she heard a younger, stroppy version of herself storming about the house, she realised it was a memory. She watched as her younger self barged into the room and marched through Kosum's body as if she was a ghost.

Kosum continued to observe her as she threw a fit of rage at her mother's expense. Kwanjai walked into the room, only to be met by more screams from young Kosum before slamming the door in her mother's face. Kosum knew the anger wasn't meant for her mother; it was anger directed at the world.

At that age, Kosum missed her father but didn't know how to communicate those feelings properly. Even after the awful things her mother had told her about him, Kosum couldn't help but miss him, and she couldn't help but believe there was another part to the story. It still didn't make sense.

As Kosum watched her younger self cry into her pillow, she was transported to another memory where Kosum was even younger, so young in fact that…

"Dad," Kosum's astral form breathed as she saw her father enter her childhood bedroom. Kosum saw him there with his slicked-back, walnut-coloured locks, wearing a grey suit and his favourite burgundy tie. She knew immediately which memory she was about to watch.

It was a day when Kosum had been bullied in elementary school for having a Thai mother and an American father. The cruel kids would exaggeratively squint their eyes at her and call her names, something that now reminded Kosum of the horrid way she had acted when she first met Nkechi. It was clearly learned behaviour and instinctive to make someone else the butt of the joke instead of her.

A young Kosum sat on the edge of her bed crying into her hands. She wiped her tears away at the sight of her father, not because she was scared of him, but because she looked up to him and didn't want him to think she was weak.

Kosum's father placed his arm around her and used his velvet tie to gently dry Kosum's eyes.

"Hey, sweetie," his smooth voice whispered. "What's the matter?"

"Nothing, I'm fine, I'm strong," a young Kosum answered, trying to hide the redness in her cheeks and the puffiness of her eyes.

"I know you are. You're the strongest little girl I know. But crying doesn't make you any less, my love. Even Daddy cries sometimes and look how strong I am," he said, playfully flexing his bicep.

Young Kosum giggled at that, then she turned serious again. "So, it's okay to be sad?"

"Of course it is." He smiled.

"Okay, good, because I am sad," she said, before crying once more.

Her father pulled her into his chest, kissing the top of her head and wrapping his arms tightly around her.

"Everything is going to be okay," he whispered.

Kosum hadn't heard her father's voice in almost fourteen years, and hearing those words in the trying times that Kosum was facing meant everything.

The scene around Kosum slowly dissipated, and shortly after she heard an unfamiliar but powerful voice over her shoulder.

"Hello, my child."

Kosum turned around to see Papa Legba's lanky stature before her.

"Y-you're… Papa Legba?" she stuttered, a mixture of shock and fear.

"Yes, and you are Kosum Jenkins."

Kosum slowly nodded.

"I don't provide mental protection for just anyone, you know," he cautioned, making Kosum feel he may not deem her worthy enough to receive it.

"I understand," she answered humbly, thinking that may have been his way of letting her down gently.

"*But* you have proven yourself worthy of a place in my flock. You are a powerful young witch, and your loyalty to your friends is unwavering even if you don't always consciously recognise it," he remarked with a raised eyebrow, recounting hers and Nkechi's fight.

"Alas, that was a mere hiccup in your journey together. You have both proved more than once that you will protect each other. And with the chaotic lives you both lead, I'm sure there will be many more times to come."

"Thank you," she smiled. "May I ask why you showed me my old memories?"

"I thought it would make the pain of the cognitive reinforcement easier. You didn't feel any pain, did you?" he asked.

"What? You mean you've already done it?" Kosum asked in shock.

"Yes. I also thought you might like to hear your father's voice again. That memory had been buried by so many bad ones that you'd almost forgotten it entirely. But now it is free, you can reminisce about it whenever you wish."

"Papa Legba—" Kosum began.

"Please, call me Papa," he smiled.

"My father *was* good, wasn't he?" Kosum asked, nervous of his reply.

"I'm afraid that is not my place to say. But I feel your answers aren't much further down the path you're on."

"Okay," Kosum sighed. "Thank you, Papa, for protecting my mind."

"It was my honour, Kosum. Now then, off you go. Wake up before that wind whips off Anuli's wig." He winked.

"That's a wig?" Kosum asked, surprised by how good it looked.

"Well, I believe normally she has a weave, but I suppose

wartime calls for desperate measures," he whispered playfully.

Kosum chuckled.

"Now, no one will be getting in here ever again," he said, tapping her temple.

Before Kosum could thank him again, she was swiftly put back in control of her body, which gently floated back down onto the dewy grass.

Nicole rushed over to see how she was. "Are you in any pain?" she asked, holding the back of her hand to Kosum's forehead, feeling for a raised temperature.

"Nah, I'm good, just a little tired," Kosum admitted, feeling calmed by Papa's presence.

"And did it work?" Nkechi asked.

"He said so," Kosum smiled.

"That's wonderful. Though you should probably get some rest," Anuli suggested.

"Yeah, I'll take her up to bed. C'mon," Nicole said, helping Kosum to her feet, which instantly made her feel a bit dizzy.

"I guess he can't protect me from the hangover feeling afterwards," Kosum joked.

Everyone chuckled and Nicole escorted Kosum to their bedroom to rest for the night.

Nkechi ventured a few doors down to Adame and Evélia's house, looking for Parfait. She'd already asked him earlier if he would help put up Nicole's birthday decorations and he had agreed, but now the appointed hour of seven o'clock had passed. Nkechi knew she was especially punctual, but when it got to 7:20 p.m. and he still hadn't shown up, she thought it was a bit rude.

She knocked on the door and waited patiently.

"Nkechi! What can I do for you?" Evélia asked, looking delighted to see her. Evélia could already sense the spark growing between Nkechi and her son, even if they couldn't.

"I'm looking for Parfait. He was supposed to be helping me with Nicole's decorations," Nkechi said, trying her best not to moan to Evélia about her son.

"Honestly, Nkechi, he's always late," she said, rolling her eyes. "He'll probably be in the basement gym. You're welcome to go find him," she added, stepping aside to allow Nkechi room to enter.

"Thank you." Evélia pointed her in the direction of the basement, though it wouldn't have been too hard to decipher as it seemingly had the same layout as Anuli's house. Nkechi descended the basement stairs, hearing nothing but the clinking of weights and heavy breathing. The room opened out into a fully functional, albeit small, gym, and Nkechi saw Parfait – specifically his shirtless, sweaty and extremely muscular back…

There was a harsh light above him that made the beads of sweat on his skin glisten like diamonds. Nkechi tried to avert her gaze as she called out to him, but the headphones clamped to his ears were clearly noise-cancelling as there was no answer. Nkechi tried again, a little louder. Still no answer. Although he was wearing headphones, Nkechi began to think he was just being his usual immature self and purposely ignoring her.

Parfait kept curling each dumbbell one arm at a time as Nkechi walked up behind him. She gently tapped him on the shoulder, and he jerked in surprise, causing him to drop the weights which only just missed his feet.

"Jesus, Nkechi!" he shouted, partly due to the shock and partly because he still had his headphones on. "You can't sneak up on someone like that when they're lifting weights!"

"I didn't *sneak* up on you, I shouted you – *twice*." Nkechi rebutted.

Parfait's face was one of confusion. That's when Nkechi realised he still had his headphones on and genuinely hadn't heard her. She sassily smized and gestured her hands around her ears to signal for him to remove them.

His eyes narrowed before realising what she meant.

"Oh, sorry," he chuckled, as he took them off and let them hang around his sweaty neck. "I guess I forgot I had them on."

"Yeah, well did you also forget you're supposed to be helping me with the decorations for Nicole's birthday party?"

"*No...* Look, just let me finish this set and I'll be over," he answered.

"Ugh," Nkechi sighed, rolling her eyes.

"Hey, it's these guns that carried you out of that warehouse," he teased, flexing his biceps, which also unintentionally flexed his chest and abs too.

"Yeah, well, I'm starting to think I'd have been better off if you'd left me there," she joked.

"Oh, please. You *loved* it."

Nkechi sucked her teeth in agitation.

"Just hurry up and finish your set," she said, sassily plopping herself on the weight bench beside him as she waited.

Parfait began finishing his set and Nkechi tried not to watch. She couldn't resist though. He looked at her too and their eyes met, but neither of them acknowledged it as it was too awkward.

Once done, Parfait quickly showered. Nkechi decided she should definitely not wait around to watch that. Once Parfait was finally ready they headed back to Anuli's house.

Nkechi began climbing up the rickety ladder to the attic with Parfait close behind her. As he looked up, he saw Nkechi's curvaceous bum naturally swaying from side to side as she climbed, and although he may have found her annoying, he couldn't deny the attraction was there. Parfait tried to shake the image free from his mind, but the distraction did cause him to slip on one of the steps.

"You okay?" Nkechi turned back to ask.

"Yup," he gave an awkward laugh as he caught up and entered the attic. He didn't want to be thinking about Nkechi in that way, and thankfully the dusty cobwebbed setting helped to dampen any sexy, romantic vibes that might have naturally occurred.

"The decorations are up here somewhere," Nkechi said, looking around at the eclectic attic. "You start that side, I'll start here, and we'll meet in the middle, okay?"

"Yes, boss," he answered with a mocking salute.

Nkechi just smized at him before turning to begin searching her side of the attic.

They searched box after dusty box, most of which were filled with moth-eaten clothes and Christmas decorations which surely needed to be thrown out.

As Nkechi blew a layer of dust off one of her boxes, on the other side of the room, Parfait came across a box that read: Old Family Pics. He flicked a dead spider off the top and opened it. At first, he just thought it would be funny to find some old goofy pictures of Nkechi, but as he sifted through the photos, an involuntary warmness came over him. There were picture spanning the past thirty years; everything from Nkechi and Nicole as children to his parents with Anuli and Nkechi's parents. They couldn't have been much older in the photo than Parfait and Nkechi were now.

He could see how in love his parents were. Even now, whenever they disagreed or had an argument, their love was present. They were always there for each other, even if they weren't on speaking terms. It often annoyed Parfait how 'lovey-dovey' his parents were, especially when they acted as a united front to complain about him. But seeing Nkechi's loving parents beside them in the photo, reminded Parfait how lucky he was still to have them. Of course, they could be harsh, but they only did it out of love for him. Or at least he knew his mother did – the jury was still out on his father. Parfait felt like everything he did was a burden to Adame.

He looked up from the picture to see Nkechi on the other side of the room with a dusty forehead. He gave a soft laugh, seeing her in another light. He didn't feel sorry for Nkechi, and she certainly didn't need his pity, but he did begin to admire her.

Despite everything that life had thrown at her she was still a positive, kind and incredible young woman.

Parfait folded up the picture he'd been admiring and put it in his back pocket, along with a few others of his parents he wanted to keep hold of. He didn't think Anuli would mind, considering they were just collecting dust. Just before he closed the box, another photo caught his eye. He pulled it out, smiling.

"Hey!" he shouted.

"What?"

"Come here, I have something to show you."

"If this is some stupid prank, then no. Just save time and find the decorations, we're already late doing this because of you," Nkechi moaned.

"Just get your ass over here."

"Ugh, fine!" Nkechi got up and patted her dusty hands on her thighs as she walked over to Parfait. "What is it, then?"

"I thought you might like this," he said, handing her a delicate photo of her with her parents

Parfait watched contentedly as Nkechi's eyes shone at the sight of the picture. It was torn around the edges and most of the colour had faded, but it was the first picture Nkechi had ever seen of the three of them together.

"Where'd you get this?" she asked breathily, growing tearful.

"In this box. You'll probably find more in here," he answered, dragging the box to her feet.

"Thank you." Nkechi instinctively wrapped her arms around him. She hadn't thought Parfait capable of being so considerate.

Their hug lasted longer than either of them had expected. Being in each other's arms, during such a perilous time, felt homely, though a moment later Parfait broke the now awkward tension.

"Erm, we should probably get back to finding those decorations, huh?"

"Oh yeah, sure," Nkechi answered as she pulled away and

caught a glimpse of his lagoon-blue eyes. "I'm just gonna take these downstairs so I can show Anuli and Nicole later," she said, picking up the box of remaining photos.

"Okay, I'll keep looking," he said, trying to disguise his blushes.

Nkechi dropped the box off in Anuli's room before heading back to the attic. To her surprise, Parfait was already making his way down with a box under his arm.

"Found them," he said.

Parfait and Nkechi spent the rest of the evening decorating together. They hung banners, streamers and balloons all around the house. They even did some baking, using Anuli's signature red velvet cake recipe, though after the flour fight, there were more ingredients on Nkechi and Parfait than in the cake. Although neither of them would admit it, there were definitely flirtatious vibes in the air that night. Or at least it seemed that way compared to their first frosty encounter.

It was the morning of Nicole's birthday, and Kosum had just awakened from her monster fourteen-hour sleep. She needed it after the ritual. After all, it's not every day you have a voodoo deity poking around your brain. Kosum felt rejuvenated, and as she rolled over and saw Nicole still sound asleep, she decided to shower her in pecks on the cheeks until she awoke.

Though Nicole's eyes were still glued shut, a smile grew across her lips as she became aware of Kosum's affections. She quickly rubbed her eyes open and wrapped her arms around her girlfriend. She pulled her in for a kiss on the lips, but

Kosum pulled away slightly.

"What's wrong?" Nicole asked, still trying to fully open her eyes.

"I get bad morning breath, according to Nkechi, and so I didn't want to gross you out," Kosum admitted, as her cheeks flushed a rosy hue in embarrassment.

"Aw, that's so cute, but I don't care." Nicole pulled Kosum in for a kiss before she could object again, and soon Kosum relaxed.

Their kisses grew in passion as their hands began to run up and down each other's bodies. They had only been wearing underwear in bed, but for what was about to happen next even that was too much clothing. They quickly stripped each other naked and their lips continued to lock passionately together. Kosum trickled her fingers down Nicole's stomach, and as she went to slip them inside her, Nicole had an idea and stopped her.

"Are you okay? Did I hurt you?" Kosum panicked.

"I'm fine." Nicole chuckled at her cute, worried face. "I was just wondering if we could try something… a bit different?"

"Well, it's your birthday so we can try whatever you want," Kosum answered open-mindedly.

Nicole reached over to her bedside draw. She rooted around for a minute until her hands latched on to what she wanted. She pulled out a dual pleasuring sex toy and showed Kosum with a suggestive smile.

"Too much?" Nicole asked tentatively.

Kosum shook her head with a cheeky grin, before taking Nicole's hand and placing the toy deep beneath the covers where it wouldn't resurface again for quite some time.

While Nicole and Kosum were making the most of their double bed, a few houses down the street, Parfait woke up in a hot sweat, panicking as he sat upright in bed. He breathed heavily and blinked repeatedly in disbelief. He looked as though he'd seen a ghost or awoken from a terrifying nightmare. The reality was far from it. Parfait had had a dream about Nkechi, a hot, steamy one at that. He rubbed his face and sweaty forehead as if it would remove the image from his mind, but it only made it clearer. It was then that he looked down and noticed that he was still *excited* about said dream, with his impressive manhood pitching a tent under his thin summer blanket. Whether he admitted it consciously or not, it was becoming obvious that he wanted Nkechi.

Parfait took a cold shower to calm himself before getting dressed. Just before he headed out the door to Anuli's house, Evélia stopped him.

"Parfait?" she called out from the kitchen as she noticed him racing down the hallway.

"Yeah?" he shouted back, hopping on one leg, trying to shuffle into his sneakers.

"You off to celebrate Nicole's birthday?" Evélia asked, leaning against the kitchen doorframe as she dried a bowl.

"Yep."

"You know, you and Nkechi would make a cute couple," Evélia commented as she walked closer to him, still pretending to dry the now dry bowl.

"Ew, Mom. No, we wouldn't. Besides, she doesn't like me like that. And the feeling's mutual," he lied, feeling flustered. Was it really that obvious to everyone? Or was his mother just as intuitive as Kosum?

"Ah, of course. How disgusting it would be to date a beautiful, powerful and smart girl like Nkechi," she mocked, rolling her eyes.

"Mom, that's not what I meant."

"Very well, but for the record, you're wrong. I have an eye for love you know?" Evélia put down the bowl and towel as she noticed the collar on his polo-shirt was askew and rearranged it.

"Thanks — for the collar, not the advice," he added, making her chuckle at her son's inherent stubbornness.

I wonder where he gets that from? Evélia internally chucked to herself.

"Right, well go on, have fun," she smiled, folding her arms as she watched him leave.

Adame appeared behind her. "You're too soft on him."

"He hasn't done anything wrong. Need I remind you that you were his age once and got into much more trouble than him. Listen to Anuli, let them be kids a little longer," Evélia requested as she turned to her husband and placed her hands on his chest.

"Okay," he grunted playfully.

"Hmm, that's the man I married," Evélia smiled, teasing his lips with her thumb. With Parfait out of the house, it made for a rather scarce opportunity for them to enjoy some *alone* time. Adame lifted Evélia off the ground and raced her back upstairs to their bedroom where they made love more passionately than they had done in quite some time.

Parfait entered through the backdoor of Anuli's house to see Nkechi sitting at the breakfast bar with a bowl of cereal. His eyes immediately widened, and he froze for a second.

"Oh, hey," Nkechi mumbled, with a mouthful of cereal.

"Hi," he replied robotically.

"You all right?"

"Er, yeah, fine." He didn't know why he was acting so weird. It's not like Nkechi had any way of knowing about his dream.

"Want some?" Nkechi offered, shaking the box of sugary puffed cereal.

Parfait nodded, still acting strange, but Nkechi just decided he wasn't a morning person. That, and the fact they didn't know each other all that well, so he could just be a bit weird in general. Not that Nkechi would judge – normal wasn't exactly how she'd describe herself, either.

Parfait sat at the breakfast bar opposite Nkechi and poured himself a bowl of the cereal that was clearly made for kids, or in this case, Nkechi.

"So, where's the birthday girl?" he asked, trying to distract himself from thinking about Nkechi and *that* dream.

"Still upstairs with Kosum, so probably…"

"Ah, got ya. And Anuli?"

"She went out to check all the outposts and grab a few more things for the party," Nkechi answered, still munching her cereal.

"So, it's just you up, then?"

"No, the girls we rescued the other day are in the other room hanging out."

"Cool," Parfait replied, slowly spooning cereal into his

mouth.

Nkechi had been trying to ignore his weird demeanour, but she couldn't any longer.

"Are you sure you're okay? You're acting weirder than usual."

"I'm fine," he said, his voice higher pitched than usual.

"*Okay…* Well, I'm gonna get ready for the party, so can you keep an eye on the girls?" Nkechi asked as she got up to put her bowl in the sink.

"Yeah, sure."

"Thanks."

As Parfait watched her leave, it was only then that he noticed she was still in her pyjama shorts and a camisole.

"Fuck, I *do* like Nkechi."

"What was that?" Nkechi asked, poking her head back round the door.

"Nothing!" he shouted.

He is so weird, Nkechi thought as she smiled awkwardly and headed up the stairs.

She is so hot. His eyes watched the staircase like a hawk for a few moments to make sure no one else appeared.

"Phew," he sighed before lifelessly shoving another spoonful of cereal into his mouth.

A few hours later the party at Annuli's house was in full swing, with teenage boys from another safe house down the road finally being reunited with the young girls. After the recent stress of their tumultuous situation, they all deserved a night to reconnect and have fun. Of course, none of them were allowed any alcohol, so thoughtfully Nkechi and the gang snuck down to the basement-cum-war room where they each had a drink and, between them, took a bottle of tequila and four shot glasses.

Kosum suggested playing a game of truth or dare, and after a little persuasion from her, everyone agreed. They stood around the war table, which was doubling as a bar.

"Birthday girl first," Kosum announced.

"Truth or dare, cuz?" Nkechi asked as she slurped her vodka and coke.

"Hmm… Well, I'm no wuss, so dare!" Nicole replied, already a little tipsy. Nkechi was pretty sure Kosum and Nicole had already snuck something stronger into their drinks earlier in the day.

"Okay…" Nkechi thought for a second. "Suck Kosum's big toe," she said, laughing.

Parfait's eyes widened and his cheeks flushed. Nkechi noticed and thought it was cute.

"Nkechi, sweet, naïve, Nkechi. That, my dear cousin, would be a pleasure." Nicole smiled.

Kosum raised her foot onto the table like a disgraced ballerina. Nicole took off Kosum's strappy high heel and wasted no time in sliding the toe into her mouth. Both Nkechi and Parfait gagged at the sight, before inevitably laughing at each other's reactions.

"Okay, okay. We get it, you love each other. Now *please* stop," Nkechi pleaded, as it seemed that Nicole was enjoying it a little too much.

"Fine," Nicole mumbled, and as she took the toe out of

her mouth there was a single strand of saliva still connecting them, causing Parfait to almost throw up.

Kosum chuckled before slipping her shoe back on without a second thought.

"Your turn next," Kosum said, pointing a drunken finger at Nkechi.

"Truth," Nkechi said.

Parfait rolled his eyes. "Boring."

"Shut up," Nkechi moaned, nudging him in the arm. "We'll see how brave you are when it's your turn."

"Oh, I have a truth for you," Kosum said. Before anyone could object, she blurted, "How *big* was Charlie?"

"Oh, my god, Kosum, too soon!" Nicole shouted, pushing her forcefully.

A fully sober Nkechi probably would've been bothered but party Nkechi was already jolly enough not to care and answered, "Annoyingly, pretty big."

Kosum cackled while Nicole looked shocked that Nkechi had even dignified her with a response.

Parfait once again blushed, looking like a deer in headlights. He couldn't help it – every time someone did or mentioned something slightly sexual, he saw flashes of his dream with Nkechi. Sitting so close to her made his skin prickle with heat and desire for her, especially in the sparkly, skintight top and skinny jeans she was wearing.

"Right, now it's your turn," Nkechi said, turning to Parfait who was still looking rosier than usual. "*Dare,* I'm, assuming?" she cockily remarked.

"Yeah, I'm no chicken," he said, puffing out his chest while trying to regain some self-control.

"I dare you to show Nkechi yours!" Kosum shouted.

"What?" Parfait's face froze in fear.

"Kosum, that's enough. Parfait, you obviously don't have to do that," Nicole reassured.

"No, he does, he has to, or he has to forfeit and take a shot," a drunken Kosum laughed.

Parfait grabbed a shot and drank it before storming up the stairs.

"Kosum!" Nkechi snapped.

"Sorry…"

"Nicole, get her some water. I'm gonna go check on Parfait. Something tells me he's not as tough as he makes out," Nkechi said as she left to find him.

"What am I gonna do with you?" Nicole asked, staring at Kosum, who looked as though she was about to vomit.

"*Love* me?" Kosum asked shyly.

Nicole lovingly rolled her eyes. "Come on, let's get a drink."

"Vodka!" Kosum cheered.

"Ha, definitely not. Let's start with water and see with if you can be trusted to move up to a soda," Nicole instructed, walking a wobbly Kosum back up the basement stairs.

Nkechi went in search of Parfait to make sure Kosum hadn't upset him. She weaved her way through the younger teens dancing to the blaring music and mini disco lights Anuli had stuck up on a high shelf. She had even conjured up a spell to create a layer of smoke on the ground. Anuli was outside on the front porch, keeping watch for any danger. All that mattered to her was that Nicole was having a good time.

Nkechi walked past the staircase and did a double take as

she caught a glimpse of Parfait. She turned back to see him sat on the top step looking rather lonesome.

With his knees curled up on the stairs and his head in his hands, it wasn't until he sensed her shadow that he looked up.

"Move up, then." Nkechi nudged him, wedging herself next to him on the step.

"Sorry about Kosum. She has no filter sometimes, especially when she's drunk."

"It's okay. That's not why I left," he murmured, his gaze firmly on the steps below.

"It isn't?"

"Well, not entirely."

"Then why did you leave?"

"Because I'm distracted, distracted because—" He turned and looked into Nkechi's hazel eyes. He could so easily have admitted to her how he felt but instead he said, "I mean, look around. We're all distracted, we're having a birthday party in the middle of a war, for God's sake."

"You know, you're sounding a lot like your dad."

"Well, maybe he's right on this occasion."

"Nah, I don't believe you think that. Come up here," Nkechi said, grabbing his hand and dragging him to the window on the landing. "What do you see?"

"I don't know," he shrugged. "It's too dark outside."

"Exactly."

"Huh?"

"It's dark outside and all of this is going on in here. When's the last time you heard singing and laughter after dark?" she asked. "This is what we're fighting for – freedom. And this," she said, gesturing towards the direction of the party, "is a reminder of that. Look, can you just wipe that moody look off your face for one night and have some fun?" she asked, pushing the corners of Parfait's mouth up to form a smile.

"I suppose, but—"

"Yeah, yeah, don't worry, tomorrow we can go back to being in the trenches. Now, c'mon, let's go dance." Nkechi held her hand out for Parfait to take. He clamped his hand in hers and she led him to the makeshift dancefloor which was just Anuli's living room with the furniture pushed to the walls.

They arrived to find a slightly less drunk Kosum grinding against Nicole. Kosum mouthed sorry to Parfait, and he gave her a smile in return. The four of them let their hair down and danced freely. Feeling a little mischievous after seeing how well Nkechi and Parfait were getting on, Kosum sneaked over to the phone controlling the music and switched to a slow song.

Nicole realised what Kosum had done as the song began to flow through the speaker. She walked over to Kosum.

"You are so chaotic. It's a good thing I don't mind a bit of chaos," she smiled as she pulled her in for a kiss.

Parfait and Nkechi stood awkwardly for a moment as the song played.

"Er…" Parfait mumbled, "do you maybe… wanna dance?"

"Sure, though I don't really know how to slow dance," she admitted.

"Just follow my lead," he said, before gently taking her in his arms.

Nkechi was shocked as she felt his arm hook around her waist. Her stomach filled with butterflies. Although she had thought him attractive when she'd first seen him, his arrogance was certainly enough to put any woman off. In that moment, however, in the softness of his grasp and with his gaze upon her, Nkechi realised she really liked him.

As they danced closer and more intensely, their thoughts became in tandem with one another:

Fuck, he's so hot.

Fuck, she's so hot.

Should I kiss him?

Should I kiss her?

Nkechi and Parfait gave in to their overthinking minds and both leaned in simultaneously for a kiss. In that moment, the room of sweaty teenagers around them melted away and it felt like they were the only two hearts beating in the room – and beating fast. Nkechi slid her hands from Parfait's impressive chest to around his neck, while Parfait held Nkechi's bum firmly within his grasp.

They opened their eyes for a fleeting second and Nkechi whispered, "Take me upstairs."

"You sure?" he checked, though hoping the answer would be yes.

"Yep," she smiled.

With that, Parfait lifted her body up against his and she wrapped her legs around his abdomen. Parfait carried her up the stairs to hers and Anuli's room. They wasted no time in undressing one another. Nkechi grabbed the bottom of his shirt and Parfait flung his arms up for her to pull it off. He then took off Nkechi's top with one hand and unclipped her bra smoothly with the other. Her breasts were freed and Parfait bit his lip in awe and anticipation.

Nkechi dropped to her knees and unbelted his jeans before pulling them down to reveal his large manhood – he'd gone commando. She looked up at him.

"I don't like underwear," he shrugged.

"That's hot," she breathed, before focusing her attention back on the matter at hand. Nkechi took him inside her mouth, causing Parfait to step back almost breathless with pleasure, his large hand gripping the doorknob behind him, bracing himself while Nkechi worked her magic. A few moments later, Parfait lifted her chin gently signalling to come up for a kiss. When she did, he lifted her and gently laid her down onto the air mattress. He kissed down her body where he pulled her lacy underwear off. Securing both of her legs over his shoulder, he reciprocated the same generous oral pleasure she had given him.

Nkechi moaned in ecstasy under his touch. He worked his way back up her body so that he could kiss her neck tenderly as he slid himself inside her. They moved together until they were hot, sweaty and satisfied.

They lay beside each other, panting for breath. Parfait was had a beaming smile as his literal dream had come to life. He felt lucky to be beside a beautiful soul such as Nkechi's and although Nkechi enjoyed herself, as she laid beside him, the same thoughts weren't in her mind.

Nkechi did like Parfait, and she definitely liked what just happened, but she was beginning to think that Kosum was right: maybe it would just be better to be under him for the time being rather than starting anything meaningful. After all, she was still having her Charlie nightmares, and she wasn't ready for anything more. She knew she had to tell

Parfait before she led him to believe something could flourish between them.

Nkechi turned onto her side to face him. Parfait turned to her too with an uncontrollable smile.

"Parfait?"

"Yeah?"

"I can't—"

"Ahh! ZOMBIES!"

CHAPTER 10

The Damned

The voodoo king had been preparing to address the remaining practitioners of his inner circle. He wanted to fill them in on his next steps for killing Nkechi and her comrades.

Since the collapse of their warehouse, the men had moved their meeting and ritual room to another more secure location. They had managed to salvage the voodoo king's throne, now placed on top of a raised altar at the back of the room, a large stained-glass window behind it. The floor was made up of worn wooden floorboards with magical symbols etched into each, outlined in chalk.

"What are we to do, sir?" one of his disciples asked.

The voodoo king stood to address them. "Seeing as you all are too weak and feeble-minded to kill a couple of children, it looks as though we're going to have to bring the damned into this fight sooner than anticipated."

"With all due respect, sir, would it be wise to waste the Army of the Damned on, as you put it, children? Would it not be better for you to dispose of them yourself?" Gaudence suggested.

The voodoo king pulled out a doll from his pocket. It looked rather scrappily put together with two different buttons for eyes, though for its purpose, it didn't need to look fancy or ornate, it just needed to be infused with a strand of hair and some powerful voodoo magic.

The voodoo king, taking his forefinger and thumb, began to squeeze the neck of the small doll, suddenly causing Gaudence to choke and gasp for air.

"I am your king, is that anyway to address your king?" he asked to a man who could barely breathe let alone respond.

"I'm guessing you haven't played chess before and therefore I'll give you the benefit of the doubt. You see, in chess the king is the most valuable piece; lose it and you've lost the war. It is also a very powerful piece able to take out any enemy in any direction within close proximity, but it's the pawns, his soldiers, who must stop him from needing to use that mighty strength. My power is obviously enough to take out those pathetic worms, but it is not my duty to venture out and seek a fight when I have pawns to do that for me. So, next time your small brain thinks of an objection, keep it to yourself."

The voodoo king released his fingers from the doll and Gaudence gasped a deep scratchy breath, trying to replenish his lungs with oxygen. The king placed the doll back inside his magically extended cloak pocket, where he kept a doll for each of his disciples. It was so he could easily dispose of them if necessary, as well as protecting himself against a possible coup.

"Who knows the whereabouts of Nkechi?" he asked.

"I do." One of the men stepped forward with his hand raised.

"Spit it out, then," the voodoo king demanded.

"We've had reports that they're—" The man stopped, too scared to utter the next words. He now regretted being the one to come forward with information. How was he supposed to tell his king that while they plotted revenge, their enemies were throwing a party?

"They're what?" the voodoo king growled, growing tired of waiting.

"Having a birthday party… We believe for Nkechi's cousin, Nicole," the man muttered.

"A party?" the voodoo king screeched in anger.

Everyone shuffled back a moment as they didn't want to be in the firing line. He marched over to the poor grunt who had supplied him with the information and lifted him by his throat. The rage coursing through his veins was too great to be satisfied by a voodoo doll. No, he wanted to feel life squirming in his hands, and that he did.

The young man panicked, and as he gasped for breath, blood pulsated around his neck. The voodoo king could feel the blood gushing beneath his skin. It soothed him to be reminded of the power that he possessed, the power to end a life in an instant. The voodoo king noticed the young man's eyes roll into the back of his head and dropped him.

His body fell limply to the ground. A fellow practitioner knelt beside him to check his pulse. There wasn't a flicker of life left within the boy. He looked up to the voodoo king with a quivering look and confirmed the boy's passing.

"No bother, he'll still serve his purpose to the cause – he'll be the final addition to the pit before we summon them."

Killing the boy had helped calm the voodoo king's aggression, so much so that he could now see a path forward.

"A party?" he chuckled. "Well then, we better not be late."

The voodoo king and his men travelled back to their now mostly destroyed warehouse. Though they no longer used it as their main point of operation, the damned still resided in the pit on the sublevels. Gaudence had made himself useful and mapped out the wreckage after the explosion to ensure there was a safe route to the damned.

They ventured through the rubble, with parts of it still crumbling as they moved close by. The voodoo king adopted the same chess analogy and ensured a few of his weakest men were front and centre leading the way, serving their purpose like canaries in a coal mine. Although there were a few loose boulders that slowed them down, luckily none of the metaphorical canaries died and they all reached a small clearing surrounding the pit. Two of the men had dragged their murdered acquaintance with them. They looked up at the voodoo king for confirmation as they halted at the pit's edge.

The voodoo king nodded in the direction of the pit and so they tossed the lifeless body into the hole, not that it would stay lifeless for long. The voodoo king allowed a minute to pass for the damned to feast on the man until he awoke as one of them – an undead monster.

While they waited, the voodoo king directed his disciples to create a circle surrounding the pit. As they carried out his orders, their faces showed a mix of emotions. Some followers were clearly long-term veterans and remained detached by the process of killing the poor man as food for the king's army. Others, however, were fearful, feeling this wasn't what they signed up for.

The voodoo king noticed the hesitant men in his herd and reminded everyone of their end goal in a bid to boost morale.

"My loyal followers, this is but the beginning of a new era. With the army of the damned, we will not only take out Nkechi and her town, we will take the entire continent. As they kill, their numbers will grow, and so will our hold on this land. We say, "No more!" to the white oppressor, it is our time to rule, and they should consider themselves lucky if we let them live long enough to be *our* slaves. Now then, if that doesn't appeal to any of you, do feel free to leave; I won't take it personally." The voodoo king stood in silence for a moment as he examined the circle of men, watching, waiting to see who would break.

Two men did indeed break. Beads of sweat flooded their foreheads as they turned to one another and bravely readied to leave.

"Ah, not the two I thought would leave but, nevertheless, you may go."

The men didn't want to look a gift horse in the mouth and so began walking back in the direction from which they had come. If they were being honest with themselves, they'd been contemplating leaving for a while but hadn't known how to.

Of course, they were foolish to think it would be that easy.

"My dear boys, where are you going?" the king asked. "The exit is that way." He smiled, pointing in the direction of the pit.

One of the two betrayers laughed nervously, while the other gulped the anxiety-induced saliva that poured into his mouth and prepared to bolt in the other direction.

"We need to run," one whispered to the other.

The nervous laughter stopped as they both turned on their heels and tried to escape. The voodoo king extracted two voodoo dolls from his pocket. He gripped each doll tightly, causing the two men to stop in their tracks.

The king turned to Gaudence and passed him one of the voodoo dolls, telling him to follow his lead to make up for his prior insolence. He did as the voodoo king said for fear of being his next victim if he disobeyed.

The voodoo king began twisting the doll's legs, causing a menacing crunch to echo around the room as the corresponding man's legs broke and swivelled around gruesomely. He then used the doll's broken legs to walk the man into the pit. It was a slow, gut-wrenchingly painful walk which caused the man to scream in agony as every muscle and bone in his body worked against his own mind.

Gaudence reluctantly followed suit, snapping the other doll's legs and marching the man behind the other. As their legs walked them into the hole, the two men grasped onto the edge of the pit, using all the upper body strength they could muster. Their nails clawed at the concrete floor, and they glared at the voodoo king with a mix of fear and hatred. An angry roar bellowed out of the pit, causing the two men to whimper and beg for their lives.

The voodoo king began crushing the doll's hands, causing the dangling men to realise they were fighting a losing battle. They turned their heads to each other once more and tried to calm the other in their final moments. They took one last gasp of air before closing their eyes and letting go. The second they stopped fighting, their bodies slid and fell into the pit where the roaring turned into a wet, sloppy sound of flesh being chewed.

"Anyone else?" the voodoo king asked, casually. There was nothing but silence in reply. He may have lost three of his followers in quick succession, but he remained unphased. He knew that back in his hometown there were hundreds of men who would literally kill to be within his inner circle. His men were as replaceable as they were deplorable and thus, he did not worry.

"Let us commence the summoning ritual," he announced.

Gaudence drew a circle upon the floor in chalk, connecting all of the men, including the voodoo king. He then drew the sacred symbol of Baron Samedi at the voodoo king's feet. He returned to his position beside the other men and, in hushed tones, they all began a chant to divert their collective power to the voodoo king.

Once the voodoo king stepped onto the symbol before him, he felt a surge of power flow through his body, fuelling him. He smiled wickedly before beginning his own ritual to garner command over the army he had been curating.

The beasts below could sense the power emanating from the voodoo king. They screamed, roared and howled in defiance. They didn't want their undead existence to be as enslaved as their earthly one, but soon they would have no choice.

"*Ta loyauté est envers moi*, Baron Samedi," the voodoo king shouted.

The damned became louder in their defiance, trying their best to fight his control. The voodoo king's eyes rolled back into his head and nothing but pure white filled his sockets. He syphoned even more energy from his followers and dropped his jaw to release a godly sound that filled the building and caused the unstable structure to shake. He uttered the phrase again and again until finally the damned could no longer resist and their moans quietened to a soft grumble as they submitted to the voodoo king.

He was now their master in death.

He released what little energy he had left back into his men, and they all simultaneously dropped to the ground with exhaustion. The voodoo king walked to the circumference of the pit to greet his new army and inform them of their task.

"Sacred army of the damned. I, your master, command you to find and kill Nkechi, and anyone who stands in your way." He dropped a single strand of Nkechi's hair into the pit and a hoard of snarls could be heard as they inhaled her scent. The sounds then softened to a communal groan as the damned familiarised themselves with Nkechi's unique fragrance and comprehended what was being asked of them.

The voodoo king waved his hand over the pit to create a spiralling staircase leading down to the bottom. The damned wasted no time in climbing their way out. Once they reached the top, the crazed rotten corpses, dressed in nothing but rags, sniffed the air for Nkechi's scent. Their eyes widened once they caught her trail, and hundreds of them bolted in the direction of Anuli's house. The voodoo king's men curled up on the floor as the damned rushed past them. After a few seconds, they seemed to relax, realising that the spell had worked. For now, they had nothing to fear.

Once the room was clear of the damned army, the voodoo king addressed him men.

"Now, we must prepare the troops. Once the damned have dealt with Nkechi and the so-called Resistance, we will take our fight to the rest of New Orleans, where our brethren can either join us or die with the rest of them!"

The remaining men, his most loyal followers, began to cheer, clap and even pound their chests with clenched fists in support of his plan.

They were all incredibly dumb if they thought it would be that easy to take out Nkechi and her family.

Nkechi and Parfait jolted as they heard the scream.

"What was that? Did someone say zombies?" Parfait asked.

"I don't know, but whatever it is, it doesn't sound good. C'mon."

They both jumped up and quickly shuffled back into their clothes. Nkechi was ready first but as she headed out of the bedroom, Parfait pulled her back. Dressed only in jeans, Nkechi had to fight the urge to stare at his still sweating chest.

Parfait swung his arm around Nkechi's waist and pulled her close to him before planting a kiss on her lips. It all happened so fast that it took Nkechi by surprise. The kiss made her feel even guiltier about the fact she knew she didn't want anything serious. She could see in his eyes that she meant more to him, and she knew the second the 'zombie' situation was dealt with she'd have to be honest with him.

Without saying another word, Nkechi tore away from his gaze and headed downstairs. Not long after, a now fully clothed Parfait followed suit, catching up as they reached the living room. No one had thought to turn off the music or disco lights, so if it wasn't for the herd of petrified teenagers in the centre of the living room, they wouldn't have thought that the party had halted.

They caught a glimpse of Nicole in the kitchen guarding the back door, and noticed that Kosum and Anuli were assessing the situation out front.

"I'll go give Nicole some backup," Parfait said, looking to Nkechi for an agreement.

"Okay. I'll go see what's happening out front." Nkechi joined Kosum and Anuli by the front door and asked for a quick catchup on the situation. What Nkechi didn't realise was that her hair had been quite ruffled by her fun with Parfait and, even in a state of emergency, it didn't go unnoticed by Kosum and Anuli.

As they turned to face Nkechi, they both immediately saw the tangled mess. They gawped at her awkwardly for a second before Nkechi felt around her hair and realised just how out of place everything was.

"Have fun?" Kosum asked, trying to keep a straight face as Nkechi fiddled with her mane.

"Oh, my god, we're not talking about this right now! What the hell is going on out there?" Nkechi stressed.

Kosum couldn't help but smirk.

"It's the army of the damned," Anuli answered with a look of worry.

"Come again?" Nkechi muttered.

"Army of the what?" Kosum questioned, neither of them having any idea as to what Anuli was referring.

"You kids would probably refer to them as zombies, but let

me tell you they are far worse than anything you've seen in the movies. These aren't just some mindless flesh-eating creatures; they're loyal to whoever summons and dominates their army. They will have a specific target, and it doesn't take a genius to work out that the voodoo king has probably picked you to be that target," Anuli explained hastily, looking at Nkechi.

"Okay, so the voodoo king has raised an army of the dead in order to kill me and, I assume, anyone who's helping me. How did he even manage that?" Nkechi asked, trying to comprehend the madness unfolding before her.

"I don't know. But the only way to eliminate them is to destroy their brain, that's where they receive their commands."

"So, it *is* kinda like the movies," Kosum joked, as the zombies made their way to the front porch.

"I guess," Anuli humoured.

"How do I kill zombie heads?" Nkechi asked, already exasperated.

"Oh, c'mon, Nkechi, get creative." Kosum smiled as she nudged her and darted off into the kitchen.

Seconds later, she returned with a swarm of kitchen knives floating above her palms. She raised her eyebrows at Nkechi excitedly before kicking open the front door and directing them into the zombies' foreheads.

"See, creative," she shouted back to Nkechi and Anuli.

Anuli looked to Nkechi. "Well, she's not wrong."

"I know," Nkechi replied, before heading out to help Kosum. So far, she had only defeated a handful of the living corpses and there were still hundreds to come, flowing down the street like a river – a sickening river full of disease, rotten flesh and entrail-soaked rags.

At the back of the house, Nicole had filled Parfait in on the ever-growing problem. He stepped into action, swiftly popping the cap off his strength elixir and downing it. He swallowed a second elixir which was a vibrant blue. Nicole wasn't sure what it was, but as he started to tear apart the zombies with his bare hands, its usefulness soon became apparent. A zombie tried gnawing at Parfait's arm but its teeth and claws didn't make a mark, let alone break the skin. It was as if the elixir made his skin as hard as steel.

Although Parfait was eliminating his fair share of zombies, there were still too many for him to corral alone. Nicole needed to think of a spell, and fast.

She began by using the cutting spell she had tried at the voodoo king's base, but it soon became apparent that zombies don't feel pain and weren't bothered by Nicole's attempt at harming them.

Nicole racked her brain as every spell she could think of was seemingly having no effect on the zombies. Then, she had a eureka moment. She closed the kitchen door, leaving Parfait alone outside for a moment as she raced up to her bedroom. She flung open her wardrobe doors and dove into the back, behind her hangers. She dug into a pile of old clothes and from them pulled out a bow and quiver. Archery was something she had picked up in an extracurricular club in high school. She loved it and was quite the shot but had to give it up when her mother needed help running the salon.

Just like riding a bike... I hope, she thought, before launching herself down the stairs. She went through the kitchen and locked the door behind her before climbing on top of the small porch roof sheltering the door. Parfait heard her clambering up onto it and turned to see her with a quiver full of arrows slung around her shoulder and a bow in hand.

"Wow, I didn't realise you were the *Katniss Everdeen* type!" he shouted out to her.

"I won't be screaming Parfait, that's for sure."

Parfait chuckled and then popped off the head of a zombie while cockily asking, "Are you a good shot?"

Nicole let her actions do the talking. She smized at him before pulling an arrow from her quiver and lining up a shot. She drew the bow back as far as it could stretch and held her breath. As she exhaled, she let the tight string slip through her fingers, and the arrow flew straight between the eyes of a zombie.

"Cool, but a little slow," Parfait jokingly mocked, while ploughing his fist into the brain of another zombie.

Nicole tilted her head at him and huffed. *Fine,* she thought as she pulled three arrows in a row and landed every shot within five seconds, barely glancing at the target.

"At least I don't have to get my hands dirty," Nicole smirked, as Parfait pulled his hand out of the zombie's head and wretched a little at the sight of the congealed brain matter that covered his hand.

"Okay, show off." He rolled his eyes and flicked his hand free of the rotten flesh before resuming the fight.

Out front, Nkechi had used her hedge witch abilities, summoning roots from the earth to stop zombies in their tracks. The vegetation circled the zombies' feet to constrict them, making them easier targets for Kosum to pick off with her knives. Kosum levitated herself into the air as her fingers danced, directing the blades from one zombie brain to the next.

Anuli stood by the door as a last line of defence, taking out any stragglers with her gardening tools. Her fork and spade were more formidable than one would think. She smacked them with her spade to throw them off balance and buy herself some time to line up a clean shot before driving the fork into their skulls. She pressed her foot up against them for leverage as she yanked the fork back out and flicked off the congealed blood, readying herself for her next victim.

Although the five of them made quite the team, Anuli knew it was only a matter of time before they became overrun; the sheer number of zombies was just too much to combat.

"Nicole, quick. My elixirs are wearing off," a panicked Parfait shouted as he struggled to fight off the two zombies latched on to either side of him.

Nicole heard his call and within a second her eyes locked onto his location. She flew two arrows at once, taking out both zombies with ease.

"Thanks," Parfait called out, a little breathlessly.

"No probs!" Nicole spotted the next group of brainless corpses heading through the back gate and reached for an arrow out of her quiver, only for her hand to come up empty. "Shit!"

Parfait turned to see what was going on.

"I'm all out!" she shouted as she slid off the porch roof and headed back inside the kitchen, with Parfait just a step behind. They slammed the door and propped their backs up against it as they braced themselves for impact.

Nicole called for her mother's help.

While Anuli ran to her daughter's assistance, out front,

Nkechi and Kosum were still working in tandem to take out as many of the damned as they could, but it wasn't making a big enough dent.

Nkechi spotted Adame and Evélia on their front porch attempting to defend themselves, but they were quickly forced back into their home by the vast numbers of mindless soldiers. Nkechi knew they wouldn't stand a chance if the hoard managed to break into their house and thus, she redirected her roots. The roots arched their way down the road, ripping through the tarmac streets with ease until they reached Parfait's house. She used them to flick the few zombies away that were trying to break in, and then grew them tenfold. Her rough roots weaved together over and again, managing to encompass the whole house in thick, woody flora. She made sure that every window and door was completely sealed off from the outside, making it look dilapidated and uninhabited and, even more importantly, impenetrable. Doing so, however, did drain some of her energy, leaving Kosum to try to pick up the slack.

"Nkechi, I'm not sure how much longer I can do this," Kosum said as her arms grew tired of aiming the slurry of knives which she flew through the air around them.

"Me neither. We need to regroup; this clearly isn't working," Nkechi replied in a worried voice.

"Girls, get inside," Anuli shouted from the front porch.

Nkechi and Kosum ran back inside the house, closing the door just in time to stop the damned getting in.

"Auntie, what do we do?" Nkechi asked, as a loud shattering crash sounded from the kitchen.

"Mom! They're gonna get in!"

Anuli didn't know where to look – there was too much to process – and if she was being honest with herself, she was just as clueless about what to do next as the rest of them. However, knew she had to pull herself together for her girls' sake and see them through this.

"Parfait, Nicole, let them take the kitchen. Come in here and start moving the furniture to barricade the doorway to the kitchen. Kosum, you help me do the same to the front door, and Nkechi… Summon Papa Legba, and beg for his help… for all our sakes."

"Yes, Auntie."

As everyone around her frantically rushed to block the entrances, Nkechi tried her best to relax and slip her consciousness into Papa's realm.

She swiftly entered the vast void and called his name in haste. Almost instantaneously, he appeared behind her.

He could sense the distress in Nkechi's voice and asked what he could do for her.

"I need to know how to defeat the army of the damned. The voodoo king has summoned them, and there are too many to fight." Nkechi looked to Papa with heavy anticipation as she eagerly awaited his wise answer. But for the first time, Nkechi saw an uneasy look upon Papa's face. He looked unsettled, even a little scared. Nkechi knew they were in a precarious situation, but the fact that even a deity was lost for words, didn't fill her with confidence.

"No, no, my child, that cannot be. You must be mistaken."

"I'm sorry, but it's the truth. Why are you so disconcerted by it?" Nkechi asked, trying to remain respectful.

"The voodoo deities outlawed that spell to humans a long

time ago. We knew it was far too dangerous to allow any single human to have rule over the dead. The only way it would be possible is if— No, even *he* wouldn't be that selfishly idiotic. Could he?" Papa paused as he questioned himself.

"Papa, what is it? I'm sorry to press you, but in my realm we're kind of running out of time."

"I'm afraid this is much worse than you fear. This isn't the work of some estranged old voodoo practitioner – this is the work of another deity. This is the work of Baron Samedi," Papa revealed ominously.

"Yes, we've believed the voodoo king has been summoning him for help for quite some time."

"No, Nkechi. The voodoo king isn't summoning him. The voodoo king *is* Baron Samedi. That is the only way this spell is possible."

"Great! How do I fight a deity?" Nkechi sarcastically voiced to the empty realm in frustration.

"I don't know. But I do know how you can stop the army."

"How?"

"To enact the spell. Baron would have had to dominate their souls until they yielded to him. They aren't as mindless as you might think. They are doing his bidding because he broke their spirit. But if you can connect to them, speak to their souls, then you might just be able to convince them to lay their bodies to rest and, in return, I'll allow them to pass through limbo and onto a peaceful afterlife."

"This sounds like a whole lot of pressure to put on me," Nkechi said, not feeling too confident about her chances.

"Nkechi, if anyone can do it, you can," Papa whispered as his body disappeared once more.

Nkechi sighed and trilled air through her lips as she tried to psyche herself up for a conversation with an army of zombies.

Meanwhile, back on the earthly realm, the others were struggling to keep the damned at bay. Rotten arms began to poke through gaps in the entrances, with crooked, deteriorated hands clawing at the air, full of anger at Nkechi's scent.

"What's Nkechi doing?" Kosum asked through gritted teeth as she used her telekinesis to hold a sofa in place against the front door.

"Hopefully saving us," Anuli answered, looking at Nkechi's still body with optimism.

Nkechi transported her consciousness to the vast misty and otherwise empty plane of Limbo, where she began her speech to the damned:

"I summon the Army of the Damned to convene with me." She looked around at the murky air surrounding her in search of their presence. A forceful wind began to swirl around Nkechi and one by one the army of angry souls appeared around her, which quickly made Nkechi feel unsettled. They glared at her with anger and frothing mouths, though they didn't understand why they hated her so much for it was only the voodoo king, or rather Baron Samedi, who made them feel that way.

"Please, hear me," she begged, as they closed in around her. "I know you are angry; I know you're in pain. Your bodies are being used against your will; I know you feel it. So, I beg of you to rebel one last time, fight the voodoo king's hold on you, fight it and return your bodies to peace. Allow your bones to be once again at one with the earth and rebirth into something new. Do this, and Papa Legba, the *true* deity of the dead, will allow you all safe passage through Limbo and you will never be at the mercy of anyone again."

Nkechi watched cautiously, unsure if she had swayed any of them.

One of the damned spirits took a step closer to Nkechi, stopping a foot away from her. She held her breath and stood firm as she looked into the poor soul's eyes. Thankfully, it gently tilted its head towards her in a nod of agreement.

"Thank you," Nkechi breathed, with an acknowledging nod of her own. With that, the wayward souls dispersed as one back into the murky mist.

Back at the house, the clawing and banging from the damned had only worsened in Nkechi's absence. All of the younger teens from the party huddled in the centre of the living room; the high-pitched screams and cries from them were almost deafening. Anuli tried her best to calm them, but it was useless. They could see how bad the situation was and were old enough to know that they could die at any moment.

As the hoard of zombies mounted on the other side of the barricades, the gang knew it was only a matter of seconds before they would break through. Nicole had her back pressed against a table that had been flipped on its side at the kitchen door, while Kosum was finally about to pass out after holding the sofa up for so long.

Kosum turned to see Nicole and mouthed, "I love you," before falling to the ground with exhaustion and allowing the sofa to drop too. Nicole's eyes widened and, without a second thought, ran to her girlfriend's aid, abandoning Parfait, who couldn't hold the table alone.

Both entrances opened, allowing the zombies to flood in.

They snarled and gnashed their rotten teeth as they entered. But before they could take another step, they came to a grinding halt. All of them froze and the air fell silent.

Anuli and Parfait had arched their bodies over the teens to protect them while Nicole sat with Kosum's unconscious body in her arms. The prolonged, eery silence caused them all to finally look up at the zombies, at which point they slowly began to turn around, march out of the house and down the street. They would eventually all return to the original place of their burials and become one with the earth once more, with Papa finally allowing their souls to pass on to paradise.

"What's happening?" a tearful and confused Nicole asked.

"She did it! Nkechi did it!" Anuli answered with a sigh of relief.

Nkechi awoke back in her body in a panicked state.

"Did it work?" she called out.

"Yes, I believe so," Anuli confirmed as she got up and poked her head out of the now broken doorway to see the army retreating into the distance.

"How did you do it?" Parfait asked, impressed.

"Papa said they needed to be reminded of who they were and be inspired to reclaim their bodies and souls in order to break free from the voodoo king's grip on them. He also assured them safe passage out of Limbo."

"Well done, cuz," an exhausted Nicole congratulated as she began to gently wake Kosum in her arms.

"You are inspirational, my sweet," Anuli smiled. "Though I think if this ordeal has taught us anything, it's that we can't wait around for the voodoo king to strike again. We need to take action. This last week has made it clear that we are no longer safe anywhere. This war needs to end, and now."

Although Nkechi was glad to have successfully defended against the army of the damned, it had come with another burden: discovering the voodoo king's true identity.

Nkechi had no idea how to defeat him nor how to break the news to everyone that the person they were fighting wasn't a man at all, but a god.

CHAPTER 11
The Master Plan

The past few hours had been spent trying to fix up as much of Anuli's house as possible and ensuring that all the teens were accounted for. Everyone was exhausted. It was the early hours of the morning and Parfait was finally readying to head home to get a couple of hours sleep before the sun rose. Nkechi walked him to the now dilapidated front porch.

"Well, that was certainly a memorable night, huh?" Nkechi smiled, though a little awkwardly as she knew she was just building herself up to let him down gently.

"You're not kidding. Hey, didn't get any bites or scratches, did ya?" he asked as he lifted her chin and softly turned her face to either side to examine her neck.

"Looks like you're all good," he smiled, answering his own question. He let his thumb linger on her chin. Nkechi could see he was about to lean in for a kiss and she couldn't hide the guilt.

"What's wrong?" he asked.

"Just a little cold," she said, trying to brush his affections away as she rubbed her arms and faked a shiver.

"Here, take my jacket," he sweetly offered, swinging the coat off his back and readying it to caress her shoulders.

Nkechi had an involuntary flashback to her first date with

Charlie when he'd offered his jacket to her. The memory only confirmed in her mind that she wasn't ready.

She did like Parfait, and perhaps they would've made a good match, but it was unfair to her to start something when she knew she wasn't over Charlie. It was also unfair to Parfait to build a relationship on lies. He was turning out to be a much nicer guy than Nkechi ever imagined, and he deserved better than playing second fiddle to a crazy ex-boyfriend, a dead one at that.

Nkechi stopped him before he could place his jacket around her shoulders. Parfait looked confused.

"Parfait," she muttered, slowly lowering his arms, "I'm sorry, but I can't get into anything new right now. I'm still haunted by my last relationship and I need time to heal and look after myself before I can even consider letting someone else in again."

"Oh." Parfait sighed, a little speechless. He had only just accepted his feelings for Nkechi, and now their relationship was being cut short without being given the chance to see if it could grow.

"Listen, I understand. I don't want to push you into something you're not ready for. I'm sorry I was such a moody dick when we first met," he chuckled, trying to play it cool.

Nkechi sniggered. "It's okay. You know, it's kind of crazy that you won me over at all. I mean my first, second *and* third impression of you weren't great to say the least."

"Thanks," he said, rolling his eyes.

"But for what it's worth, I have actually come to really like you."

"Thank you," he smiled, trying not to lose himself in her

eyes.

"Promise me things won't be awkward?" Nkechi asked, sensing his lingering gaze.

"It won't – we're good. Besides, I'm pretty sure we're gonna have quite the distraction planning to take down the voodoo king and all."

"Oh yeah, about that… When I spoke to Papa Legba about the damned, he told me that the voodoo king is in actual fact the deity, Baron Samedi," Nkechi explained flatly.

"Oh shit."

"Yeah, I know. I'm gonna fill everyone else in tomorrow."

"I'm sure that'll go down a treat," he smirked. "Anyway, that's tomorrow's problem. Right now, we should *both* be getting to bed."

"Yes, you're right. Goodnight, Parfait."

"You forgetting something?" Parfait asked, making Nkechi feel awkward as she assumed he meant a kiss. Had he not been listening to their conversation at all?

Nkechi raised her eyebrow. "Huh?" she muttered.

His eyes darted down the road to his house still securely contained within Nkechi's roots.

"I'm kinda locked out, and you're the key," he laughed.

"Oh, my god. Sorry, I totally forgot!" she chuckled.

Nkechi held out her palms in the direction of the house and closed her eyes. She pictured the roots returning to the earth, and so they did. Parfait watched, in awe of her powers as the flora shrank and retreated to the soil they grew from, though it was a shame Nkechi couldn't retarmac the road she'd torn up to grow them in the first place.

"Lovers or not, you're pretty incredible, Nkechi." Parfait

left her with that as he cautiously descended the broken porch steps and swaggered back to his home where his worried parents were finally able to emerge and greet him.

Nkechi sniggered to herself as she watched Parfait squirm under the shower of forehead kisses he received from his mother.

Upstairs, in Nicole's room, she and Kosum were engaging in some loving pillow talk.

"So, Nkechi told me about how badass you were, flying and stabbing brainless bitches left, right and centre," Nicole said, playfully poking Kosum in the stomach.

"Yeah, well, Parfait told me about the whole Katniss thing you had going on, so I guess we're both pretty badass. I never knew you were an archer!" Kosum playfully poked her back.

"I guess there's still a lot we don't know about each other. And it's gonna be hard again when you go back home," Nicole admitted, looking a little solemn.

"I like to think of it as a good thing," Kosum commented.

"Kosum, are you being positive? Maybe I *was* bitten by a zombie," Nicole joked.

"Shut up! Look at it this way: most couples spend the first month or two getting to know each other and then after that, that's it. I like the idea that we get to stretch those first few blissful months out a little longer."

"Okay, that is quite a cute sentiment, but I'm surprised it came from you," she laughed.

"Oh, my god, why does everyone think I'm incapable of being nice? I'm not a total bitch, ya know!"

"Oh, but I do love your mean side, so don't lose it," Nicole teased, poking Kosum again, which gradually progressed into a tickle fight. They wrestled each other in bed, Kosum cheating by using her telekinesis to push Nicole away with her pillows.

"No magic!" Nicole playfully growled, batting the pillows away and launching herself on top of Kosum with her fingers between her ribs. Kosum was wriggling under Nicole's touch.

"Yield!" Nicole instructed.

"Never!"

"Fine, you asked for it," Nicole jested before unleashing her full strength on Kosum.

"Ah, okay, okay. I yield!" Kosum panted.

Nicole, having straddled Kosum, released her fingers from Kosum's midriff and leant in for a kiss, as she whispered, "I love you."

"I love you, too," Kosum smiled, before waving her hand to flick the covers back over them both so they could engage in some other fun that would surely leave them both breathless.

Back downstairs, Anuli sat alone in the kitchen sipping some hot tea. She was contemplating whether the war was even worth it. Of course, deep down she believed it was, but she couldn't help torturing herself at the thought of the losses, and the lasting affects the war could have on the younger generation. As she sat stewing, feeling melancholy about the whole ordeal, she was joined by Adame and Evélia.

After reuniting with Parfait and knowing he was safe, they had decided to check on their oldest friend. Thanks to Nkechi who had sealed them inside their house, they hadn't had to battle the damned as Anuli had.

"Don't look so glum, Anuli," Evélia's soft voice spoke as they entered the room.

"I'm sorry," Anuli apologised as she turned to see them. "It's just that now we're so close, I'm scared of messing everything up. Everyone expects me to know what to do, but I don't. I didn't have a clue how to deal with the damned, and who knows what else the voodoo king has planned for us next."

Adame knew that 'I told you so' wasn't going to help and he didn't want to add to her guilt, so he said, "This isn't all on you, my old friend. We know we rely on you too much but if we do fail—"

"Which we won't!" Evélia interrupted, nudging her often senseless husband in the arm.

"—then it will have been a pleasure fighting by your side. You may not have known exactly what to do, but you took charge and put the people in the right places to fight. That's what good leaders do."

"Thank you, Adame. That is surprisingly comforting coming from you," she sniggered, which also made Evélia chuckle. "Would either of you care for a drink?"

"Please, though don't waste your time boiling water. It's been a long day, and I think we deserve something a little stronger, don't you?" Evélia proposed.

"Indeed," Adame seconded.

"Okay, but just a couple, we need our wits about us tomorrow." Anuli gave in and grabbed a couple of whiskey glasses that were left, most of which had been trashed when the zombies took over the kitchen.

The three of them engaged in a nightcap and enjoyed each other's company for an hour before heading off to bed.

As Anuli entered her bedroom, she tried to tread carefully

so as not to wake a sleeping Nkechi. What Anuli didn't know was that Nkechi was stuck in another nightmare about Charlie, and so when the creaking floorboards woke her up, she was rather relieved.

Nkechi rose up in bed in a sweaty panic. She instinctively flicked her blanket away and widened her eyes as she looked around the bedroom.

"Sorry, dear, I didn't mean to wake you. Are you okay?" Anuli asked, noticing the fearful look on Nkechi's face.

"Yeah, I'm fine," she lied, trying to hide the terror on her face.

"Come on now. You're not too old for nightmares, I get them too. Was it about the voodoo king?"

"Er… yeah." Nkechi lied again. She didn't see the point in telling Anuli; it would only distract them from the more pressing task at hand. Nkechi didn't want to be a burden to anyone, especially her aunt.

"Don't worry, my dear, we will all be stood beside you ready to fight."

"Thanks."

Anuli turned over and snuggled into bed, but before she could get to sleep Nkechi softly called out for her:

"Auntie?"

"Yes, dear?" Anuli answered, rolling over and looking down to face Nkechi.

"When I was seeking Papa's help, he warned me that the voodoo king is in fact Baron Samedi."

"The deity?"

"Yes."

"I see," Anuli replied calmly. She could sense Nkechi was

scared and didn't want to alarm her. The last thing Nkechi needed was to start doubting their chances against him.

"Nkechi, god or not, we are going to win this war. And do you know why?"

"Why?"

"Because we have something worth fighting for. Now get some rest and we'll figure out our next steps in the morning."

"Thank you, Auntie. Goodnight." Nkechi lay back. She could still smell Parfait on her pillow. It was a rather soothing smell, and it made her feel safe as she returned to slumber.

Anuli also finally lay back in bed, but as her head hit the pillow there was no soothing scent filling her mind. Instead, she stared at the ceiling and pondered how on earth they were going to defeat a god.

The next morning, everyone was readying to meet up in the war room. The sky was overcast, smothered in a dull, grey blanket of cloud – certainly not New Orleans's typical summertime weather. It was almost as if Mother Nature knew of the forthcoming battle and allowed the sky to reflect everyone's worry.

The core members of the Resistance filtered down into the war room one by one until all except Parfait were there.

"Where's Parfait?" Nkechi asked. She worried his absence might be her fault for breaking up with him the night before. Not that it even was a breakup – they hadn't actually been dating.

Nkechi now contemplated whether it had been a wise

decision. Perhaps she should have waited until after the war was over. Then again, there would be no telling whether any of them would survive it.

"We're not sure, Nkechi. But I *am* sure that he'll show up; he knows how important this fight is.

"He informed us last night that the voodoo king is Baron Samedi," Evélia explained, hopeful that her son hadn't indeed run away.

"Sorry, who's Baron Samedi? Do we know him?" Kosum asked, now seemingly being the only one still out of the loop.

Though Nicole hadn't been told either, she knew the name from learning about the voodoo deities as a child.

"He is a voodoo deity," Anuli answered.

"Oh, awesome. So now we just have to defeat a fricking god?" Kosum voiced sarcastically.

"So, what's the plan?" Nicole asked, in the hope that someone in the room might have an idea.

Thankfully, Anuli did.

"Some spies of our own have informed us of Baron Samedi's new location and security set-up: he's staying in one of the mansions on the border of our two towns where one of the murdered elders once lived. There are two guards at the main entrance, a further four behind the front door. Another four will be guarding Baron's private quarters and there'll be at least another ten practitioners roaming the corridors on high alert. We will split up into teams and then—"

Suddenly the room froze. Anuli's lips were still pursed mid-sentence, even the tiny molecule of spit that flung from her mouth was still in midair. Everything and everyone were statuesque, like time had stopped.

All except Nkechi.

Nkechi looked around, puzzled. She waved her hand in front of Kosum's face to see if there was any reaction, but nothing. She took a step closer to the war table at the centre of them all, when her head became filled with a high-pitched noise which almost deafened her. She dropped to her knees and screamed as she clamped her hands over her bleeding ears. The sound slowly dropped off and was replaced by the harrowing, base of Baron Samedi's voice.

Nkechi shook her head to try to rid him from her mind, but it was no use. Back in the safety of his base, he was once again siphoning the abilities of his followers to overpower her.

"Nkechi, I know of your feeble plan to storm my stronghold, and you must know by now who you are dealing with. Thus, I will give you one opportunity to save your family. Come alone within the hour and we can end this once and for all. Do this and I will spare your little merry band of witches. Try anything stupid and I will see to it that you all meet your demise."

His voice finally left Nkechi's head, his words ingrained into the forefront of her mind.

Time resumed and everyone turned to see Nkechi on the ground trying to recover. Kosum noticed the blood that trickled down her cheek from her ear.

"Nkechi! What happened?"

Nkechi was too stunned to speak. She had a pounding headache, and everything now seemed a little fuzzy. As her eyes refocused on the room, she noticed Kosum's hands held out in front of her ready to help her up. She allowed Kosum to pull back onto her feet.

"Are you okay?" Anuli asked, placing the back of her hand to Nkechi's forehead. "Nicole, go get a damp cloth."

"I'll be okay, I just need a second," Nkechi answered, trying to ease the discomfort in her forehead.

Nicole returned with the cloth and gently mopped up the blood on either side of Nkechi's face. Nkechi explained to everyone what had happened in the fleeting moments that they were frozen in time.

"Well, we're obviously not letting you go in alone," Kosum announced.

"Too right," Anuli firmly agreed.

"But what about what he said? Ya know, the bit where you'll all die if I don't go alone! He gave me his word that you'd be safe if I did what he asked."

"Nkechi, he's a crazed god – his word doesn't mean shit. For all we know you could go off alone, he'd kill you and then of all of us, too," Nicole retorted, trying to help Nkechi realise they weren't dealing with someone who could be trusted.

Baron Samedi had proven himself to be a coward who fought dirty. From the very first moment they had landed in New Orleans, every attack had been unjust and underhand.

"Yeah, I guess so." Nkechi sounded deflated.

"So, what's the plan now?" Evélia asked the room.

"We stick to Anuli's original plan – it's the best one we've got – and—"

"No…" Kosum interrupted. "Sorry, I don't mean to cut you off, but I think I have a better idea."

"There's no time for half-baked ideas!" Adame growled, clearly disgruntled at being questioned.

"Oh, be calm, dear. Let the girl speak," Evélia said,

silencing her husband and gesturing to Kosum to continue.

"We let her go in alone." The start of Kosum's plan was met by incredulous faces; even Evélia looked a little regretful at having allowed her to speak. "Or at least we let Baron think that," she added. "Nkechi hands herself in to the front guards who will escort her to him, leaving a small window of opportunity for the rest of us to infiltrate. Then Nkechi just needs to keep him talking, which from what we've already heard of him shouldn't be too hard – he certainly has the ego for it. While he's distracted, the rest of us can enact Anuli's plan. We take out the guards one by one until finally we're all in place and can take Baron by surprise and kill him – or whatever it is you do to stop a deity," Kosum concluded with a proud smile.

"Hmm, I'm not sure about this," Adame doubted, resting his folded arms across his chest.

"Well, I think it's a great idea," Nicole voiced in support of her love.

"I concur. It sounds like the best plan we've got. Kosum, since it was your idea, you should take the lead," Anuli commanded, smiling at Kosum with pride, as if she was her own flesh and blood.

"Oh, okay, thank you."

Adame let out another groan but Evélia gave him a playful slap on the arm and a stern look.

"Fine, let's put the kid in charge. What's the worst that can happen?" he said moodily.

"If we're all agreed then, Nkechi, as long as you're feeling up to it, you should probably go get a head start. Just keep him talking," Kosum reminded her.

"I'm all right – I just need to walk it off. And besides, like you said, it shouldn't be too hard to keep him talking," Nkechi said with a lopsided smile.

"Good luck," Nicole called as Nkechi headed up the stairs.

"She won't need it," Kosum said nudging her. "She'll have us."

"I'm so glad you made up. It was really weird you guys not being glued-at-the-hip besties," Nicole commented.

"Yeah, me too." Kosum smiled. "Right, the rest of us need to gear up. But someone needs to stay here."

"Why?" Adame rolled his eyes. He knew letting Kosum be in charge was a mistake.

"Because someone needs to protect the kids. For all we know this could be another ruse to distract us while they abduct them again," Kosum explained.

"She's right. I'll look after them," Evélia volunteered.

"Great. Now, Adame, you need to find Parfait. We'll need his strength in the end fight," Kosum said.

Adame groaned at the thought of having to babysit his son.

"Like Parfait could do anything to stop Baron Samedi. He barely—"

"Adame Okoye! For once in your life stop putting our son down. You will go find him and tell him just how amazing he is. Then you will bring him to help Kosum and the girls, or Papa Legba help me I will divorce you and send your ass into limbo!" Evélia raged.

She had no idea why Adame had become so incredulously stubborn and loveless towards Parfait, but she wasn't going to stand for it any longer.

"He is *our* son and he is perfect just the way he is. He has nothing to prove to you, so get off of your high horse and do something useful."

"My love, I'm sorry…"

"I don't want to hear another word until Parfait is stood beside you, the voodoo king is dead, and we are all safe."

"But—"

"Go!" She huffed, turning away from him with her arms crossed.

Adame slumped off up the stairs, feeling embarrassed and angry. At first, his anger seemed aimed towards Evélia, but after he'd had some time to cool off, for the first time in a long time Adame had clarity. He could see the husband, the father, the *man* he'd become, and he didn't like it. Living under the voodoo king's rule for so long had taken a toll on him, but that was no excuse. Everyone in the town had experienced the same hardships, though the women even more so as they had to deal with the lewd behaviour of the voodoo king's men.

Adame had been weak and unthoughtful when it came to his son, but no more. As he walked the streets, pondering where is only son might be, he had a sudden revelation and sprinted off in the direction he hoped Parfait had gone.

With Adame on his way, Evélia left the group, wishing them luck on their quest while she prepared to fortify the house. In her house she grouped together the local youth and placed them upstairs. She placed a protection spell over the house to magically seal all possible entrances and then made herself a calming peppermint tea and sipped it as she sat at the base of the stairs, alert, ready to protect the children with her life.

Anuli, Kosum and Nicole left the war room to prepare themselves for the fight ahead. As Anuli turned off the light, she hoped the next time she entered her basement it would be to store some wine or old junk, not to plan another attack.

Kosum and Nicole got changed into black combat outfits teamed with chunky boots. They were still fashionable, of course. Kosum may have been on a journey to better herself, but that didn't mean her fashion sense had to suffer.

Nicole headed out front to start up the car and, as Kosum tried to follow, she was called back by Anuli.

"Er, is everything okay?" Kosum asked, a little worried.

"Yes, dear. I just wanted to give you something. You've been a rock to both my girls this past year, especially for Nkechi when I couldn't. You're a part of the family now, Kosum," Anuli smiled with glassy eyes.

"Thank you, Anuli. But you don't need to give me anything. I love them both, no matter what."

"I know you do and that's why you deserve it. Here," she said, revealing an athame. "After the damage you caused with those kitchen knives last night, I couldn't imagine anyone better to have this in battle." She placed the athame in Kosum's hands. "It was hand-crafted by my great-grandmother and imbued with her magic."

The short magical dagger was beautiful. The handle had been expertly carved from deer horn and the blade was five inches long with a sharp edge on both sides. The cool grey metal was symmetrically curved like an hourglass, tapering to a fine point. It had been magically hardened by Anuli's great-grandmother to withstand great force and be strong enough to cut through steel.

"It's stunning. But I can't take this. Nkechi or Nicole should have it," Kosum insisted, feeling overwhelmed.

"As I said, you are the most suited to it. They have the blood of their ancestors running through their veins – they don't need a material object to connect them to their ancestry. Think of this as your christening into the family."

Kosum's eyes began to well up as she accepted Anuli's kind words. "Thank you, Anuli."

"Call me Auntie, everyone else does," she said, bringing Kosum in for a hug and squashing her into her bosom.

They gently pulled away and Kosum apologised for crying on Anuli's chest.

"It's fine," she chuckled, wiping Kosum's tears away with her thumb. "Now c'mon, our girls need us."

"Yes, let's go."

CHAPTER 12

The Last Stand

Nkechi made her way to the main entrance of the mansion that now doubled as Baron Samedi's base of operations. Anuli's informant had been correct thus far as Nkechi noticed the two guards at the entrance.

As soon they caught a glimpse of her, the guards readied themselves for attack.

Nkechi held her hands up and called out, "I accept Baron's terms."

The guards didn't relax their stance, even a bit. Baron Samedi had made them aware of his offer and warned them that Nkechi may try to trick them.

One of the guards waved her over, shouting at her to keep her hands in the air. Once close enough, the second guard slapped a pair of handcuffs on her wrists.

The guard waved his hand over them and whispered, "*Lier.*" The handcuffs magically tightened, pinching Nkechi's skin as they did so. After a quick flinch of pain, Nkechi remained silent. She was sure enough of her power that she felt she would be able to break out of the magical lock when the time came.

Kosum's plan seemed to be working so far as the two guards began escorting Nkechi through the mansion. She tried her best to stay vigilant and take note of anything about the house that might be useful for their fight or escape, though she didn't see anything particularly noteworthy. It was simply an old, characterful New Orleans-style house, except for the fact that it was full of magical bigots, of course.

They took Nkechi into a large room on the first floor. It was full of portraits of Baron Samedi, each as grossly egotistical and distasteful as the next. There wasn't much else in the room other than his ornamental throne salvaged from the warehouse and a desk close to the back wall.

Not the décor I'd have gone with, Nkechi thought, chuckling to herself. She then refocused as she looked around carefully for any other entrances or exits. There were two seemingly ordinary doors in both corners of the back wall, behind his throne.

Just then, Gaudence emerged from the left door to see who had entered.

"I'm here to speak to Baron Samedi," Nkechi announced.

"Very well. One moment." Gaudence left to fetch his master who had been once again enjoying the fruits of his many female companions.

"Sorry, ladies, we'll have to cut our time short. I have business to attend to," Baron said, before snapping his fingers and allowing them to dress his naked body.

Baron Samedi and Gaudence returned to the room where Nkechi was awaiting them. Gaudence opened the door for his grace to enter.

"Ah, Nkechi." He grinned, his arms open as if greeting an old friend.

"Hello, Baron," Nkechi greeted him blandly.

"Don't look so glum. I know it must pain you that you couldn't defeat me, but at least you made the sensible choice to surrender."

"I didn't *have* a choice," she replied testily without looking at him. She didn't want to feed into the attention he so clearly craved. Instead, she thought it would be more fun to be dismissive and wind him up a little. After all, she had to keep him talking until Kosum and the others arrived.

Kosum, Nicole and Anuli reached the stronghold just in time to watch Nkechi enter. Before the door could close and relock itself behind Nkechi and the guards, Kosum used her telekinesis to fly her athame across the street, wedging its thin blade between the doors, leaving them open by a slither.

"Nice one, Kosum," Nicole whispered enthusiastically.

Anuli didn't say anything but gave her a nudge and a look of appreciation. It solidified in her mind that she had done the right thing in giving it to Kosum, and she was glad to have her as a part of the family.

The three of them ran across the street as quick as they could to spend as little time out in the open as possible. They stood on the outside of the door and pondered how they could get in unnoticed. If their intel was correct, then they'd be immediately encountering four guards at the very least. For all they knew, there could be ten of them standing guard in the entrance hall. Nkechi handing herself in might also change the guards' positions inside.

"What do we do now? I know this was my plan, but in

theory it was a lot easier. If that room's full of goons, we can't go in guns blazing because that will alert Baron and he could kill Nkechi there and then." Kosum felt the heavy weight of everyone's lives on her shoulders.

"Calm yourself," Anuli said as she placed her hands on Kosum's restless shoulders. "It would seem it's time for a little voodoo magic to help us out. Nicole, I'm going to give you sight of the spirits."

"Mom, you know that spell always makes me feel queasy afterwards," Nicole moaned.

"We don't have any other viable options, I'm afraid. Nkechi can't stall him forever."

"Fine."

"You got this!" Kosum quietly cheered, showing Nicole a soft smile of encouragement.

"Okay, just get it over and done with."

Anuli took a deep breath and placed her index and middle fingers on Nicole's temples. She gazed into her eyes and whispered, "*Vue de morts.*"

Nicole's eyes turned a pearlescent blue which refracted in the daylight. She turned to the door and the spell allowed her to see through it. All inanimate objects were a dark grey, with anything living taking on a yellowy silhouette. In the entrance hall she could make out three guards and, as she turned her gaze to the first floor, she saw multiple figures dotted around the house. There were too many to differentiate Nkechi and Baron Samedi, but at least now they had a little more insight as to what they were getting themselves into.

Nicole explained what she saw, and Anuli rescinded the spell, allowing Nicole to see normally again. Or at least a version of normal, as her vision was blurry, making her nauseous as she predicted.

"This will take care of the first three," Anuli said, pulling a little cloth pouch tied together with twine from her pocket.

"What is it?" Kosum asked.

"Yeah, someone fill me in, considering I literally can't see it!" Nicole groaned.

"A sleeping dust bomb of my own creation," Anuli smiled, proudly turning it in her hand to admire her work. "I'll throw it through the door, and it will knock them out without the ruckus of a fight."

"Your mom's awesome," Kosum said to a still queasy Nicole.

"Yeah, yeah, she's great, whatever. Let's do this. My right eye is starting to clear up now, so yay me," she said, attempting to roll her eyes, tough for all she knew, her eyes could have been glaring in different directions.

Anuli pulled a box of matches from her pocket and lit the short piece of twine emanating from the top of the pouch. Kosum then grabbed her athame and they opened the door a little further, just wide enough for Anuli's hand to slip through. She flung the bomb into the centre of the three guards and Kosum retracted her athame as they waited to see if it worked.

"Huh?" one of the men stuttered as the cloth pouch rolled between his feet.

"What's that?" another of the idiotic men blurted, bending down to get a closer look.

"You dumbass, it's a—"

The ball of powder exploded before them, coating each

of their faces with enough sleeping dust to knock out an elephant. They simultaneously drunkenly fell to the ground where they would stay for a twelve-hour slumber.

Hearing the thud of the men falling, Kosum poked her head through the door to check the bomb had worked. Once she saw the three men knocked out, she opened the door fully and waved the others to follow her in. They made their way up the stairs where they began to sneakily take out as many guards as possible, all while Nkechi kept Baron talking.

"There's always a choice, Nkechi," he smiled smugly.

"You realise the good guy usually says that line, right?"

He cackled for a moment which confused Nkechi.

"Do you really think that you're the *good guy* in all this?" he said in a mocking tone.

"Do you?" Nkechi retorted.

"I don't believe it's that simple."

"You've murdered people!"

"As have you."

"In self-defence!"

"So, you say. To me, it seems that you're just as wicked as I am. Besides, haven't our people suffered enough? Isn't what I'm doing just delayed self-defence?" he questioned, hoping to disrupt Nkechi's moral compass off course.

But she saw beneath his twisted words; she knew the difference between them.

"Otherwise known as revenge," Nkechi commented, starting to irritate him.

"Call it what you like. But I'm the only one brave enough to avenge the past. The Western world needs to pay for what they have done to us. It's time *they* feel the tail end of a whip against their back; time that *they* are brought to their knees in agony, time that *they* feel the pain of hundreds of years' worth of oppression."

"You can't punish innocent people for something their ancestors did!"

"Innocent?" he laughed. "Tell me, Nkechi, if it weren't for your gifts, would you feel totally and completely safe in this world as a young, black woman?"

"Well, no… Look, I'm not saying the world is perfect. But the scales need to be balanced, not tipped from one extreme to another. If you do that, you'll be as unjust as the white supremacists!"

"I don't expect you to understand. You didn't live through it; you didn't have to stand by and watch as our people died. The other voodoo deities just provided you with rudimental magic in the hopes you would free yourselves. None of them cared enough to get their hands dirty. But I did – I do! In the early days of New Orleans, I saw this flesh bag," he said, gesturing to his body, "about to be killed by his master. So I permanently possessed his body so that I could save as many of our people as I could. Now I have the power and loyal practitioners to rework the entire world, and I'm not going to let a little girl stop me now."

"I understand that your original reasons were noble, but you can't possibly fathom the amount of pain and suffering you'll unleash upon the world."

He huffed at Nkechi's rebuttal. "You see, that's where you're wrong. I am a god – I *can* fathom the world and everything in it. It is *you* childish mortals that can't *fathom* what it takes to reshape a world. It is *you* who can't see the bigger picture!"

Nkechi paused for a moment as she pondered the heinous crimes he had committed and just how exactly they were favouring some kind of bigger picture. She then asked the question she'd been wanting to ask for a long time. Part of her was scared to know the answer, but knowing this could be her last chance to ask it, she bit the bullet and asked, "What about my parents? Why did they have to die?"

"Surely by now you see that their union was a disgrace? They represent the very opposite of my core values – fraternising with the enemy and creating an abomination such as you, no less." He chuckled.

"Look at you, neither black nor white, just a dirty mix, an albeit powerful one but dirty nonetheless. Once your cold corpse is beneath my foot, I'll move on to the rest of your disgraceful family, and then when there's no one left to oppose me, I will finally take pleasure in ravaging every disease-ridden town in this country. I won't stop until every white man, woman and child are either enslaved or dead."

"You will be stopped; *I* will stop you!" Nkechi raged.

"And how exactly do you expect to do that?"

Nkechi gave a smug smile as she yanked her wrists apart in a burst of energy to break the handcuffs. Except she couldn't. Nkechi's eyes widened with embarrassment and shock. She thought she'd easily be able to break through a pair of handcuffs. She looked down examining them in confusion, then heard Baron once again cackling at her expense.

"Oh my, Nkechi. You're even more of a novice than I

thought," he said, laughing continuously. "My men placed a binding spell on those cuffs the second you willingly put them on. Your magic is useless as long as you're chained up."

Nkechi began to shake her hands in a futile attempt to break them apart, hoping this was just another of his lies. But after trying a few spells of her own, none of which working she finally gave up.

"Bring her to me," he demanded.

The two guards that escorted Nkechi dragged her to him.

"On your knees," he instructed.

"Never!" Nkechi scowled.

He flitted his gaze to his men and Nkechi was swiftly kicked in the back of the leg, dropping to the required position.

"Ah, perfect. You know, Nkechi, if you didn't have such tainted blood and look, well, like that, you could've made a good and powerful wife," he said as he lifted her chin with his finger to examine her closer.

She turned her face to try to be free of his touch, but he grabbed her throat with force and brought her back into his eyeline.

Nkechi spat at him, causing him to jump back in disgust. The commotion gave Nkechi a chance to glance towards the back of the room where thankfully Kosum had just slipped through unnoticed.

Kosum crouched behind a desk, popping her head up briefly to make eye contact with Nkechi. Nkechi looked up for a moment to see that Gaudence was trying to help the Baron clean his face, but a stubborn and proud Baron threw him to the ground.

Nkechi gestured her handcuffs to Kosum, who quickly thought of a way to break them.

But before she could do anything, the Baron's attention was firmly back on Nkechi.

"I've had enough of you. Any last words?" he asked, forging a green, glowing ball of energy between his palms.

Nkechi panicked; she could barely take her gaze off the pulsating light that was about to end her life. But then she caught another glimpse of Kosum mouthing something behind him. Nkechi's eyes squinted slightly to see Kosum's arms above her head.

Nkechi turned her attention back to Baron. "I'll be saving those words for someone worthy of hearing them, but thanks for asking." She smiled, raising her manacled hands above her head. The second her hands stretched the handcuff chain taut, Kosum's athame flew through the air, breaking the chain, along with the binding spell.

Nkechi let out an energy burst of her own, knocking back everyone in the room.

Kosum's athame returned to her side as she ran to join Nkechi. Baron got back on his feet. He glared at Nkechi with a searing anger. He was sick of being embarrassed by her, sick of losing the upper hand to her, and sick of being bested by an eighteen-year-old girl.

Baron gave an angry look at Gaudence, signalling him to get some backup.

"You two, keep them busy," he barked to the two guards who had originally escorted Nkechi before cowardly retreating behind his throne.

Kosum looked to Nkechi, nodding at the two guards

before them.

"I'm gonna let you take them out. You've had it easy so far."

"That's fair. Besides, I have a new spell I wanna try," Nkechi smiled, as Kosum stepped to the side.

"*Ne dis rien de mal*," Nkechi whispered.

Nothing happened at first, but as the two men tried to utter a spell of their own, they couldn't. Their mouths looked as though they were sown shut. All that they could do was groan as their lips wriggled in fear and panic.

Nkechi then uttered, "*Délire*," as if it was a throwaway word, but it sent them into an even deeper state of hallucination. Their muffled screams sent a chill down Kosum's spine. They clawed at their faces, trying to pry their lips apart until they drew blood and dropped to the ground in agony. Once on the floor, Nkechi and Kosum turned their attention back to Baron.

He was about to slip through one of the back doors when Gaudence's body flew through it, knocking Baron to the ground as Nicole and Anuli came bursting through after him.

"Sorry, it looks like you're out of backup," Nicole taunted, closing the door behind her.

"There's nowhere left to run, Baron," Anuli said, he still crouched on the ground plotting his next move.

As Baron regained his bearings, a weakened Gaudence foolishly stretched out his hand for his master's aid.

"Master, hel—"

Baron cut off Gaudence's plea as his large hand smothered his face. The veins along the back of his hands and arms began to glow green as he sucked the life force from Gaudence until his was nothing but an empty husk.

"Surrender," Nkechi demanded.

A still hunched Baron broke into insane laughter as he rose up from the ground.

"Enough!" he yelled. "I am a god, and you will treat me as such!" With a snap of his fingers, all four of them dropped to their knees and became frozen in place. Baron rubbed his hands together, causing green sparks to fly between his palms. As he pulled them apart, a wooden staff materialised from thin air. Once fully conjured, he grasped it with both hands and slammed it into the walnut-brown floor beneath.

Four green flames came to life and danced along the floor, each heading towards them. As the flame trails reached them, each were surrounded by a circle of fire.

They all slowly became breathless and, with the twist of his staff, Baron started to siphon their magical energies into himself.

"You may have taken my willing batteries away from me, but you four contain more than enough power to keep me going." His facial orifices opened and allowed their magical energies to flow into him, the power of each showing as an emerald green light leaving their bodies which then flowed into him.

Their necks jolted as their magical essences were draining from their faces. Anuli fought the force tugging at her essence just enough to look over at Kosum and mouth, "Athame!"

Kosum saw the athame in the corner of her eye, laying on the floor beside her. She used every bit of willpower she had left to flick her wrist and send the athame straight into Baron.

The dagger plunged deep into his chest. He gasped a loud

voice breaking breath that broke his concentration and thus the energy-siphoning spell. He buckled and finally fell to the ground, his hands cradling the handle of the blade.

The girls took a moment to catch their breath before getting back on their feet to ensure the deed was done.

"Nice work, Kosum," Anuli smiled from across the room.

"Yes… well done, Kosum," Baron said with a slow clap. "Though you must know it'll take more than that to kill me," he chuckled. "I am much more than the mere flesh I inhabit. I am a god; I am pure energy. You cannot destroy me, foolish girl."

He slowly pulled the blood-soaked dagger from his chest and threw it to the ground. It clanged against the floor and flicked his crimson blood upon the walnut-brown floor.

The mood in the room dropped once more – no one knew how they could kill him – but Nkechi knew how to buy them some time.

"I'm gonna try something crazy, you guys figure out how to kill him and make him stay dead," Nkechi said hastily.

Her eyes glazed over as she focused all her energies on Baron. She took his consciousness into a vast white plane – Papa Legba's plane. Baron's body contorted and he clawed at the wall as Nkechi ripped his consciousness from his earthly vessel.

As they both appeared against the vast white backdrop, it only took a second for him to realise where he was.

"Well done, Nkechi. But you know you're not strong enough to keep my consciousness here for ever," he smiled at her smugly.

"Oh, I know, I'm just stalling while the others figure out a way to stop you," she rebutted, nonchalantly.

Baron swiftly ignored Nkechi and called out into the endless abyss, "Well, come on out, Papa. This is your realm after all, you could at least be a gracious host."

Papa graced them with his presence, materialising in front of them both.

"Nkechi," he greeted with a respectful dip of the head. "Baron," he said bluntly, barely willing to give him eye contact.

"Ah, Papa Legba, the most cowardly of all the voodoo deities," he mocked.

"Ah, Baron Samedi, the most selfish and reckless of all the voodoo gods."

"Papa, you—"

With the snap of Papa's fingers, Baron disappeared. Nkechi instantly looked worried, thinking he might've jumped back into his vessel on the earthly plane.

"Papa, where did he go?" Nkechi panicked.

"Worry not, my child. This is my realm; he has no power here. I simply sent him to the furthest corner of it so we don't have to listen to him spouting lies. I assume you brought him here because you're stuck and need to buy time?"

"Yes. Thank you, Papa. How long can you keep him here? I can already feel my hold on him slipping."

"Not long, so use your time wisely. I sense help is on the way, but a big decision will have to be made."

"Okay, thank you."

"Now go, I will do my best." He turned to walk away.

"Papa, wait… I know Samedi isn't exactly a saint, but a few things he said did have me wondering."

"Yes?" Papa prompted.

"Why didn't you help our people back then? Why didn't you stop the pain and suffering?"

Papa's face dropped. He always suspected that one day Nkechi might ask one of the big questions, he just hoped he might've had more time to prepare an answer. After all, it's not easy to explain the morality of gods to a mortal even if they are a witch.

"Nkechi, it isn't our place to interfere in earthly affairs. If we took charge every time there was confrontation on Earth, we would become overlords. There would be no free will. And though free will can bring out the worst in some people, it also allows people to be the very best they can be. There would be no love and kindness without pain and suffering. The tables did turn an unfair advantage back then. That's why we made magic available to balance the scales and give our people the opportunity to rise up and fight back, which they did. But it was never our place to do more. I know that might not bring comfort to you, but it is the way of the gods – it always has been and always will be. Baron Samedi is simply on a power trip. Sure, he might say his interests are for our people, but he has always been deceptive and selfish. He was never content just being a god. He thinks he has the right to rule over humanity. I and the others do not."

"I see," Nkechi muttered a little solemnly. She understood where Papa was coming from, but she still didn't totally agree with his reasoning. Whether they were in agreement or not didn't matter right then as Nkechi had to return to her body and help the others plan Baron's demise once and for all. Now that was something they did agree upon.

"Now go, you don't have much time," Papa said, waving his hand and sending Nkechi back to her body.

Back in Baron's mansion, while Nkechi was talking to Papa Legba in his realm, Adame arrived with Parfait and somewhat good news to share.

Parfait burst through the doors to see Nkechi still in her unconscious state.

"Oh, my god, what happened? Is she okay?" he flustered, checking her for injuries.

"She's fine. Nkechi's keeping him busy while we rack our brains to figure out a plan," Kosum explained.

"I think I can help with that. I've been doing some research into voodoo deities. It said that they can't be killed—"

"Yeah, we've just had to find that out the hard way," Kosum interrupted.

"But it did say that they can be trapped."

"How?" Nicole asked hastily.

"We need to extract his essence from his body – or whoever's pour soul that body used to belong to – and transfer it into a spellbound witch or practitioner so that his abilities are rendered useless."

"And where are we gonna find someone willing to do that?"

"Right here. Me," Parfait professed.

"What?" Adame choked.

"Oh, c'mon, Dad. You've spent my whole life telling me how I'm not good enough and how I need to live up to my name. So, if you still think I'm unworthy of being your son after this, at least I won't be sane enough to remember."

"Sane enough? What do you mean?" Anuli questioned

before Adame had the chance to respond.

"Whoever hosts Baron Samedi will spend the rest of their life fighting for space in their own mind."

"Don't be stupid, you are not doing that!" Adame exclaimed.

"Yes, I am, Dad! Please, just let me be useful to you for once in my life."

Adame began to tear up. Seeing his son so desperate for his approval that he was literally willing to sign his life away, was unfathomable to him. He always thought he was pushing him for the better, he never realised he was pushing him over the edge of a cliff.

Adame walked up to Parfait and placed his hands upon his son's shoulders.

"Parfait, you are my son, and I am so sorry that I've made you feel this way. You're an incredible young man and I am so immensely proud of you. You deserve far better than the way I've treated you. I'm just sorry it's taken this long for me to realise it, that it's taken me this long to act like your father. *I* will be the one to host him."

Parfait went to object but Adame placed his finger over Parfait's lips.

"I've lived a good life. Your mother has made me the happiest man in the world. I want you to have a chance at finding love," he said, with a subtle glance towards Nkechi.

"But Mom wouldn't let you do this if she was here."

"She would, son. We both know that she'd – *we'd* – do anything to save you."

"But, Dad…" he teared up.

Adame tightened his grasp on his son's shoulders. "Parfait,

it's okay. I will always be with you. Now, I promise this is the last time I'm going to tell you this," he smirked, "but you need to pull yourself together. We may have a plan in place, but it will still take all of us to pull it off."

Parfait wiped his tears with the cuff of his jacket and sniffed back the snot trying to escape his nose.

"Okay, Dad. I love you."

"I love you too, son."

"How does this work exactly?" Nicole asked.

As she did, Nkechi returned to her body and opened her eyes.

"Parfait! You came."

"Of course. You didn't think I was gonna let you have all the fun, did ya?"

Nkechi gave a goofy smile, forgetting the world around her for a moment.

"Right, Nkechi. You will need to separate Baron's soul from his body," Parfait stated, refocusing her attention.

"How?"

"Like you did with Charlie," Kosum pointed out. "Remember, you have a god-mode of your own."

"Yeah, but that also left me knocked out for a couple of days, *remember?*"

"Yeah, but you're an even stronger witch now. I have faith in you, Nkechi, we all do."

Nkechi looked around, and everyone in their own way looked confident in her abilities.

"All right fine. Then what?"

"Kosum, Nicole and Auntie will use a binding spell on my dad and then I will use this transfer potion to entrap Baron inside him," Parfait explained, holding up a vial full of a black tar-like substance.

"And then what?" Nkechi asked.

"That's it – we win."

"What? No, that can't be it. That isn't a win if we don't all make it!"

"Nkechi, it's okay. I know the sacrifice I must make," Adame said bravely.

"There must be another way," Nkechi demanded. Seeing Parfait's solemn face hurt her. She still couldn't help feeling that somehow this was her fault.

"I'm sorry, dear, but they're right. It is our only option. This is the unfortunate reality of war. Often not everyone makes it, but their selfless sacrifice will always be honoured and remembered," Anuli explained, trying to comfort Nkechi.

"Besides, I can think of worse ways to go than being remembered as a hero," Adame joked tenderly.

"I guess…" Nkechi muttered, feeling defeated and not much comforted.

"Guys, he's stirring awake. It's now or never!" Nicole warned.

"You got this. *We* got this," Kosum whispered affirmingly to Nkechi.

Nkechi took a moment to regulate her breathing and free herself of the anxiety thumping in her chest. She floated into the air like a goddess, a swirl of wind beneath her. Her hands became engulfed in bright orange flames. Her eyes glazed over to an opaque white as she easily gained control of Baron's dazed body. She threw him into the centre of the room and encased him in a pentacle that she scorched into the floor around him. She stood him up and froze his limbs in an outwards starfish position.

"What are you doing?" he gasped.

"Ending your long overdue reign of terror," a godlike Nkechi replied. "This vessel never belonged to you, and it is time you returned it."

Roaring flames began to circle Baron as water simultaneously filled his lungs.

"Now start the binding spell!" Nkechi shouted as she prepared herself to peel Baron's essence from his body.

Anuli began reciting the spell, and once Nicole and Kosum had listened a few times they joined in, shouting it in tandem:

"*Liez cette magie et laissez son vaisseau être vide.*"

"I summon the power of all voodoo queens past and present. Heed my call: allow me to be a vessel of your essence; aid me in silencing the god who desires to rule over us all. Let us prove it is us who make gods what they are, and it is only us who can take them off that pedestal."

Nkechi felt the help of her fellow witches; she could hear the voices of those she had summoned. Voodoo queens across the world and beyond whispered their affirmations to her as they fuelled her with enough energy to rip a god from his earthly vessel.

Suddenly, Nkechi heard a voice she recognised. It was her mother, and although it was amongst a hundred or so other voices, Nkechi could recognise that voice anywhere. Hearing her mother's voice reassuring her, gave Nkechi the last push she needed to beat a god at his own game.

She once again spoke, but this time with the voice of a hundred women – powerful, immovable women.

"Baron Samedi," her voice bellowed, echoing around the room, deeper than usual. "With the power of my sisters and mothers, I banish you from this earthly body."

Though his body remained stiff, Baron screamed in agony as his essence was torn from the man he had inhabited for the past few centuries.

"Now, Parfait!" Nkechi shouted as she felt herself losing control over his energy.

Parfait popped the cork off his vial and threw it into the air. The thick viscous liquid turned into a sparkling black dust that scattered into the air, covering Baron's wispy, glowing essence suspended above them. Parfait then began to recite the words, "*Transfert d'energie.*"

He chanted over and over again until slowly Baron's floating essence was pulled into Adame's chest.

Nkechi dropped to the ground and rendered herself unconscious from the exertion of energy, as the last strands of Baron's life force was consumed by Adame.

He too dropped to the ground, though much livelier than Nkechi as he wriggled and writhed with pain. He tried to fight Baron for control of his own body, but it would seem he was losing the inner battle as he continued to twist and turn upon the floor. A single tear slipped down Parfait's cheek as he watched his father contort in agony, knowing there was nothing he could do to help.

Suddenly, Adame rose, his gaze darting around. He glared at them, snarling, almost rabid, with a mixture of fear and confusion in his eyes. He cracked his neck and blinked rapidly, seemingly trying to calm the frantic look on his face before speaking.

"Ha-ha, fools! You'll never be free of me," Baron's voice bellowed from Adame's lips. He reached out his hands and splayed his fingers to perform some kind of magical feat, but nothing happened.

"What? What is this?" he asked in confusion as he looked at Adame's hands, wondering why they didn't do as he commanded.

"Your energy has been spellbound and trapped within this body for eternity. You will never cast a syllable of magic again," Anuli announced.

"What? No! You can't do this to—"

Anuli blew a handful of sleeping dust into his face, knocking him out mid-sentence.

"I think we've heard enough from him. I'm sorry, Parfait, but we will need to imprison your father's body to ensure any leftover followers can't reach him."

"It's okay, I understand the sacrifice he made. I just wish we had more time together, knowing what I know now."

"Know that he is proud of you," Anuli said, placing her palm on Parfait's tearful cheek.

"I know."

Parfait picked up his father's body and readied to take him back to a Resistance holding area.

"Nkechi, are you okay?" Kosum asked, kneeling down beside her, trying to shake her awake.

"Yeah," she mumbled weakly.

"Can you walk?"

"I think so," she breathed, struggling to get up.

"That's a no, then. Nicole, help me get her up."

Nicole and Kosum took an arm each and propped up

Nkechi between them. They led the way, the group finally leaving the mansion and its terrors behind.

A few hours later, Nkechi was fully conscious. She was snuggled up on the couch between Nicole and Kosum.

Anuli was over at Parfait's house helping him break the awful news to Evélia.

"I can't believe we did it," Nkechi said in disbelief.

"Well, I can. Look at us, I knew all it would take is a couple of badass witches and a hunky guy to take down a god," Kosum said brazenly.

"Oh yeah? I'm pretty sure you crapped your pants when you first heard that he was a god," Nicole teased.

"I did not!" "Anyway, all that matters is that we did it – together," Nkechi intervened.

"Exactly." Nicole smiled, wrapping her arms around the two of them.

"Speaking of togetherness, I should probably call my mom to tell her the good news that we'll be coming home soon."

"Okay," Nkechi and Nicole replied in tandem.

Kosum walked into the kitchen to call her mother in private. As the phone rang, Kosum gave a sigh of relief. It had been the longest summer of her life, and it wasn't even over yet. But knowing she was heading home to the comfort and safety of her Manhattan penthouse with her mother, filled her with a calming sense of joy.

Finally, her mother picked up and Kosum belted out, "Hi, Mom!"

CHAPTER 13

The Fireplace

Five days earlier

"Ana, I need your help with something," Kwanjai requested with a worrying look.

"Anythin'," Ana confirmed, reaching out to hold Kwanjai's hand. "What is it?"

"I need to go home first, then I can show you."

Kwanjai got off the bed and instantly buckled over in pain, scaring Ana. Ana lifted Kwanjai's loose top to see that her stomach was still plastered in reds, blues and purples from the blast that almost ended her. It was like looking into a galaxy, except it was missing the highlights of all the stars twinkling.

"Jesus, Kwanjai! You need more time to rest," Ana instructed, jumping to her aid.

"No, I've rested long enough. I've waited long enough. I need to solve this once and for all."

"Solve what? What's goin' on?"

"You'll see."

A reluctant Ana helped Kwanjai to her car and drove them both back to Kwanjai's penthouse. Kwanjai seemed to be handling the pain much better now, or least so she pretended to.

As they entered the apartment, Kwanjai made a beeline for

the fireplace much to Ana's confusion.

"It's in here," Kwanjai said, slightly giddy.

"Kwanjai, are you sure you're all right, darlin? You're talkin' about a fireplace." Ana wasn't sure if Kwanjai was thinking straight, if at all.

"Just come over here," Kwanjai politely demanded.

"Okay," Ana smiled, while internally thinking, *I knew I shouldn't have let her out yet. She sounds like her brain's turned to mashed potato.*

Ana kept the unconvinced smile on her face as she slowly walked over to her friend, who was clearly in need of help. Ana just wasn't sure if it was help from a friend or a therapist she needed.

Kwanjai waved her hand over the fireplace and, with a little puff of dust and sprinkling of rubble, it cracked open. It had got a little wedged in place through lack of use. The fireplace opening was a foot wide. Kwanjai, being slim, slipped through easily, just as she always had. When Ana tried to follow, however, her posterior and chest proved to be quite the obstacle.

"Wow, Kwanjai, ya really didn't think about us curvy girls, did ya?" Ana joked as she pressed down her breasts to squeeze through the gap.

"Sorry," Kwanjai chuckled. "To be honest, I didn't think I'd ever show this to anyone else, but I guess my second closest friend is allowed that privilege," Kwanjai teased.

"Second closest? Gurl, you better be messin' with me!"

Kwanjai just laughed in response, though it did cause her stomach to cripple again in pain.

"Don't make me laugh anymore," she pleaded.

"I won't, I promise. Just as soon as I squeeze my juicy ass through this gap."

Once into the tiny hidden room, Ana was shocked to see what looked like some strange shrine-cum-police investigation board dedicated to Kwanjai's late and abusive husband. Although the fireplace had turned out to be a real room, the sight didn't fill Ana with confidence about Kwanjai's mental state.

"Kwanjai, what is all of this?"

"My research," Kwanjai answered bluntly.

"Well, I can see that, but what in heaven for?"

"Fred."

"Kwanjai, sweetheart, what's there to research? We're the ones that, ya know, *ended* him."

"Yes, I know that. Now stop looking at me like I'm fresh out of an 1800s mental institute."

"Sorry," Ana replied, sounding a little calmer but still unsure how to react.

"I always thought it was strange how quickly everything changed within him, and it seemed so suspicious. But in the moment, there was too much fear and emotion to truly contemplate it. Then the grief meant I couldn't see clearly, either. But this past year, I've finally been piecing together what happened, and I've almost worked it out."

"Kwanjai, there's nothin' to work out. I'm sorry, but sometimes that's just what happens. People you think you know, show their true colours. Look at my husband – we were blissfully married and then one day he decided he was gonna have an affair. It's neither of our fault that they changed. They did it themselves, and we don't owe them anything."

"Ana, I really don't mean to be rude but, for one, it's not the same, and two, I know Fred would've never acted that way of his own free will."

"Well, that was rude, but I'll let you off considerin' you've been in a coma for the last six weeks," Ana huffed, with her Southern accent breaking through even more than usual. "So what? You think someone brainwashed him?" she asked, her arms folded and avoiding Kwanjai's eye.

"Kind of. Look here. I was retracing his steps before the first time he lashed out, and as luck would have it, I found this on one of the suits he was wearing at the time," Kwanjai said, holding up a silver strand of hair under the light.

"Margaret!" Ana growled.

"That's what I thought, but I couldn't be sure. That's why on the night of Charlie's death I didn't attack Margaret too heavily on the girls' behalf. I knew I was harbouring my own case against her, and I didn't want a wrong accusation to spook her before I could make her pay for what she'd done to me. Of course, she got spooked anyway and now no one knows where she is, *and* I still don't have proof that it's even her hair."

"Well, I don't know how we can find her, but I do know a spell that can identify that hair."

"You do?"

"Yup." Ana spotted a box of matches on the side. "Pass me those," she requested.

Ana held the strand of hair in one hand and asked Kwanjai to light a match and place it into her other.

"Spirits neither lost nor found burn this witch's name into the ground." As she recited the spell, she slowly singed the hair. The long, smouldering strand floated down to the ground as it burned. When it hit the floor, beneath them several smouldering paths carved into the ground in different directions until finally they spelled out Margaret White.

"Looks like your suspicions were right."

"Yes, but *how* did she do it? Mind control, a spell, a potion?" Kwanjai contemplated aloud.

"Oh no," Ana gasped, as she came to a hurtful realisation.

"What? What is it?"

"Kwanjai, I'm so sorry. You must know I had no idea she would use it on Fred."

"Ana, what did you do?"

"Around that time, Margaret asked me to make her a rage potion. I didn't think much of it at the time, but in hindsight I guess I should've realised when you started to tell us about the abuse. I'm so sorry." Ana stated, looking at Kwanjai for forgiveness.

"Ana, why did you make her that kind of potion, anyway? You must have known that even if it hadn't been given to my husband, nothing good would've come from it."

"I know, but it was a different time. I was still the new one in the group, till you came along. Margaret had done me a lot of favours in helpin' my business get off the ground, and when all she asked for in return was one little potion, it seemed like I'd got off lightly. So I did it."

"One *little* potion that ruined my life!" Kwanjai said angrily.

"Kwanjai, please don't be like this. You know I love you and Kosum like family. Nkechi too now. I'd never knowingly do anything to hurt any of you."

"I know, but intentional or not, you are part of the reason I wake up every day with a piece of myself missing." She sighed. "At least now I know I was right and my judgement of his character was never wrong. I guess the same can't be said for my judgement of you."

"I will do anything to make it up to you."

"You can start by helping me kill Margaret."

"What? Kwanjai, are you sure that's what you want? You're not the revenge type."

"She turned my husband into a monster, and along with the rest of the coven convinced me to kill him. She's the reason my daughter has no father. So yes, I am sure… Just think yourself lucky you've been a good enough friend to me over the years not to meet the same fate."

Ana gulped the nervous saliva gathering in her mouth. She'd never seen Kwanjai this hell bent on anything before, let alone murder.

"Okay, so how do we find her?"

"I don't know, but annoyingly she is a smart witch and likely won't have left a shred of evidence to help us find where she's hiding out. We're going to need some help."

"The gurls?"

"No, they have enough problems of their own to deal with. We need someone with just as much disdain for Margaret as we do. We need Blair."

Kwanjai and Ana decided to rest for the night. Kwanjai didn't want to admit it to Ana, but she had definitely overworked herself. She knew she'd need another night's sleep to muster up enough energy to track down and eliminate Margaret.

Ana retired to the spare room, and though it was as comfortable and luxurious as a guest bedroom could possibly be, she didn't get much sleep. She felt stupid, like she'd been taken advantage of. She knew what most people thought of her when they looked at her and heard her talk – country bumpkin with nothing going on in her head. No one ever looked beneath her shell to see that she was a strong businesswoman, loving mother and powerful witch. Well, one person did, but now Ana knew that she'd let down the one person who truly saw her. She just hoped that given time, they could go back to normal as she instantly felt lonelier without the reassurance of her best friend.

It was the early hours of the morning and Ana still hadn't fallen asleep. She couldn't stop the tears from flowing and soaking the satin pillows beneath her head. She felt overwhelmed with guilt.

Across the apartment, Kwanjai also hadn't got much rest as her mind was far too busy contemplating Ana's actions and the way she'd reacted. Kwanjai did believe Ana when she said she would never intentionally hurt her or the girls, and technically they had only just met when it happened. It's not like Ana had done it now when they had an *almost* airtight friendship.

As Kwanjai lay back and tried to fall asleep, she heard the muffled whimpers coming from Ana's room. She turned over onto her side and opened her bedside draw. She pulled out a picture of her and her husband on their wedding day. Now knowing that Fred was indeed the kind and loving soul she'd always thought he was, she knew that if he were here now and the roles reversed, he wouldn't allow Ana to torture herself like this. Kwanjai knew she couldn't allow her friend to be in such pain. She kissed the picture of her late husband and propped it up against the lamp on her bedside table.

Punishing Ana now wasn't going to change the past, and Kwanjai was sick of living in the past. Once Margaret had been punished, it would finally be time for her to say goodbye to her husband properly. Then perhaps she would be able to move on and look to the future, a future where she would certainly need her best friend.

Kwanjai let out a little huff of air and slammed her arms down on top of the duvet, before kicking it off and sliding into her slippers. She stretched and yawned as her exhausted and bruised body walked across the apartment to Ana's room.

The cries grew louder as Kwanjai got closer to the guest bedroom door. She opened it ajar, letting a little light through, alarming Ana. Ana jumped up and flicked her bedside lamp on, only to see Kwanjai standing in the doorway.

Kwanjai looked at Ana, her hair ruffled, and face soaked in tears and snot.

"Kwanjai, I'm so sorry," Ana sobbed.

"I know." Kwanjai walked over to the bed, climbed in and pulled Ana's head to her chest.

"It's okay," she whispered, as Ana continued to sob and plead for her forgiveness. "Shh, of course I forgive you. I love you, Ana. One mistake doesn't destroy the years of support and friendship you've given me."

"Thank you."

With them both feeling like a weight had lifted, they finally managed to fall asleep in each other's arms.

The next morning, Kwanjai and Ana were on their way to Blair's house. Ana drove under Kwanjai's instructions as she'd never met Blair before. Though she had some idea of what she was like from Kwanjai's accounts over the years, she was feeling a little worried as to how Blair would react to her. It had been made clear that apart from Kwanjai, Blair wasn't keen on the Manhattan coven of witches. Although Ana knew herself to be a beautiful, strong woman, she still had her moments of feeling insecure, and this was seemingly one of them.

"So, do you think Blair will be okay with us showing up unannounced like this?" Ana asked, glancing at Kwanjai before returning her gaze to the road. "Especially as your last encounter with her didn't end so well," she added.

"I'm sure the mutual hatred of Margaret will soon soothe any uneasiness," Kwanjai joked.

"Yeah," Ana chuckled awkwardly. "But what about me?" she asked, keeping her eyes on the road, too embarrassed to look at Kwanjai.

"What about you?" Kwanjai questioned, confused.

"Do you think she'll be okay with me?" she asked sheepishly.

"Ana, it's not like you to care so much about what people

think."

"I know, but it's just you're my best friend and she's your friend, so I want her to like me."

"That's sweet, but I'm sure she will find you just as charming as I do."

"Thanks, doll." Ana smiled, feeling less nervous.

"Take the next right, then keep going for a mile and we'll be there," Kwanjai instructed.

As they pulled up, Blair stood on her front porch arms folded, awaiting them, having sensed their arrival.

Kwanjai got out of the car first and, as Blair saw her, she turned to enter the house, leaving her front door open as an invitation to follow.

"Not much of a talker, then?" Ana joked.

"She chooses her words carefully," Kwanjai answered honestly without realising it made Ana feel criticised for talking too much.

Kwanjai led the way into the house where Blair had already set up a pot of tea at the coffee table. They sat on the sofa across from Blair who was pouring them a cup of tea each.

"Kwanjai, how're you?"

"Well, I've certainly had better days."

"Ah yes, the girls told me about your coma. I'm sorry there was not much I could do to help, though seeing you up and about now, I assume means they managed to source some more of the Hecate herb. How long have you been awake?"

"For about a day. And thank you for aiding them in their quest to help me."

"Not at all. But Kwanjai, you shouldn't be out and about so soon."

"I did tell her that," Ana pointed out, nudging closer to the edge of her seat and trying to involve herself in the conversation.

"This is Ana," Kwanjai said, introducing her.

"Ah, the famous potion-brewer for the Manhattan coven. A pleasure."

Normally such a title would've made Ana feel proud, but given the recent revelations, it didn't exactly sit well with her.

"Thank you. It's a pleasure to meet you, too." Ana smiled thinly.

"Blair, I need your help," Kwanjai requested.

"Again? Kwanjai, you're always business and no pleasure these days. It's that city – brainwashes you all if you ask me. When's the last time we had a proper catch up?"

"Er, er," Kwanjai stuttered, caught off guard by the reprimand.

"Is it an urgent matter?"

"Well, not technically no. I'm sorry. Of course, let's just have a chat first," Kwanjai said, wanting to appease her. "So, how're the girls?" she asked.

"They're maturing into womanhood very nicely. Their abilities are also coming along amazingly; I'm quite sure there isn't much else I can teach them. No doubt I'll be an empty nester soon enough," she chuckled, though Kwanjai doubted it would be any time soon, what with her twins always glued to her hip. Kwanjai didn't like to judge, but they did always seem a bit cossetted.

Nothing like Kosum.

"You should join the coven when that happens," Ana blurted, without thinking.

"You know, I'm not sure I'd fit into that environment very well, I'll stick to my open fields and fresh air. But thank you for the offer, most kind of you Ann."

"Oh, it's Ana."

"Of course, sorry, Ana." Blair smiled, almost a little too full-cheeked.

"Where are the girls, anyway?" Kwanjai asked, sensing the awkward tension between her two friends. She was beginning to think that perhaps Ana's worries were right. People have different friends for different reasons, and they shouldn't always mix.

"They're out running some errands. How are things at the coven? Margaret and Gweneviere still spearheading their outdated garbage beliefs?"

"Well, funny you should mention that as it's partly what we came here to talk to you about," Kwanjai began, pausing as if asking permission to carry on with her 'business' talk.

"Very well, pray tell." Blair gave in with a playful eye roll.

"Margaret and Gweneviere left the coven in a hurry, and we need to track them down. Well, one of them at least."

"Whyever would you want to find them? Surely, just be grateful they left!"

"Trust me, I'd love nothing more than to forget the pair of them, but I can't let Margaret get away, not after what she did."

"Oh, come on now, Kwanjai, don't be vague. What did she do?"

"Well, you remember what happened with Fred all those years ago?"

"Yes, of course. It was a tragedy, dear."

"I've always known that something was wrong, that Fred acted entirely out of character, but I didn't know why. Now I've finally uncovered the truth: Margaret slipped him a rage potion."

"Jesus! Why would she do that? I mean, I know she's a bitch who has all the grace of a cow in labour, but *that*… That's something else."

"No doubt to trick me into asking for the coven's help, and therefore making me feel indebted to them so they could use my luck magic for the coven."

"Where did she get such a potion?" Blair asked, casually taking a sip of her tea, feeling she already knew the answer.

Ana shrivelled up inside with guilt. As she was about to take responsibility and admit her mistake, Kwanjai commented:

"That doesn't matter."

Ana looked at her friend with a thankful smile.

"Okay, so what exactly are you going to do when you find her?"

"Kill her! Or at the very least maim her," Kwanjai spat angrily.

"Kwanjai, this isn't like you," Blair said, sounding shocked and a little disappointed.

"You heard what she did to me, right?"

"Loud and clear. But if you kill her, you'll be just as guilty of wrongdoing as Margaret."

"I strongly disagree!" Ana piped up in defence of her friend.

"Well, of course you would. Everyone knows you're a bunny boiler who has her husband drugged up on love potion twenty-four-seven," Blair remarked, suddenly throwing caution to the wind.

"You bitch! At least I don't flounce around in the mud all day actin' like the real world don't exist!"

"That's enough! Both of you!" Kwanjai demanded.

"Blair, I'm not asking for your moral counsel right now. I'm asking, as a friend, if you will help me locate the woman who ruined mine and Kosum's life. Will you do that for me?"

"Only if you promise to think about what I said."

"I do."

"And how exactly is *she* goin' to find her?" Ana asked, her arms folded sulkily.

"By the art of plant divination. There are perks to 'flouncing around in the mud all day'," she said slyly at which Ana rolled her eyes.

"Plant divination?" Kwanjai questioned sceptically.

"I'm a hedge witch, dear, the earth and I are one, especially the land I lovingly tend. There's a tree whose roots stretch across the whole of my grounds. It remembers every soul who's walked across it, and it can use its connection to plants all across the continent to divine where someone is. So as long as Margaret hasn't gone overseas, we should be able to find her."

"Well, here's hoping," Kwanjai mumbled, worried her only shot at finding Magaret could be gone if she has.

"Wait, so that means you can stalk me now, too?" Ana asked.

"Technically, though it's quite the exhausting task, and I wouldn't want to waste my energy on such trivial matters," Blair retorted.

Kwanjai clapped her hands to break the tension.

"Right, shall we go see this amazing tree, then?"

"Yes. Follow me." Blair swiftly walked out the back door.

They followed Blair into the garden, the tended areas soon giving way to a thicket of trees. She looked like a goddess with her long auburn hair and floral flowy dress, gliding through the wooded area barefoot. For Kwanjai and Ana it was more of an awkward tiptoe as they tried not to step on the muddy patches of ground that Blair seemingly didn't bat an eyelid at.

They managed to catch up with Blair as she stopped before a grand tree. Its thick twisted trunk was an ashy brown and over two metres wide. Hundreds of branches grew out of it, high into the sky, enveloping them all in its cumbersome shadow. Each branch was littered with a plethora of lime-green leaves that were almost perfectly circular in shape, resembling lily pads.

"Okay, that is a cool tree, I'll give ya that," Ana reluctantly commented, in awe of its beauty.

"It's called a pathfinder tree. There are only a few in existence, and they're thousands of years old. Hedge witches back in the old days used pathfinder trees to help villagers find lost children. I've only had to ask for its help once – when the girls were young, they ran off and I couldn't find them. Thankfully, the tree showed me the way."

"That's amazing. So, how does it work?" Kwanjai asked.

"It's simple I just need to connect with the tree and be open to its guidance but, like I said, it can take its toll on a witch. So I'll need you to help me back to the house afterwards."

"Of course, it's the least we can do. Thank you again for this, Blair, it means a lot," Kwanjai said appreciatively.

Blair smiled and tipped her head respectfully, though it

was tinged with disappointment. Blair hoped that Kwanjai would reconsider her actions when she found Margaret. But she promised she would do her part and wouldn't interfere any further.

"Now then, I will communicate with the tree, and once it has located her, I will announce the coordinates. Make sure you write them down as I can't guarantee I'll remember them once the connection is broken."

"Okay. Ana, you text me the address so we both have it, and I'll be on standby to catch Blair if she falls down afterwards."

"You got it, Kwanjai."

"I guess there's nothing left to do but begin," Blair said, rubbing her hands together to warm them before placing them on the tree.

Blair shuffled her feet to widen her stance and placed her palms against the bark, softened by a mossy coverage. Suddenly, the moss reacted to her touch, gentle tendrils growing animated and wrapping themselves around Blair's hands, allowing them to sink beneath the trunk's surface and solidifying her connection to the tree. She then leant her cheek against the trunk and whispered: "Margaret White."

The tree awoke and began to pulsate, sending powerful neurological signals into the ground through its roots, connecting to every living flora in North America. The waves of energy flowing through the ground beneath them were powerful enough to make Kwanjai and Ana's legs tremble. Within mere seconds of pulsating, the direction of the energy waves reversed. Margaret had been located and now all of the signals were being redirected to the epicentre of the tree, and Blair.

Blair's head thrashed backwards as the tree fed her the knowledge she desired. Blair began barking out the coordinates as her head continued to whip from side to side. Kwanjai rushed over, Blair's pupils hugely dilated to the point where that was all could be seen.

"Are you getting this?" Kwanjai shouted at Ana.

"Yes," Ana replied as she hastily punched the last digits into her phone.

The spell was complete and the tree released Blair's hands, causing her to fall into Kwanjai's arms.

"Help!" Kwanjai shouted as she struggled to keep Blair upright.

Ana slid her phone back into her pocket and, albeit reluctantly, aided Kwanjai in escorting a dazed Blair back to her house.

Once back at the house, Kwanjai knew the least she could do was wait with Blair until her daughters arrived home. She made her a cup of tea, with Ana even adding a few of her own ingredients to help Blair recuperate faster. Although they might not have seen eye to eye, one thing they did have in common was that they would both do anything for their friend, and Ana respected that about Blair.

A few hours later, Blair's daughters arrived home and took over caring for their mother. Ana briefly said her goodbyes, before waiting in the car to give Kwanjai and Blair a moment to be alone.

"Thank you for everything, Blair."

"You're welcome. But Kwanjai, remember what I said," she mumbled, still half dazed.

"I will."

Blair smiled before allowing her eyes to rest once more as she lay upon the sofa. Her daughters let Kwanjai out and she joined Ana in the car.

Ana typed Margaret's last known coordinates into her sat nav and asked, "You ready?"

Kwanjai looked determinedly at the dirt track ahead of them and firmly nodded.

Thirty minutes into their two-hour journey, Kwanjai mulled over Blair's words. Kwanjai knew Blair was right, violence wasn't the answer, but she hadn't yet thought of another way to get justice. It's not like she could tell the police that Margaret used a magical potion to make her husband an abuser, forcing her to kill him! Even if somehow Kwanjai did manage to frame Margaret in a mortal way, her legal expertise was the best in the country – she'd never see the inside of a cell.

"She's right," Kwanjai said above the music blaring in Ana's car.

"What was that, darlin'?" Ana shouted.

Kwanjai turned the volume down to almost silent in the car as she reiterated:

"I said Blair was right."

"About what?"

"Killing Margaret would just bring me down to her level. I don't want that; I don't want Kosum to think of me like that."

"So, what are we gonna do when we get there, then?"

"I don't know yet." Kwanjai paused and turned to Ana.

"She was right about you, too. Don't you think it's time you stopped using the love potion?"

"But what if he leaves me? I'll be alone," Ana said, tearing up as she tried to concentrate on driving.

"Isn't an honest life better than the lie you're living in? Ana, you're smart, talented and beautiful. If he doesn't want you, then screw him! You deserve someone who loves you wholeheartedly. You don't need to settle for some Stepford husband crap. It's time to set him free; it's time to set yourself free."

Ana considered what Kwanjai had said about not wanting Kosum to see her in that light, and Ana definitely didn't want her children to think of her as some kind of mind- controlling monster. Kwanjai was right, perhaps an honest life was preferable, even though it might be painful.

"Okay, I promise when all this is over, I'll stop makin' potions that affect anyone's emotions. I don't think they help anyone."

"I think that'd be best," Kwanjai smiled, placing her hand on Ana's knee.

"You do realise you'll have to be my wing woman when we're on the lookout for new husbands, right?"

"Ha-ha! But I don't know if I'll ever want another husband, though, my Fred was perfect." Kwanjai paused to try to swallow her sorrow. "But I'll certainly help you find Mr right… Wait! That's just given me an idea how we can punish Margaret."

"How?"

"Margaret's wife, Jane, doesn't know about magic, does she?"

"No, but what's that got to do with anythin'?"

Then Ana's eyes suddenly lit up as she realised Kwanjai's plan.

"Oh shit! You sure about this?"

"Yep. We're going to tell Jane all about Margaret's double life and exactly what she uses her 'gifts' for."

"Okay. Well, I'm back on board with the revenge plan," Ana said. "Also, you've been using your luck magic for our businesses to succeed for years. Maybe it's time you reversed that a little, for Magaret at least."

"Ruin her marriage and career? Ana, you are bad!" Kwanjai teased.

"I know, but it's better than our original murder plan."

"True."

They both chuckled before turning the music up for the final leg of their journey.

Ana's car pulled up outside their destination, a rather lavish house on the outskirts of New York.

"I guess she thought it would be smarter to stay close rather than flee far away," Ana commented.

"Yeah, but she wasn't smart enough to see this coming, was she? Come on, let's go."

"But how do we know if Margaret's home?"

"Oh, I'm past caring, she can sit there and listen to the story time too if she wishes but either way, I'm ending this now."

"Damn! You know, you're more like Kosum than I ever

realised."

"You mean she is more like me. I think that's what scares me most about her," she chuckled.

Kwanjai walked up to the front door of the luxurious home, Ana behind her. She rang the doorbell quietly so as not to raise any suspicion.

A few moments of anticipation later, the door opened to reveal a woman a little older than Kwanjai and Ana. Her brown hair was styled in a bob and she had deep crow's feet around her eyes, which is probably to be expected when married to Margaret. "Hello, how might I help you?"

"Is Margaret home?" Kwanjai asked politely.

Jane wrapped a long lilac cardigan around her tightly before answering.

"No. And she won't be back for a few hours yet. Can I pass on a message?"

"Certainly," Kwanjai smiled.

Jane, being the good hostess and housewife she was, invited them in for a coffee while they chatted, unaware of the devasting news she was about to hear.

Kwanjai and Ana spent the best part of an hour filling Jane in on all the details of Margaret's secret life. Jane admitted that she'd always been suspicious of Margaret's work, but she could never have begun to imagine it would include magic and such heinous crimes.

"We'll see ourselves out," Kwanjai said, leaving a tearful Jane to sit with her thoughts while they returned to the Jenkins Hotel to digest everything that had happened.

Kwanjai did feel bad leaving Jane in such a state – she didn't deserve it. But ultimately it was Margaret's secrets and lies that had hurt Jane, not Kwanjai's truth.

Ana stayed with Kwanjai for the following few nights as she still wasn't feeling 100%. They hadn't heard any news from Margaret, but assumed she was busy trying to piece her life back together. What with Kwanjai also retracting any active luck enchantments on Margaret's business, she surely had a lot of angry phone calls coming her way.

One evening, while Ana was preparing dinner, Kwanjai's phone which was upside down on the kitchen counter rang. Kwanjai glared at it for a moment in worry.

"Pick it up, then," Ana moaned, not thinking anything of it.

"What if it's Margaret?"

"Oh, please, I doubt she's going to ring you. Just turn it over and see who's on the caller ID."

"Yeah, okay." Kwanjai walked over to her phone and slowly turned it over, squinting at the screen, anxious as to who it might be. But when she saw the letter K, her face lit up as she knew it was Kosum. She hadn't heard from Kosum for a few days and assumed that she and Nkechi were busy dealing with the voodoo king.

"It's Kosum!" Kwanjai beamed, shaking her phone having still not answered.

"Answer it, then!"

Kwanjai swiped her finger across the screen to answer.

"Hi, darling."

Ana watched Kwanjai's smiling face as she tried to make

out what the conversation was about. The gaps were soon filled when she heard Kwanjai offer to pick Kosum up.

Kwanjai put the phone down and turned to Ana with an even bigger smile on her face.

"Well?" Ana said, raising her eyebrows, awaiting the news.

"They're coming home tomorrow. My baby's coming home!" Kwanjai shouted, before wrapping her arms around Ana, who was trying to stop the dinner from burning.

Ana tossed the wooden spoon to the side as she gave in and embraced her friend.

"Let's get takeout," she smiled.

CHAPTER 14
Anything for You

Kosum was pacing Anuli's dilapidated living room, on the phone to her mother, while Nkechi sat patiently at the bottom of the staircase, waiting to hear how she was.

"Okay, thanks, Mom. 'Bye."

"How is she?" Nkechi asked.

"She sounds good, almost back to normal. She said that she and Ana would pick us up from the airport tomorrow."

"Okay, good, because I'm still traumatised by our last cab ride!"

"Yeah, that'll teach me to be nice and hire an independent."

"You know, I don't think that's the lesson to take from that encounter," Nkechi chuckled.

"So, any plans for your last night? Maybe a bit of action with Parfait? You know, it was pretty obvious what you guys had been up to the other night."

Nkechi's cheeks flushed with embarrassment.

"Firstly, that's none of ya business, and secondly, I called it off with him. Don't get me wrong, it was great, but I'm not ready for anything more at the moment."

"That's all right. I'm proud of you for getting back on the horse," Kosum teased, playfully nudging Nkechi's arm.

"Thanks. Listen, I'm gonna head out for a bit. I have

something I need to do."

"Are you all right?"

"Yeah, I'm fine."

"Okay. If you need me, I'll be—"

"Yeah, getting jiggy with Nicole! It's just as obvious when you two have been at it as well," Nkechi teased.

But her comment didn't bother Kosum, who just shrugged almost proudly as she went in search of Nicole.

"Text when you're on your way back," Kosum shouted from the top of the stairs.

"Will do!".

Oh, my god, I sound just like Mom, Kosum thought. The idea of becoming like her mother would've previously made Kosum shudder, but given everything that had transpired over the last two months, she now felt differently. Kosum loved her mother and was just grateful she was still here, even if she was overbearing and annoying at times.

Nkechi looked around her childhood home, still in its trashed state from the attack of the damned. The only thing to have survived unscathed were the helium balloons from Nicole's party still bobbing about. Nkechi watched as they drifted around the room carelessly. It reminded her of her tenth birthday in their tiny New York apartment. Even though money had been tight, her mother always spent a little more for Nkechi's birthday, with decorations and a decadent cake that the two of them would happily finish off. On her tenth birthday, Nkechi's mother got her two huge helium balloons in the shape of a one and a zero. The ballons lasted for weeks, bobbing around the quaint apartment, her mother often having to bat them out of the way when she made dinner.

Nkechi was pretty sure that if there was an apocalypse, cockroaches and helium balloons would be the only survivors.

This thought gave Nkechi an idea.

She ran upstairs to grab her backpack and stuffed a few supplies inside it. She did so as loudly as possible to try to drown out the sound of Kosum and Nicole who were certainly *celebrating* the town's victory.

Nkechi gathered up all the balloons by their dangling ribbons and headed to a nearby lake she'd loved to visit as a child; the very same lake where Kosum and Nicole had shared their first kiss. She walked out to the middle of the bridge that stretched the full width of the lake. With the balloons secured to her wrist so that she didn't accidentally let go of them, Nkechi pulled a sheet of paper and pen from her bag and leaning on the wooden railing she wrote a letter to Charlie. She still wasn't over him – not that anyone could blame her – but she was ready to move on. Thus, she decided to take Alex's advice and say goodbye to the Charlie *she* had known and loved.

Dear Charlie,

I'm sorry for what happened to you as a child, I truly am, and perhaps if we had met earlier in life I could have helped you and shown you the love you needed to feel.

But now isn't the time for what could've been, now is the time for the future, and I'm afraid I can't carry you with me anymore. I did love you, and to go from seeing you almost every day to knowing I'll never see you again hurts like hell. But I also know that in time that pain will fade, as will the haunting dreams.

Thank you, Charlie, for being my first love; thank you for showing me how to love. Thank you for making me feel seen; thank you for filling me with confidence about the way I look. And although it may have all been a façade, I thank you for it as the ignorance was truly blissful for a while.

I'm sorry you only ever saw the world through a cracked and distorted lens, like so many others do, because if you stop every now and then, you'll see that there's so much more this world and its people have to offer.

Anyway, I'm probably rambling now, and as this letter is more for my benefit than yours, I'll stop writing.

Charlie, my love, I bid you an everlasting and final farewell.

Nkechi rolled up her letter and tied the balloon ribbons around it tightly. She held it clenched in her hands for a moment as she looked out onto the peaceful lake under the clear, summer night sky. As a single tear fell, Nkechi relaxed her hand, letting go of the letter and letting go of Charlie.

As the sun rose over New Orleans, Nkechi's hometown was about to experience its first full day of true freedom in over ten years. Once again it would be a safe place to raise a family, a safe place to be unapologetically oneself, and a safe place to rebuild a lost community.

As Anuli packed her car with the girls' luggage, Nicole and Kosum said their goodbyes.

"I wish you could come with me," Kosum pouted.

"Me too. But I think my mom's gonna need a lot of help rebuilding this place," Nicole said, rubbing her hands along Kosum's arms.

"I know. Maybe we can see each other at Halloween?"

"Yeah, I'd love that," Nicole smiled.

"And Thanksgiving?"

"Yep!"

"And Christmas?"

"Don't push it," Nicole teased.

Kosum pulled a face and playfully tried to pull away, but Nicole swiftly brought her back, close enough that they couldn't bear to resist kissing one another.

"Is that a knife in your pocket or are you just happy to see me?" Nicole joked as she felt something jabbing her thigh.

"What?" Kosum blurted, confused. "Oh," she smirked, "it's the athame your mom gave me. She said I could keep it. It's an heirloom, and apparently I'm a part of the family now."

"Kosum! That's amazing!"

"So, you don't mind me having it?"

"Of course not! I just can't believe she gave it to you. She must really love you – she barely talked to any of my other girlfriends."

"Well, I *am* pretty extraordinary," Kosum bragged, dramatically flipping her silky hair over her shoulder.

"That is definitely one word I'd use – as well as sexy, funny, high maintenance, mean—"

Kosum placed her finger on Nicole's lips.

"You should've stopped at funny!"

"But I love all of you, not just the good bits."

"Cringe!"

"Shut up, you love it," she said, pulling her in for one last passionate kiss.

"Oh," Nicole jerked as the athame jabbed her side once again, "maybe you should store that somewhere else."

"Good thinking. I'll slide it into my boot for now – never know when I might need it."

"Hopefully not for a long time," Nicole smiled, placing her lips back on Kosum's.

Meanwhile, Nkechi had been helping her aunt load the car when a familiar voice called her name. She turned around to see Parfait walking across from his house.

"Weren't you going to say goodbye?" he asked, genuinely affronted.

Nkechi stuttered, feeling a little chastised.

"W-well, I didn't know if it would be awkward."

"Nkechi, it could never be awkward. Besides, the least you could do is thank me for saving your ass. Without me you'd still be fighting a god," he said smugly.

"Okay, I'll give you that… By the way, you do realise what you did back there, right?"

"An ass whipping? Damn straight."

Nkechi chuckled. "No, you moron. You performed a spell when you transferred Baron's life force into your father. I think that makes you the only guy left that can do that, right?"

"Yeah, I guess I did. I hadn't really thought about it like that, you know, what with me being a little distracted with enslaving my father. But I guess I should keep practising, maybe even with a few of the other guys around town."

"You definitely should. Who knows, maybe one day you'll be able to give me a run for my money," she teased.

"Maybe, but I think I'll stick to the smaller stuff for now."

"That's fair. So, how is your mom dealing with everything? Is she coming out to say goodbye?" Nkechi asked with a lopsided smile. She still felt incredibly guilty that she hadn't been able to find another way to stop Baron.

"No, sorry, Nkechi, she's not coming out. She's still pretty devastated about Dad. But she did tell me to say that your mom would've been proud of you, and that she knows you did everything you could to avoid the outcome. She still thinks you're our saviour," he chuckled, scratching his head awkwardly as he relayed his mother's words.

"Thanks, Parfait, though you're just as much a saviour as me."

"Thanks," he smiled.

"Parfait?"

"Yes?"

"I've been wondering this for a while now. If our parents knew each other, how come we hadn't met before?"

"We had."

"No, I definitely would've remembered someone as cocky as you," Nkechi joked.

"Well, I wasn't as cool back then. But we did hang out for a while before you and your mom left town. Imagine me with braces, glasses and none of this godly muscle," he said in jest as he flexed his arms.

"No, that kid's name was Perfect, and he was actually nice."

"Seriously, Nkechi?"

"What?" She continued to stare at him with a tilted look of bewilderment.

Parfait stood with his arms folded as he watched and waited for her to come a sudden realisation. Her expression slowly turned from one of confusion to one of understanding. Parfait smirked watching the cogs turn on her face.

"Oh, my god, I don't think I've ever felt this dumb in all my life – parfait is French for perfect!" she blurted. "And to think I got an A in French!"

"Yeah, and you literally do all of your spellcasting in French too," he added, rolling his eyes.

"But wait, why did you start saying your name in French?"

"I always did. You just had trouble saying it when we were kids, so I said you could call me Perfect."

"Well, I guess you did have a bit of your ego back then, too," Nkechi teased.

"Definitely not! Ya know, I kinda had a crush on you back then, but I was way too geeky to do anything about it."

"We were both geeky. The only cool one was Nicole."

"True."

They chuckled for a moment until they fell silent.

"A part of the reason I was so cold when you came back was because – and I know it wasn't your fault - I really missed you when you left. You were my only friend, and life was shit growing up in the town under the voodoo king's rule."

"I'm sorry I forgot about you, Parfait. But my mother did meddle with my memories as a kid and perhaps I just got confused. I promise it wasn't intentional nor malicious."

"Don't worry, I know you're not capable of that, especially not when you were a kid," he smiled.

"If it makes you feel any better, I grew up pretty lonely too. It was just me and Mom against the world."

"Yeah, I mean no, it doesn't make me feel better," he chuckled awkwardly. "I guess the voodoo king ruined a lot of lives, huh?"

"You can say that again. But thanks to us, he's gone."

"Indeed." Parfait smiled again at Nkechi as he tried to take a mental picture of her, not knowing when they might cross paths again.

"Your hair looks good," he said, gently running some of the wavy locks through his fingers.

Nkechi blushed, feeling the back of his hand brush her cheek. "Er… thanks. Nicole gave it the works last night. It was well overduc."

The silence crept in once again and remained for a moment as neither of them knew how to say goodbye. Eventually, Parfait placed a kiss on Nkechi's forehead, smiled and headed back home. Nkechi watched contently as he walked away. Although she might not have been ready just yet, something in Nkechi's mind told her that their story wasn't over.

The girls finished packing the car and Anuli drove Nkechi and Kosum to the airport, where she helped them offload their luggage, and said her goodbyes.

"Girls, I think of you both as my honorary daughters. Thank you for everything. I'm not sure what would have happened had you not shown up when you did. Know that you both have a home with me, should you ever need or want one."

"Thank you, Auntie," they replied in tandem.

She pulled them both towards her, squeezing them tightly.

Once she reopened her arms, she said goodbye and watched as they entered the airport where they could start the final leg of their summer journey.

After almost getting arrested at customs for Kosum's athame, Kosum treated them both to some brunch. Thankfully Nkechi had done some swift possession to get them off scot-free. As they tucked into their food, Kosum was still adamant that before summer was over, she was going to take Nkechi to a remote island full of eligible men.

During the final bites of their bacon-filled croissants, the Tannoy announced that an earlier flight to New York was available.

"We should get it, then we can show up at the apartment and surprise them," Kosum said with a mouthful of croissant.

"Okay, but we need to hurry. C'mon, let's go," Nkechi mumbled, shovelling in her last mouthful and jumping out of her seat.

Back at the Jenkins Hotel, Kwanjai and Ana were busy making the penthouse as inviting as possible for the girls' return. Kosum had informed her mother of Nkechi's living situation and of course Kwanjai had no qualms about housing her.

They cleaned Kosum's room and made up the spare room that Ana had been staying in for Nkechi. Ana had been out shopping to make the girls a hamper full of their favourite treats, while Kwanjai had been busy preparing Kosum's favourite Thai dish, Tom Yum Goong, a traditional Thai soup which was somehow sweet, sour and spicy all at the same time.

The time seemed to be flying by; they had one hour left before Kosum and Nkechi's plane landed, or so they thought. They got ready to set off, but as Kwanjai grabbed her car keys, there was a heavy knock at the front door.

"Did you order room service again?" Kwanjai moaned to Ana. "I told you that's only for the hotel guests."

"No, I promise. Since you told me off for orderin' that cheese wheel the other night, I haven't ordered anythin' else since. Though it was a damn good cheese wheel, and I do think I deserve another," Ana pouted, placing her hand across her stomach. "Oh, my god, I bet it's the girls. No doubt they landed early and thought they'd prank us or somethin'."

The heavy knocking persisted.

"Jeez, they're probably cranky from the flight. Oh, I know – you answer it, and I'll go dish up some of the soup for them."

"Okay," Ana smiled.

Kwanjai headed back into kitchen while Ana prepared her fake surprise face as she answered the door. She looked through the peephole, but they must have been standing too close to the door as she couldn't see who it was.

Ana grasped the handle and, as she turned it, the door blasted off its hinges. It knocked Ana to the ground and rendered her unconscious. Kwanjai heard the thunderous noise and came running in with a bowl of soup in hand.

"Margaret! What the hell are you doing?" Kwanjai shouted, shocked by the sight of Ana laying on the ground, partially trapped under the front door.

"What I should have done a long time ago – eliminate

you two ungrateful vermin," she said, before telekinetically gripping Kwanjai by the throat and throwing her against the wall, the bowl of Thai soup Kwanjai had lovingly made for her daughter launched across the room with her. The living room filled with its deliciously sweet scent as the bowl smashed onto the hard wooden floor.

The sudden surge in Margaret's power took Kwanjai by surprise. Up until then, her powers would've been more useful in a pub quiz than a brawl.

"You ruined my life! She's left me! She hates me, and it's all because of you!" Margaret angrily shouted. "What was it, huh? Tit for tat?"

"Margaret, you are the reason my husband is dead. And your deceitful nature is the reason your wife left you. All I did was help her to see the truth," Kwanjai answered, still pinned to the brick wall behind her.

"Yeah, you hateful bitch!" Ana shouted, having now woken up. She tried to shimmy her way from beneath the door, but with a wave of Margaret's hand, Ana's lips became glued shut, causing her to scream internally as she panicked.

"How are you doing this?" Kwanjai growled.

"Well, though I may not have been the one behind those experiments, it turns out that Charlie was on to something. Seems like soon anyone will be able to acquire such power."

"What are you talking about?"

"Oh, it doesn't matter now," she laughed.

Margaret saw the broken shards of the ceramic bowl on the floor and raised them, floating them an inch from Kwanjai's neck.

"Any last words?"

As Kwanjai's fear translated into tears and sweat which flowed down her face, the elevator pinged.

As the doors opened, Kosum saw her mother and Ana in peril. She didn't hesitate as she dropped her bags and ran in.

"Kosum!" her mother screamed.

Kosum's eyes flicked between her mother and Margeret for all of a millisecond before she instinctively pulled her athame from her boot and flew it straight into Margaret's chest, who had turned to face her.

Margaret was stunned and, for the first time in her life, speechless as the intense pain burnt into her body. Her arm dropped, releasing Kwanjai and the ceramic shards from her telekinetic grasp. Blood began to pour from her chest, soaking the cream blouse she was wearing. Her wide, shocked eyes were fixed on Kosum.

Kosum was breathless, shocked by what she'd just done. She couldn't help but stare back and watch as the life drained from Margaret's face. Margaret fell, and as her lifeless body thumped upon the floor, Kosum finally understood Nkechi's argument: she really would do *anything* for her mother.

EPILOGUE

A week had passed since Margaret's death. Kosum had spent most of that week in bed. Kwanjai explained to her about the fireplace and her father, and that Margaret had come for revenge. As she attempted to reassure Kosum that her actions had been right in the moment, she only heard snippets of her mother's speech as the guilt was deafening.

She finally understood the melancholy feeling Nkechi had described after killing the professor and Charlie, and she knew it wouldn't go away easily.

Of course, Kosum had never liked Margaret, but nothing could prepare her for seeing her life fade in front of her eyes. Nkechi also tried her best to console Kosum, but she knew from her own experience that Kosum would have to come to terms with it in her own time.

Another few weeks passed, and it was nearly the end of summer. The dark nights began to outweigh the light days, and it was almost time to return to college.

Kwanjai had begun forcing Kosum to get up and dressed in preparation for returning to school. There was also a coven meeting approaching that she would need to attend, being a member of the inner circle. The meeting was to discuss the source of Margaret's new powers, as well as the new and powerful witches popping up all across New York, thanks to

Charlie's research.

Reluctantly, Nkechi had been working with Trish to find some answers. Of course, Nkechi would've much rather worked with Kosum but Kosum barely had the motivation to brush her teeth most mornings. So, alas, Trish it was. Despite their differences, Trish and Nkechi had made progress. They had managed to trace the new black-market powers to a woman called Isabella – Charlie's former maid.

In the wake of Charlie's death, Isabella, feeling like his true mother, decided to carry on his work and maintain his legacy. Just before he died, Charlie had perfected his formula for giving mortals magical powers. Isabella had been the one to clear Charlie's apartment, taking all his research with her so that she could train herself to recreate the serum. Isabella was unknowingly creating a new breed of witch – unnatural, unsolicited and extremely dangerous.

The time had come for the coven to face the witches of New York and their fear of the growing problem.

Kwanjai, Ana and Trish were already in their thrones, while Nkechi dragged Kosum along to meet them.

"C'mon, Kosum, it'll be okay. I'll be sat right next to you."

"Okay. But I'm not saying anything."

"That's fine. Now come here, I'm gonna run a brush through your hair. We can't let everyone think your standards have dropped now, can we?" Nkechi joked, trying to cheer her up.

"Thanks, Nkechi."

Nkechi and Kosum took their seats just before the New York witches filtered into the room. Many witches who had raised their concerns at the beginning of summer about how they would be protected without Gweneviere, now had good reason to be worried.

The sea of disgruntled witches began to call out, with no care for rules or decorum. They wanted answers. Everyone agreed that these new witches couldn't be allowed to roam freely with such unknown powers and the community of witches wanted to know exactly what the coven were going to do about the ever-growing problem.

Kwanjai, now back to full strength, commanded the room.

"Please, everyone, calm down! Nkechi and Trish have made progress with the problem we're facing."

"Pfft, what's Trish going to do? Fuck them to death? Everyone knows she's just an Indignus," someone shouted.

Trish's cheeks flushed a deep shade of red. She wasn't normally a prude, but a stranger shouting out a comment like that shocked her. She was used to the usual discrimination towards her. Like the way Gweneviere felt about a Marcidus, many people didn't feel an Indignus should be allowed a seat at the inner circle. They saw them as a second-class witch because they had to siphon energy from others to fuel their magic.

Although Trish and Kwanjai didn't always agree, Kwanjai wouldn't stand for that kind of discriminatory slander against any of her fellow witches. Kwanjai had dealt with her fair share of ignorance in New York and she wasn't going to let those same people infect and spread hate like a disease in her community.

"Let me reassure you that Trish is a very valued member of this coven, without whom we wouldn't have the information that we do. Anyone who has a problem with Trish, feel free to leave the safety and protection of the New York coven. If you remain, I ask that you show some humanity and respect. Witches are supposed to be an inclusive species – need I remind you of the awful trials our ancestors had to endure because of their differences? They did not go through all that for us to turn on and berate each other now."

One man got up and left but no one else followed.

"Good riddance," Ana commented.

Trish gave Kwanjai a look of thanks.

"Now then, Trish, Nkechi and Kosum will be tackling this issue head on. We will bind any of these new unnatural witches and find the source of these black-market dealings! So unless anyone has any further objections, this meeting will be adjourned until we have further updates."

The room remained silent for a moment until Kwanjai gestured for them to leave. Kwanjai seemed the perfect replacement for Gweneviere. She was a kind and passionate leader, but with a firm command of her audience.

Ana, Trish and Kwanjai left, leaving Nkechi alone with a silent Kosum.

Nkechi could see Margaret's death was continuing to plague Kosum's mind and tried her best to pull her out of her slump.

"I guess we're not gonna have time for that sexy island holiday after all," Nkechi joked, poking Kosum in the arm.

"Huh? No, I guess not," Kosum replied.

"Hey," Nkechi said, pulling Kosum in for a hug. "We'll be okay. *You'll* be okay. I promise, it gets easier."

"I hope so."

That brings the second chapter of Nkechi and Kosum's story to an end, but as always nothing is ever simple in their life. It would seem that even after Charlie's death, they're still dealing with the aftermath of his legacy. But will they ever overcome it?

INDEX OF SPECIES... continued

Ogres

Ogres are a humanoid species that evolved from their giant counterparts thousands of years ago. Giants coexisted with humans and many other magical creatures for quite some time without any issues. Humans even glorified female giants for their beauty and great stature. However, as time went on, humans became less tolerant of the magical world, often blaming natural disasters and diseases on magical creatures. As hateful, fabricated stories of giants eating human children began to spread, it wasn't long before humans turned on the entire giant race. The giants were hunted almost to extinction. Small groups retreated to the forests dotted around Great Britain. Over time, interbreeding became their only way to survive, though it took its toll on the gene pools through each successive generation.

Ogres became the result of hundreds of years of interbreeding. Shorter than their fifteen-foot ancestors, ogres were riddled with deformities and faces that became more disfigured with each generation. They also succumbed to diseases much faster due to the lack of gene diversity in their blood. Their much shorter lives meant less knowledge could be passed down to the next generation, and thus they became increasingly more ignorant.

In these modern times, ogres have lost all sense of morality.

They skulk around the enchanted forests of Britain feasting on deer, horses, and hikers who stray too far from the designated path. They live alone and are aggressive towards all other forms of life that dare to cross their path.

The Damned

The damned are an army of undead voodoo practitioners and witches that could be summoned by a voodoo king or queen. The voodoo deities, however, deemed it to be too powerful an army for any one mortal to command, and thus banished the spell used to summon them, making it only known by the gods themselves.

Once awoken, the army is loyal to their summoner and will enact whatever actions their master sees fit.

The damned have an insatiable hunger for flesh, and a bite from one of them, if left untreated by an antidote, can infect and transform a human into one of them. They are faster and smarter than your average zombie though, and the only way to eliminate them is by destroying the brain, whether through trauma to the head or simply decapitation. Their sheer numbers, however, would probably overrun you before you could take the time to carefully shoot each one.

This is all theoretically speaking of course, because no god would be crazy enough to summon them, right?

The *Madame Voodoo* trilogy will conclude with...

MADAME VOODOO
AND THE
NECROMANCER

ABOUT THE AUTHOR

A.W. Jackson is a 26-year-old barista with nothing but determination and a dream to tell their stories to the world! In 2023, they stepped down from their full-time job as a manager, in order to focus on writing. They also published their first novel that same year, *Madame Voodoo*, followed by a prequel *The Pudding Lane Witch*, released in 2024.

Keep up to date on all things *Madame Voodoo* by following A.W. Jackson on socials:

Instagram: @awjacksonauthor
TikTok: @awjacksonauthor